NIGHT SHIFTS BLACK

THE HOLD ME SERIES
BOOK 1

ALY STILES

Night Shifts Black
Copyright © 2016 Aly Stiles (Alyson Santos)
All Rights Reserved

Cover design by Books and Moods

ISBN: 978-1-961197-00-8

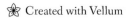 Created with Vellum

A NOTE ABOUT NIGHT SHIFTS BLACK

Dear Reader,

Thank you for your willingness to take a chance on my words. When I wrote this book as part of the healing process in my own battle with depression, I never imagined it would have the impact that it's had. Hearing stories from readers who also struggle with mental illness (or their loved ones) has meant the world to me, and I'm so glad this book has helped others to feel seen and understood. Whether or not you like the story itself, I hope you can sense the heart and soul poured into it.

Happy reading, and remember to never curb your compassion. Just a small act of kindness could save a life.

Love,
    Aly

Just a simple picture. Innocuous to anyone else, but horrifying to those who recognize that ugly, battered, vacant diner chair.

1

DAY ONE

I'd be lying if I said I don't notice him enter the restaurant. We all do. It's impossible not to.

He isn't drop-dead gorgeous or anything. In fact, I can't describe a single trait I haven't seen before. He's not particularly tall, nor is he memorably short. His hair is messy in an intentional kind of way that makes you think he cares a little, but not too much. At the very least, he used to care and old habits die hard. He's dressed similarly, casual, but uncomfortably so, like this is his one pair of jeans in a closet full of suits. Although really, his jeans are too expensive to count as jeans anyway. He hasn't shaved in a couple days but it suits him and makes you pretty sure it's an intentional look. No, it isn't any of that.

It's the way his eyes scan the café. The chairs, the walls, the ceiling. The way what should be a very confident young man cowers in the entrance, the cold air blowing in behind him, interrupting our breakfasts with his personal drama. Stan Hemford even mutters something about moving in or moving out, but I don't worry about Stan. I can only stare at our intruder's clenched fists and the way they mirror his set jaw. He's here, but he doesn't want to be.

And then, his eyes seem to find what he's looking for.

Me.

I almost choke on my tea as he begins his approach, and my brain launches a frantic index of the last few years, trying to piece together why I'd have any role in this person's life. Maybe he kind of looks familiar, but I don't think I know him. He isn't the type you'd forget so I believe myself. In a brief moment of absurdity I even consider the possibility that this is a real live hit. But he doesn't look like a hit man, at least not what a girl who's spent most of her life in a rural Pennsylvania town imagines a hit man to look like. He looks more like the guy who would hire the hit man. Actually, he looks like the actor who would play the guy who hires the hit man. A hit man? That's my working theory? I swallow.

"I'm sorry to bother you," he begins with an obvious accent, which is actually the first thing about the scene that doesn't surprise me. Nothing about him fits here, at this place, in this moment. It's all so foreign that, for a split second, I feel like I don't fit either.

"Can I help you with something? You look lost."

His eyes change again, filling with a heavy sadness. Fear, maybe. No, terror. I don't move. Everyone is watching us.

He shakes his head. "I'm not lost. I was just hoping I could have your chair for a bit."

"My chair?"

"There are many others available."

"True."

There's one right across from me. I really don't have a good reason not to move, nor can I imagine denying the simple request with him looking at me like that.

"Sure, no problem."

I push my saucer across the table and stand with great ceremony. He stares at me in shock, maybe a hint of amusement, as I skirt around him and drop to the other side of the table.

"This ok?" I ask, and when his lips twist into a slight smile, something beautiful happens to his face. But it's gone so quickly I actually feel sad.

"You're very literal."

"You're the one who interrupted my breakfast."

He nods but doesn't apologize, and I suspect he suddenly forgets about me. He's far away now. I watch his face as he studies the chair, his eyes tracing each detail. The chipped paint, the frayed fabric of the seat. He reaches out and touches it, tentatively at first, and his fingers caress the back, gliding over the bumps and cracks. I fight my instinct to say something, to interrupt the awkward encounter between this stranger and a piece of cheap diner furniture. The defensive humor slips to my tongue, but catches on my lips. Again, it's his eyes. There's something there. Something deep. Something shattered. I'm not even sure he's here to sit.

After a long pause, he bites his lip and backs away.

"Thank you," he mumbles before breaking for the door and disappearing with the same impact with which he arrived. The audience is glued again, and I hear Stan mumble something about punks and hippies.

I stare after the stranger as well, maybe even with a little regret that I hadn't been more memorable. While it's clear I'm not part of his life, I'm suddenly afraid this odd event will make him part of mine.

My server approaches with an apologetic smile.

"Sorry. I should have warned you."

"Warned me?" I ask, still watching the door as if he'll return and explain the mystery so it doesn't explode into something that will haunt me after I leave.

"Yeah. It started on Monday. You haven't been here since. Third day in a row. Same time. Same table."

"What do you mean? What started?"

"What you just saw."

"He comes in and stares at this chair?"

She shrugs. "Basically. Just stands here and looks at it. He touched it today. That was new, I guess. What are we gonna do, though, right? It's not like he's breaking any laws. Just acting weird is all. Can't arrest a guy for being weird. Well, unless he's naked, too. You think I'm kidding, but that happens. At least this one is just weird."

Weird? That word seems dissonant to me. Part of me can't help but wonder about the weird naked guy, but just a small part. The rest is still invested in our current, clothed weirdo. No, not a weirdo. The name just doesn't work. I would need a lot of words to describe what I'd just witnessed in those brief seconds, but "weird" isn't one I'd choose.

"He seemed so sad."

"I don't know. Maybe. We get all kinds in here. None of my business as long as he doesn't disturb the guests. Sorry if he bothered you."

"He didn't."

"You want a refill?"

I nod and instinctively study the vacant chair across from me.

2

DAY TWO

I never eat breakfast at Jemma's two days in a row, but I knew the second I left yesterday that I'd be back. I'm not a nosy person by nature, but I am an observant one. And I certainly can't ignore things the way a lot of people can. I sense I'm exposing myself to a world I might regret, but judging by the amount of time I've spent reviewing every detail of that strange encounter, I'm pretty sure I'm already stuck in it.

So I go back. Request the same table. Settle into the chair across from the important one this time. I'm grateful I have a different server, Darryn with a "y," so he doesn't recognize what I'm doing because I'm embarrassed for some reason. I don't want anyone to know why I'm here. No one except the stranger, anyway. I need to know why he's sad. Why he's afraid. Why he's ok being weird when he's clearly not. I need to understand the chair.

I was very intentional in my decision to leave his chair open when I sat on the other side. I wonder if he'll notice. I order my tea and pretend to study the menu, but really, I'm watching the door, waiting. It's the wrong angle to view the door from this side, however, so I'm forced to scan the rest of the restaurant with each peek. I notice a few other familiar faces around the room and can't help but wonder if they're waiting, too. Stan is here, still too close to the entryway so he'll be cold when the stranger enters and hesitates in the opening.

He's a little later today. Just a couple minutes, but enough for me to think that he's not some kind of obsessive sociopath who times his fixation on a rigid schedule. This chair routine is part of his day, but it's not the only part of his day. I take some comfort in that, although I'm not sure why. This has nothing to do with me.

Like yesterday, the hostess doesn't even ask him if he'd like to be seated. She knows why he's here and watches with a vigilance that's ready to call for help if necessary. Her hand seems poised to reach for the phone as he does his search.

And that's when it occurs to me that he's not searching. He knows where to go. He knows what he will find when he gets there. He's not looking. He's bracing.

He starts toward my table again and then stops abruptly. I can't tell whether he's annoyed, upset, or pleasantly surprised to discover my obvious intrusion into his life. He's dressed similarly to yesterday, but different enough that I realize this casual style may be new to him, but it's now permanent. As I study him with the same intensity he studies me, I also notice he's younger than I first thought. He's been aged, but not by time. If I had to guess, I'd say mid to late twenties. I'm terrible at guessing, though, so I decide not to.

"You're back," he says quietly.

I still can't interpret his reaction.

"So are you."

I motion toward the chair. "This might be my table, but you can have the chair."

"Thank you."

Oddly enough, he doesn't even look at it today. In fact, he sits at the neighboring table as though he's completely abandoned his mission. I'm disappointed, and again, startled by my strange reaction. I suck in my breath and grip my teacup.

"Mind if I join you?" I ask, before it actually occurs to me that's weirder than anything he's ever done. I kick myself.

He glances at me, but doesn't seem nearly as surprised by my question as I am. Then I realize it's only because he's distracted. He doesn't care about my question.

"Sure," he mutters. I suspect it's more out of politeness than a desire to allow me access to his life, and I quickly regret my impulsive request. He doesn't really want me here, that much is obvious, but neither can I back out now in any reasonable way. At this point, I'm committed to picking up my saucer and sliding across the narrow aisle to his table.

"I'm Callie, by the way."

"Luke."

"You're not from around here, are you?" I cringe.

Nice work, Callie.

There's that brief smile again, and my embarrassing cliché is momentarily forgiven.

"No, I'm not. Are you the law in these here parts?" he teases back, and now I'm officially hooked.

"Sorry. I know. That was probably the worst thing I could have said."

"I can think of worse."

"Do you come here often?"

This time the slight smile becomes a full-on grin.

"As often as you, apparently," he responds.

"You must think I'm stalking you."

"Are you?"

"A little." Before I can control it, my gaze shoots to the chair, and his smile fades.

I wish I could take it back. I wish I'd been strong enough to stop it, but we both know that's why we're here. We both know we're connected for no other reason.

Neither of us says a word. I have no way of knowing if his mind is in the same tailspin as mine, but I sense it probably is. I'm sure his head goes to places most of us could never understand.

The server approaches and seems surprised to find us together.

"Can I get you something?" he asks Luke. I don't miss his quick glance in my direction, but he doesn't let it linger long enough to force me to respond.

"Toast, please," Luke answers.

"White, wheat, or rye?"

"Rye."

"You got it. What about you? Still fine with just tea?"

I glance at Luke. I am, but a cup of tea isn't long enough. "Actually, I'll take an order of pancakes. Small stack."

"Hash browns or fruit cup?"

"Fruit."

"Bacon?"

"No thanks."

"Sure thing."

He shuffles off to fulfill our orders, and I'm suddenly nervous at the thought of being alone again with Luke. I'm nervous because he's enigmatic, and beautiful, and sad, and debatably weird. Although clearly not as weird as I am I've learned.

"No bacon?" he asks.

I'm relieved he's forgiven me for my earlier chair blunder.

"I wanted you to think I'm healthy."

"You care what I think?"

"Maybe. I don't know. I'm not sure yet. Just covering my bases in case it turns out that I do."

I'm rewarded with another smile. "Fair enough. I don't want to know how I rate with my rye toast."

I shrug. "I'm reserving judgment until I see what you put on it."

This time he actually laughs, and now I'm sure he was someone else once. He would have occupied this whole restaurant wing with his fancy suits and perfect hair, surrounded by a crowd of admiring acquaintances. This is a man who wasn't alone until recently. His magnetic laugh wouldn't have allowed him to be alone. He must not laugh anymore.

"That's a lot of pressure for a condiment," he observes.

"There has to be a marketing campaign in there somewhere."

"Maybe, but what about you? Pancakes come with many possibilities as well."

"True. You'll just have to wait and see."

He nods, and I fight with my brain to keep the conversation flowing. I know if it stops, he will get lost in himself again and retreat to that place I can't go. I don't know why it's so important to me that I prevent that from happening, but when I see his eyes move to the right, a small ember of panic begins to ignite. I'm losing.

"Do you live in the city?" I ask, drawing him back to earth.

He seems to have to shake something before he can respond. "No. Well, not really."

"Just visiting?"

"Kind of. What about you?"

"Yes, I do, but I've only been here a few months."

He nods. He's being polite again. Polite does nothing to help me.

I need to bring him back to the café, this table. "You know, Stan's been watching you like a hawk."

"Stan?"

I motion to the table by the door with my eyes.

"Ah, yes. He's the one who needs a jacket."

"I think he's amazed you actually stayed this time."

"He's not the only one."

Surprised, I go to meet his gaze but he's not looking at me. That wasn't a flirtatious comment. He's not even referring to me. I might be partially responsible for his shocking delay for toast, but I'm just an excuse. Maybe even a roadblock. I'm still not entirely certain he wants to be here right now. The way he fidgets with his fork and absently bounces his knee, it's like he's already left the café and his body doesn't understand why it can't catch up.

"Look, I'm sorry. I'm afraid I'm being rude. I don't mean to be. I'm just..."

He doesn't finish. He can't. Not because he's going to cry or anything, he's just not good at this sort of thing anymore. Conversation.

I understand and smile to let him off the hook. He seems relieved, and I watch as his grip relaxes on the fork for the first time.

"We don't have to talk. I'm kind of tired anyway. Late night," I explain.

He nods and rubs his eyes as if commiserating. I can tell he knows late nights, too.

"Thanks. It's not personal."

"Oh? I didn't think it was until now."

He smiles, but his eyes aren't in it this time. I've definitely lost him and know he's counting the seconds until he can finish his toast and escape. He's regretting this, staying, participating in life again. I feel like I've been whacked in the stomach but I don't blame him. He doesn't owe me anything. This is my fault, not his. I have mercy on him.

I look at my phone and force a curse. "I'm so sorry. I didn't realize what time it was. I actually have to be at work in ten minutes," I lie. "Don't hate me, but I have to run."

Our eyes do meet this time, and for the briefest moment, I think he knows what I'm doing. I don't know how or why I think that, but he almost seems grateful for my sacrifice.

"Sure, no problem."

"Here." I slap some bills on the table and force the most genuine smile I can. "Breakfast is on me."

He shakes his head, but it's instinctive. "That's not necessary. It's the least I can do for making you move...twice," he adds.

"Really. I wouldn't feel right forcing you to pay for food I didn't even eat. But it was nice to meet you...Luke." The dramatic pause before his name sounds awkward, but it doesn't seem right to leave him, maybe forever, without making our goodbye personal.

He appears to notice my embellished farewell. He almost seems disturbed by the sound of his name, like he's not used to hearing it anymore.

"Thanks. You too. Callie."

I grin at his pronunciation. It's not quite right with an "a" that sounds more like an "o," but I like it better the way he says it. Now, I don't want to leave. I'm not sure I can, but I have to. I don't belong here, in his world.

I get the sense no one does.

3

DAY THREE

It's another three days before I finally go back. I wanted to go the next day, and the next, but I used all the strength I had to let my will overcome my compassion. I wasn't ready to face that chair, whatever it is. Whatever he is. This fledging relationship built on a mutual understanding that there isn't one. It felt like I'd be breaking one of our rules if I went back too early. Like I'd be pushing for a place in his life when he clearly doesn't want me in it. If I waited, though, just a couple days, even, then we could blame it on chance. It wouldn't be fair for him to claim my favorite café and force me out permanently. He'd understand that and have to respect the fact that I'd reappear eventually.

So here I am. Day three.

I take the table beside the one with his chair again. The same one where we almost shared breakfast last time. When I see him enter, my pulse quickens. I don't know if it's attraction. Probably. How could it not be? But it's also something else. Fear maybe, that he won't accept my presence. That he's spent the last few days in this spot without me, relieved I've disappeared and left him in peace.

My fear dissolves into a rush of something else when he nearly smiles and heads straight for our table.

"You're back," he says, removing his jacket and placing it on the back of the chair. His vintage t-shirt is thin today, and I notice the hint of tattoos peeking through the light-colored sleeves. He's also muscular, more than I would have thought. Not obsessively so, like he spends every waking hour working on his body, but naturally, like he lives a life where it's inevitable. I can't help but wonder what fills his hours when he's not in Jemma's Café staring at that chair.

"The tea here is second to none."

He smirks and drops across from me. "If this is going to be a regular thing, you'll have to do more than drink tea. It's a little too obvious."

My heart soars. I don't even know why, unless it's because it's the first time he's acknowledged that I've made an impact.

"I almost had pancakes last time."

"Almost. Just so you know, I didn't stay for the toast either. I'm surprised they let us back in."

I smile. "We paid for our wasted food. Did we leave a decent tip?"

"Since you emptied your wallet on the table, I think we covered it."

"How do you know I emptied my wallet?" I ask.

"I watched you do it. You almost threw in a couple receipts, too, until you stuffed those back in."

"Yeah, but..." I don't finish. He's observant, like me. I wonder how many other things he's noticed about me. That I'm left-handed? That my hair is darker than what seems natural for my skin tone? That my eyes are too big for my face, but really all my features are, so maybe they work together anyway. I realize there are a lot of things people could observe about me, and consider how one-sided my approach has been to forming my world.

"I was in a hurry," I explain.

"Right, because you were late for work."

"I was."

"Yeah?"

I swallow. "Yeah." I look at my phone and wince. If I had been late that day, then I'm really running behind today. "I have staggered hours?"

He grins and nods. "Ok."

I return his smile and clear my throat. "Fine. You caught me. I actually make my own hours."

"I see. Then technically you could have been late, if you'd decided you were."

I like his observation, for many reasons.

"Technically."

"Well, that's helpful then. Now I don't have to be offended that you ditched me."

"Ditched you? Please. I was doing you a favor by leaving, wasn't I?"

His smile fades, but this time he doesn't totally retreat to that dark place that makes me regret approaching his wall. This particular withdrawal is more introspective.

"Maybe."

"So what are your hours, then?"

"I guess I make my own hours as well."

"Self-employed?"

"Are you?"

"Yes," I say.

He nods. He didn't answer my question. He doesn't intend to answer my question. I wonder if it's the question itself, or a deeper flaw. I doubt he will answer any of my questions, so I decide not to ask any more for now.

"I'm a writer," I continue, accepting that if we're going to talk, it will have to be about me.

That seems to interest him, and I know I will have to make this topic seem a lot more glamorous than it is. I don't usually worry about other people's opinions, but now I want to impress him for some reason.

"A writer, really? What do you write?"

"Everything I can. A lot of it is to pay the bills, but some is to keep me sane."

"I'm more interested in the part that keeps you sane."

I expected as much and lean forward. I'm disappointed when the server prevents my response.

We place our orders, and the server eyes us with subtle suspicion. I don't blame him, given the fact that we walked out on him the last time we were here together. I wonder again if Luke sat here alone the last two days without me. I wonder if he ordered anything. I wonder if he wondered where I was. I doubt it, and the thought makes me sad.

"Poetry mostly."

"Poetry?"

"The part that keeps me sane."

"I see. Interesting."

"What about you?" I kick myself. No questions. I wait for him to shut down, but this time he doesn't.

"No poetry. Not exactly, anyway."

"Novels?"

He smirks. "No. Maybe one day."

"Can you give me a hint? My next guess will be travel brochures."

He smiles. "Song lyrics."

Suddenly, it hits me. I don't know how I missed this. "You're a musician," I guess.

He seems disturbed. "Used to be, but yeah."

All of a sudden I want to look at the chair, but this time I'm able to stop myself. There's no way I'm messing this up.

"Used to be?"

"Used to be."

"Is music something that ever really goes away?"

He visibly shrinks.

Stupid! I'm furious with myself.

"Yes. I wouldn't have thought so, but yes, it can."

We're silent, both letting that thought settle around us, deep into the cracks of our tenuous alliance. Me wondering what it would take to break a musician of his music. Him wondering...I have no idea.

At least I understand his hair now. And his clothes. And the fact that he doesn't really fit in here. He never wore suits like I'd originally thought, but he also doesn't wear jeans like the rest of us. I know my head shouldn't go where it does, but the thought blasts through before I can stop it. I wonder if he's a musician I would know. "Musician" could mean anything, but there's something about him that makes me think he's in a tier I'd recognize. I think back to that strange glimmer of recognition when I first saw him.

But I don't ask, for once managing to hold my destructive question inside.

The silence continues, although it's not awkward this time. I like that we don't have to talk. I like that simply watching his eyes work the room is enough to replace any need for conversation. I find it fascinating that he's ok with my presence, but doesn't really need me here. Part of me thinks I could be anyone, and he'd be sitting in the same position, tattooed arm resting on the table, fingers absently exploring the napkin.

Fingers that used to explore a piano, or guitar, or flute. I want to know which one and think maybe that's a safe question.

"What instrument did you play?" I ask, breaking the silence.

It was safe enough, and he comes back to me.

"Guitar mostly, but we all played everything."

"In a band?"

He nods. I sense that I shouldn't go any further.

"Not an American band, though," I tease.

He smiles again. "Actually, yes. Don't let the accent fool you."

"So it's just a fake one?"

My joke startles him, but he likes it. "My accent? No, it's real. It didn't hurt my image as a frontman either."

Another clue. "I'd imagine not. I have yet to meet a girl who is anti-cute-musicians-with-accents."

"No? I have," he returns with a grin.

"Really?" I ask, skeptical. "I'm going to go out on a limb and guess they were anti-something else."

This time the grin spreads into his eyes, and I actually catch my breath for a second.

"You're probably right about that."

It's then that I notice it. The ring. My heart stops.

I don't know how I missed that as well, and it makes no sense that I'm disappointed. It's not like this is a date, or any hope of a date. This isn't even about that. Maybe that's the problem. This is more than that, and the fact that he shares these moments with someone else the other 23 hours of his day hits me harder than it should.

But I don't ask. I don't say anything. I actually pretend I don't see the dark band on his left hand, even though I'm captivated by the way it encircles his finger, a finger perfectly refined by years of creating art. The ring is a work of art in itself, nothing like I've ever seen before. It suits him. A musician's ring. A ring a rockstar would wear after marrying the exotic lingerie model most men would kill for.

I say nothing, afraid if I do he'll think I'm suggesting something I'm not. I'm afraid he'll feel guilty and he hasn't done anything wrong.

Our breakfast arrives, and I can almost sense our server's relief that we're still here to receive it this time. He hovers a little longer than necessary, reciting a list of possible additions to our meal no one over the age of seven should need to review. We assure him we're fine, and he finally backs away, still watching as if expecting us to disappear before he can return with the check.

"His life will never be the same," I whisper when he finally accepts that his job of delivering our food is done.

"I fear you're right," Luke responds. "Should we apologize for last time?"

"I don't know. That might freak him out even more."

"We don't want that. We'll just have to regain his trust over time."

My knife stops cutting. I know I shouldn't, but I look up anyway.

He clears his throat. "I'm sorry. That was forward."

Forward? That was amazing.

"I have nothing better to do in the mornings if you don't," I reply as casually as possible.

I hate that I suddenly think about the chair. He does, too, and glances over. We both do. We stare at it. We stare at it until he finally shakes his head and closes his eyes. His knife hovers over his plate. He doesn't move, doesn't speak, doesn't explain. He just remembers why he's really here and it's not to have breakfast with me. He's betrayed himself. His chair.

"It's ok," I say quietly. "Luke, it's ok."

He opens his eyes and this time they're clouded. There are tears there, threatening. He's fighting them so hard his knuckles are white on his utensils. I notice that. I notice everything about him at that moment. I'm also powerless to do anything but watch and it kills me.

He laughs, but there's no humor now. He swats at his eyes and I can't tell if he's angry or simply embarrassed. It might be neither. I have a feeling it's too complicated to classify. I don't know where to begin, he's given me nothing to work with, but the one thing I can do is just be. I'm good at that.

I'm quiet. I wait. I put down my fork, mirroring his action. He stares at his, but that I don't do. I can't look away from his face. From the pain and sadness and fear. It's horrifying and beautiful at the same time. His instinct is telling him to run. I watch his eyes trace the path from the chair to the door. His leg has shifted to clear the base of the table. He's poised for flight, but not in a weak way. He's not going to run for the exit. He has enough control, enough strength to make a graceful escape. He will form an excuse, maybe coupled with an apology, offer one of his priceless smiles. Then with a calm stride, he'll be gone. Dignity intact. Strength unquestioned. Another confusing shift for our server.

I can't let that happen.

"Did you want the jam for your toast?"

"Excuse me?"

"I'm not sure why he put it on my side of the table if you're the one with the toast. Here."

He hesitates, not sure what to do with me and my resistance. I hold my breath. The chair. The door.

"Sure," he says finally.

I smile as if I expected that response, even though I still can't breathe. "I'm going to guess blueberry."

"Orange marmalade, actually."

"Really? Ok, wow. So first you ordered eggs with your toast today, then you chose orange marmalade. I may have misjudged you."

"You assign a lot of value to people's breakfast choices."

"We're in a café. What metric would you suggest?"

The smile returns, genuine this time, and it has a strange effect with the redness still influencing his eyes. It's haunting, in a way. One of those images that I'm afraid will affect me at a later moment, when I least expect it.

"You're right. That's fair. Although I notice you went with pancakes, fruit, and no bacon again."

I don't know why I'm surprised he remembers. It was only three days ago.

"I'm pretty predictable."

"I'd argue that."

The comment warms me, but I let it go. He isn't trying to start a conversation; he's trying to end one.

We stop talking, using our engagement with this cheap breakfast as a shield against another grenade that could destroy everything we've just spent three days building. And to think, this used to be my favorite place for tea. Now, it's my favorite place for pretending to eat pancakes.

I watch my plate clear. Quickly at first, then slower as my stomach fills up. There's something sad about our pace. I know it will be time to leave soon. Time to go back to my apartment and try to work on the part of my life that doesn't include the magnetic puzzle sitting across from me. Time for him to return to whatever it is he does now that he doesn't have music.

The server returns, almost stunned we've not only accepted our meal, but consumed it.

"Can I get you anything else? We have several fresh baked goods. Coffee?"

Luke shakes his head and gives his polite smile. Not the real one. I wonder if he even knows how many he has.

"Thanks, but I'm full. This was great."

The server nods and turns to me. I offer an apologetic look. "No, thank you."

"Ok. I'll get your check."

"Thanks," Luke replies. "You sure you don't want anything else? My treat this time since you paid for the last one."

I give him a similar response, but decide not to argue about the bill. He's right. I did cover the last breakfast. And then some.

It's time.

My legs feel heavy as I force a casual front and push up from the table. I reach for my jacket and find myself struggling with the zipper. I don't think it's on purpose, but maybe it is. I don't want to say goodbye yet. I don't want him to know that.

"Thanks for breakfast," I say.

"You're welcome. Thanks for breakfast on Tuesday," he responds.

We exchange a smile. More than a smile.

I begin counting the minutes until tomorrow.

LUKE DOESN'T SHOW the next day. I order my tea to save face, but I'm beyond disappointed. I entertain all kinds of irrational thoughts. Silly things that only an over-analytical writer could invent. He'd think I'd lost my mind if he were here and I actually shared any of them with him. I wouldn't blame him.

But he's not here. He never promised he would be.

I sip my tea, staring out the window. I can't stare for long until my gaze crosses paths with the chair. It's still vacant. In fact, I realize I haven't seen anyone in it since I'd been an unknowing trespasser. I think it will be strange watching someone sit in it. Irreverent somehow. It won't be his or her fault. The intruder won't know the blasphemy they're committing. I imagine what would happen to Luke's face if he were here eating his toast with orange marmalade and all of a sudden someone sat in the chair. I can almost see the darkness settle over his features, the internal battle that rages every time his present clashes with that part of his past. My instinct wants to call it "his chair" but I don't think it is. There's a ghost there, in that chair.

The hair rises on my arm as I study it, only five feet away. I could probably touch it and even make it look like an accident if I wanted to. I don't know why I'd want to. It's Luke's chair, not mine. I don't touch it. I don't have that right.

4

DAY FOUR

It's hard to admit I'm relieved to see the distinctive leather jacket when I enter, but there's a flood of something rushing through me, so I have to acknowledge it. He's switched sides at our table. I only see the back of his head because he wasn't watching for me like I watched for him yesterday and the day before.

I approach slowly, still not entirely confident he will welcome my presence. If I go in casual, it will be easier to fake a retreat when he recoils.

"Callie."

"Luke."

"You up for some pancakes?" he asks, and a huge weight lifts from my shoulders.

"I don't know. Maybe I'll surprise you today."

He likes my challenge and pushes back my chair with his foot.

"Try me."

"Did you order yet?" I ask.

"Just coffee."

He was waiting for me. At least, I hope he was. I don't think I'll ever know for sure.

"You want some tea?"

I nod. I do love my tea. I love that he knows it. "Tea would be great."

Our server isn't Darryn with a "y" today. It's Shauna, the woman who filled me in about Luke's chair obsession on that first day. I'm not surprised I remember that though. I seem to have every detail of Day One etched into my brain.

"Hi, Shauna."

"Morning. Tea?" she asks. She knows me better than Darryn. I'm not sure why Darryn's had so many of her shifts lately. Maybe she's had other obligations. I realize that I don't know enough about Shauna. I should know why she was off. She knows I like tea.

"I've noticed Darryn's been on a lot lately."

She sighs. "Yeah, I've been picking up the evening shifts instead. The sitter decided to take some classes, so now I have to work when my husband Jake's at home, since I can't have the sitter during the day."

"How many kids do you have?"

"Two. Maddie's four and Mark is two."

Maddie and Mark. That's sweet.

She leans close. "Hey, sorry to make you wait, but I have to go check on Stan's omelet before he calls the FBI."

I chuckle. "No problem. Tea would be great. We'll give you our orders after you take care of Stan."

She delivers a grateful smile, and I don't miss the look she casts at Luke. She wonders about him, too. Wonders about the chair. Wonders why he now stays and eats breakfast. Why I'm special. In other words, she wonders the same things I do.

I feel Luke's gaze after she leaves, but I'm not prepared to meet it. I don't know if it will be admiring or curious or accusatory. I could make a strong case for all three. If I avoid it, it doesn't matter. Except it does matter. I know it matters. Even more than I'm prepared to admit at this point. Eventually, I look up, but after all the debate, I can't read his expression anyway.

"Shauna seems nice."

"She is."

"You've obviously been coming here for a while. Well, for the few months you've lived in the city at least."

"A few times a week."

"Really."

He does the math, and I redden.

"I come more often now." I have nothing to lose.

He doesn't respond, but he doesn't run screaming either.

"Where did you live before this?" he asks finally, and I breathe a sigh of relief.

"A small town. You've never heard of it."

"Try me."

"Shelteron, Pennsylvania."

"You're right," he replies.

"Told you. We don't even have a stoplight. Well, we do, but it only flashes yellow so I don't think that counts."

"So what, you graduated high school and had to escape the small town to go make a name for yourself in the big city?"

I bite my lip and look at my hands. "No. Nothing like that. I'm older than I look."

I have his interest now. He's not the only one with secrets.

"How old are you?" he asks.

"Twenty-three. How old are you?"

"Twenty-seven."

"You're younger than I thought."

"How old did you think I was?"

I panic when I realize I lied. I did think he was twenty-seven. Well, about that anyway. I don't even know why I said what I did, and now I'm stuck.

"Twenty-eight."

He smirks and leans back. "Sorry to disappoint you."

"I'm not disappointed. Twenty-seven is a fine age."

"So's twenty-three."

It's the years in between that are rotten. We both think it. I look at the chair. I can't help it.

He clears his throat. He doesn't want to cry in front of me again. "Anyway, since you're the expert, what's good here besides the eggs, toast, pancakes, and tea?"

I pick up the menu as if I'm actually going to have the presence of mind to read it. My head is still spinning.

"Um...there are fresh baked goods," I suggest, thanks to Darryn's recitation at our last meeting. Unfortunately, he remembers that, too, and his lips spread into a grin.

"You've never had anything other than the pancakes and tea," he charges.

"I have!"

He crosses his arms. "Really. Like what?"

"The fruit cup."

This time he laughs, and we invite some glances from a nearby table. They're not annoyed, though. In fact, they are curious, intrigued even, and I notice them paying more attention to us now. Well, to Luke anyway. I'm startled by the sudden glimpse of what he was. What it would have been like to enter a room with him and leave with fifty new friends. His laugh does that. His eyes...

I stare at my menu. I'm not ordering the pancakes today.

"The omelets are good, too."

"According to whom? Stan?"

I shrug. "He's here every day. I'd say that's pretty reliable testimony."

"Should we do it?"

"Do what? Order omelets?"

"Yeah. You get bacon and cheese. What should I get?" he asks.

I like this game for some reason. "Western style."

"Ok, deal. Hash browns or fruit cup?"

"Hash browns for me, fruit cup for you."

"Toast?"

I shake my head. "Not for you, unless you get wheat and put strawberry jam on it."

"Fine, but you have to drink coffee instead of tea."

I wince. "Coffee?"

He raises his eyebrows, and I sigh.

"Ok, fine. Coffee. Cream, no sugar."

"Deal."

He holds out his hand. I take it.

I do an admirable job of pretending the handshake is exactly what he intended it to be, and when Shauna returns, we place our orders. She is confused why I don't touch the tea she just brought and order coffee instead. She also doesn't understand why, when I instinctively order a fruit cup, Luke jumps in and changes it to hash browns. She's especially confused when I apologize to him for messing up my own order, but she's a good sport and promises to be right back with my coffee.

"Living on the edge today. I don't know if I can handle all this excitement," I say after she leaves.

"Wow. So Sheltertown really was a small town, wasn't it," he teases.

"Shelteron," I correct. "And yes, it was."

"They didn't have coffee there, I presume?"

"They only have orange marmalade in England?"

He grins. "You think I'm English."

I blush. I do. Well, I did.

"I guess that means you're not."

He shakes his head. "No. South African." I also think he might regret embarrassing me. "Don't worry about it. I get that all the time, believe me. Especially here."

"Yeah, I know. Ignorant Americans."

"I didn't say that."

"You were thinking it."

"Really? You know me well enough to know what I'm thinking?"

No. I know him well enough to know I have no idea what he's thinking.

"So you weren't thinking it?"

He smiles and shakes his head. "No. I really wasn't. I've lived here since I was fourteen. My accent isn't a true South African accent either. I can't blame anyone for not being able to place it."

"What brought your parents to the United States?"

His eyes shift. Uh-oh.

"As fate would have it, nothing, actually."

I go into triage mode. "Well, then. At least I understand your love of oranges."

He laughs again, but I sense it's more from relief that I let the parent comment slide. "Oranges? You know nothing about South Africa, do you."

"Sure, I do."

"What? Name one thing."

I tap my fingers as I think. "Um...it's in the southern part of Africa."

He grins. "It's true."

"Don't ask me for something else, though."

"After that response, I wouldn't dream of it."

I give him a look and his return smile plunges deep inside of me.

"Fine, smarty-pants. Then name one thing about Shelteron."

"Anything?"

"Anything."

"Ok. Well, it only has one traffic light. I should say, a light that flashes yellow, anyway."

I scrunch my nose. I want to laugh. I don't know why I don't. Maybe I'm afraid I won't stop.

"Am I wrong?"

I smile instead. "No."

I notice his hand resting on the table. It's further on my side than seems natural, his sleeve a little long and covering his wrist all the way to the middle of his palm. I want to touch it. To feel the warmth of his fingers. Or maybe they'd be cold. My fingers are always cold. That would be awkward, my cold hand stunning his. I abandon the idea of reaching for my glass and causing an accidental collision. My eyes rest on the ring, and I freeze. He caught me.

The warmth disintegrates as he draws his hand away and tucks it in his lap. I wonder if he'll explain. I want him to tell me the truth almost as much as I don't. I don't want to be reminded that he's someone else to someone else. I don't dare to speak. There are no words for this.

"I was married."

Was. Divorced? Widowed? I don't know how to ask. He's not going to offer. But he's no longer someone else's someone else. That much is obvious.

He shakes his head. "Anyway, let's not do personal stuff, ok?"

I nod. "Sure," I say, as if there's any other response I could give. I'm not here to marry him. I'm here...the chair. My heart starts beating faster. Is she the ghost? I want to look at it as if there would suddenly be new clues after this revelation. I have to look, but I can't. He doesn't either. I watch his eyes instead, waiting to see where they go. They're staring at his hand. I can't see it anymore, but I'm sure he's looking at the ring.

He still wears it.

My heart shatters.

He's widowed.

I try to catch my breath. I want him to know that I know, but I don't know how to tell him without words. Useless, volatile words that I can command at will on paper but seem to hold me hostage in conversation.

He's too young to be widowed. Way too young to be widowed for long. He needs to know that. I clench my fists. Of course he knows that. It killed his music.

Shauna brings our meals, and I thank her for both of us. I know Luke won't. In fact, I'm surprised he's still here. I study his face in silence, watching him consider his omelet. I imagine him wishing he'd ordered toast like usual, but then I realize how silly it would be to think about toast when you have a dead wife. I don't know how to talk about dead soul-mates to twenty-seven-year-olds.

"Luke..." I have to try.

"I said no personal stuff."

"I know."

It's my turn to study the omelet. I need hot sauce. At the very least, ketchup. I signal Shauna. Like everything I could request at Jemma's Café, hot sauce is no problem, and she'll bring it right back.

Luke still hasn't moved. He's lost in his head now. I'm not sure he even remembers that I'm here. He definitely doesn't care.

And then, it happens.

Before Shauna can return with the hot sauce, the hostess seats an older couple beside us. I watch Luke tense as the man takes his seat. No, not his seat, the ghost's seat. The hostess even casts a quick glance at Luke, and I can't tell if she's concerned or gloating about her decision. She certainly understands enough to acknowledge what she's done.

I suck in my breath, waiting, fearing, watching Luke, anticipating something, but I have no way of knowing what. His blue-green eyes absorb every square inch of the table beside us. I can even see his muscles constricting through his shirt, contracting as he clenches his fist, already punishing the couple for a sin they can't possibly be liable for. But they are, and I understand that, even though I want to rescue both sides from an unjust war that can't occur.

"You want to go?" I ask. I'm sure the concern in my heart is all over my face, but he's not looking at me. He's looking at them. "Luke, we should just go."

"What am I doing? What have I done?" he rasps, shoving back from the table.

I'm stunned. Hurt, but also afraid, as he charges from the restaurant. I don't know what he has to run to apart from me and his chair, but I'm terrified it's only going to make things worse for him.

I can't follow him, I know that. I have no right to offer comfort. I'm only part of his life when he's here, at this table. He hasn't invited me into the rest, but Shauna comes rushing over and prevents such a mistake anyway.

"Are you ok?" she asks, staring at the door just as Luke disappears through it.

"Fine," I say. "It wasn't about me." I glance over at the table beside us and notice the couple whispering to each other. They're watching the door as well, and suddenly I'm angry at their gossip. They don't know. I don't even know. They're not allowed to judge him. I hate them for judging him. Shauna follows my gaze, and I'm pretty sure she understands my message.

"I told Ailee to leave that table open while he's here," she mutters. "I'm sorry."

I want to tell her that it's ok. That it's not a big deal, but it is. There are plenty of other empty tables in the café. It's not packed. It's not ok.

"His name is Luke," I say, drawing Shauna back to the conversation.

"Luke."

She says it like that information answers a lot of questions for her.

"He's a musician. Or was."

She nods. "I can believe that. He's pretty cute, actually."

He is, but it seems silly to talk about stuff like that right now. I try to smile. "I hope he comes back."

"I was surprised when he started talking to you. He didn't talk to anyone until you."

"Did anyone ever try to talk to him?"

No. That's obvious. She just looks away and shrugs. It's not her job to talk to customers if they aren't customers. I know that. I can forgive her. It still hurts.

"Are you going to finish your meal?"

I should. The only thing stopping me is the fact that I'm no longer hungry. "Can I get it to go?"

She smiles. Again, she seems to understand. I wonder why she didn't try to talk to Luke. Maybe it wouldn't have come to this. Maybe he wouldn't have needed me and would be getting to know Shauna instead. I go cold at the thought. I can be a very selfish person.

"I'll get a box. You want his, too?"

I look at his untouched plate. I do, but not because I want

to eat it. I just can't stomach the thought of leaving it to be
discarded by a heartless busboy.

"Sure. I'll pay for both, don't worry."

"I'm not worried, Callie."

Surprised, I somehow manage to thank her. I'm not sure
how she knows my name. Maybe she knew his, too, and just
pretended not to. It has to be hard to spend your days around
people pretending not to know them.

I glance over at the invading couple. They've now relaxed
and are scanning the menu. I think of Luke. His ring. His eyes.
The anger slipping into his face.

He hadn't run that day he encountered me in his chair. I
wonder what changed.

I'M NOT surprised when Luke doesn't show up the next day. I
don't intend to stay long either. I stop by the table, check in
with Shauna, then move on to the next phase of my schedule.

The second day I can forgive as well. I never lost a
spouse. I have no idea how long the grieving period is or what
it takes to recover from something like that. I figure it's probably more than two days. I still check back in at Jemma's, just
in case, this time taking my place at the table for a cup of tea.
I hope the recovery period is shorter than I imagine, and my
gaze shoots to the door every time it opens, but it's never
Luke. I see Stan, even Darryn showing up for a shift, but not
Luke.

By day three I'm starting to get concerned. I don't really
know him, but that fact brings no comfort, only leaves me
feeling incomplete. We have work to do, conversations to
explore, memories to share. I don't know Luke well enough to
need him, but I know I need to finish whatever we've started,

even if we're only two strangers who decide to remain that way. I just need it to end with a choice.

I quiz Shauna on day four, but she hasn't seen him. Even the hostess shrugs, making it clear that my problem is not her problem. Luke is a sidebar, an anecdote for her friends over a beer on the Friday nights she isn't working. He's the weird guy who comes in and disturbs the peace by staring at a chair like a freak. That is, until he started eating breakfast with me. Now, he's the freak who runs away when other people sit in a chair. She isn't going to help me.

Oddly enough, my only clue comes from Stan. Luke had taken a call after he fled that day. Stan heard every detail as the younger man hovered in the windbreak, pleading with someone to cancel something and sell the rights to something else. Since Stan knows nothing about him, the conversation makes no sense to him. Since I do, I know I have to keep waiting for him.

So, I do. Day five, day six, and day seven. An entire week I wait.

It isn't until the following week when I can finally breathe again.

5

DAY FIVE

"Callie."

I want to hug him. I actually start to rise from my chair to begin the embrace and catch myself.

"Luke."

He sighs and drops to the seat across from me. "I'm sorry."

"For disappearing for a week without a word, or giving me a heart attack?"

"You were worried about me? You shouldn't worry about me."

"Of course I was! You didn't exactly leave in a calm state. Then, nothing for days. What am I supposed to think?"

"Like I said, you really shouldn't worry about me. You can't, ok?"

Says the most biased judge in the history of verdicts.

And yes, I catch the disturbingly cryptic nature of his warning, but it's a dangerous sentence. I can't deal with that right now.

"Next time, can you at least text me or something?"

"I don't have your number."

"You could."

He nods, but doesn't ask for it. I try not to be hurt.

"I'm just saying that we were all worried about you."

"I'm still confused by that. Why would you be worried?"

I really don't have a good answer. I mean, I have answers, they'd just sound crazy out loud. He's a stranger. He's asked for nothing. I owe him nothing. He owes me even less. Why would I be worried? Because he's more important to me than he should be? That's not an answer. That's my problem, not his.

"We just were." And that was even worse than an answer.

"Really. It's my turn to go out on a limb and guess that by 'we' you mean 'you.' I can't imagine anyone else here cared that I didn't come in for breakfast."

"And what if it does?"

"Now I have to check in with the Jemma's Café patrons every time I do anything?"

He's trying to sound playful. He's not even close.

"No, of course not, but a week? Last time I saw you, you were so upset you stormed off. How am I supposed to know how you fared after that?"

He doesn't respond at first, and somehow I know what he's thinking. Why is he even here? I'm nobody, and now I'm a nobody who nags him. I hate being a nobody who nags him. I'm more than that. He's more than that. We're so much more than that.

"Well, I fared fine. I went home and cooled off. Then did some traveling. Now, I'm back."

I have to stop nagging. I force away what's left of it. "Traveling? Where to?"

Darryn arrives, and I'm not sure if his timing is perfect or terrible. "Morning, guys. Tea? Coffee?"

We thank him.

"Houston."

"Texas?"

He gives me a look. "Yes. Houston, Texas."

Ok, it was a silly question. "What's in Houston?"

"Family."

I nod. "So is that where you're from in the States?"

He looks away and shakes his head. "Kind of. She was."

It's her family.

My stomach actually begins to constrict a little. We both look at his ring. I want to touch it. To trace the intricate etchings in some absurd attempt to soothe the pain.

"What about you? Shelteron, huh?"

I sigh. "Yeah. Shelteron. I have family there. My dad, anyway. We haven't seen my mom in over ten years."

"She took off?"

I nod. "New boyfriend, new life."

"And your dad?"

"New girlfriend, same life."

"And yet, you're here."

I'm not as terrified of my own history as he is of his, but it still isn't my favorite topic.

"I am. New girlfriend isn't a gem, which is why she's perfect for my dad."

He understands, and I notice the change in his eyes. "I'm sorry."

I shrug. "Anyway, there was never anything major. It just didn't make sense for me to stick around once I didn't have to."

"Still, it's admirable that you are able to live independently as a writer."

"It's not all that impressive."

"Sure it is. It can take years to generate enough income in that profession to survive alone, especially here, and you're doing it at twenty-three."

Not exactly. I clear my throat and look away. I know the

second he says those words that I'll regret letting him admire me for a lie, so I can't let this go.

"Actually, I don't make enough to survive. The reason I could leave Shelteron was because of an insurance settlement."

"Insurance settlement?"

"Yeah." I still can't look at him, even though I feel him studying every inch of me. "But no personal stuff, right?" I remind him quickly, trying to smile to lighten the comment. I hate closing a door, but I can't go there. Not yet. If anyone would understand that...

He does. "Sorry, no you're right. It just seemed like maybe you wanted to talk about it."

It probably did. And maybe that was even true until it started coming out. That story isn't an out-loud story.

"I know. I only brought it up because I didn't want to give you the wrong impression. I didn't want to lie to you."

"You weren't lying. Having secrets isn't lying."

"Sometimes not. Sometimes it is."

It's his turn to look away and I wonder which part of this conversation is causing the problem.

Darryn brings our drinks, but we both decide to pass on food today. I'm not surprised given our rocky start to the conversation. Neither of us wants to commit to a long encounter right now.

We don't talk for a while after Darryn leaves. Luke is meticulous about opening the creamer cup and mixing its contents with his coffee. He's painfully thorough. I doubt there is a single drop of creamer that isn't transferred and completely dissolved into his cup. He wasn't so meticulous the last time he had coffee with me. To be fair, my teacup suddenly doesn't seem to sit quite right on the saucer, and I adjust it in an endless loop of futility.

It's then that I notice the four girls whispering several

booths away. I wonder if they recognize Luke as the chair-watcher, or just as a good-looking guy with an average woman who's clearly beneath him. My interest is piqued when one of them is pushed from her seat by the others, and it becomes apparent I'm about to learn the answer to my question.

She stops a few times during her approach, glancing back at her friends whose whispers and silent giggles have reached what seems like a feverish pitch to me, but hasn't fazed Luke. His back is to them. He hasn't even turned to take a peek at the commotion. I don't know how he hasn't noticed the direct attention when I can't focus on anything else.

The girl continues to move forward, and I'm startled to catch a glimpse of a pen. I can't make out the contents of her other hand, but suddenly, my blood runs cold at the prospect of what I'm about to witness. I glance back at Luke and am also surprised by his clenched jaw. I thought he hadn't noticed the girls, but it turns out I just hadn't noticed him enough.

"Hi. Um...I'm sorry to bother you. You're from NSB, right? Ok, wow...can you sign this? Please? My sister will die. She loves you guys!"

I stay calm, suddenly losing sight of everything around me except Luke's face. I watch him react, instinctively, a new smile I haven't seen yet crossing his features. It's not the fake one he uses for Darryn, or the weak one I get when he's trying to be nice but can't. It's definitely not the real one I've captured a few times that turns his entire face into a work of art. This one is some combination of all three. It's his stage smile, and it fasci-nates me.

"Sure. What's her name?"

The girl nearly shrieks with excitement and shoves the pen at him along with what I can now see is a carwash flyer.

"Um, Linny. That's with a 'y.'"

She hovers inches from him, watching each stroke of the

pen. Probably breathing in his aftershave, his shampoo. Maybe even getting a bit of the leather jacket brushing against her hip. She'd definitely be able to feel the heat of his body. She's now been closer to him than I have, and I'm forced to fight off the sudden absurd stab of jealousy.

"Here you go."

"Thank you, thank you, thank you! She will die! She's going to seriously pass out! I love your accent by the way." She looks at the flyer as if verifying it's real. "Wait, you're actually Luke from NSB? You're her favorite! She's totally in love with you!"

Luke smiles again, dismissively this time, but the girl doesn't seem to get his subtle hint.

"Thanks."

The girl is now reaching for her phone, and I have no choice. A photo op is the last thing we need right now.

"Hey, hon, thanks for stopping by," I interject, "but we're actually in the middle of something." She looks disappointed, but resigns to her fate.

"Oh, ok. Well, it was great to meet you! I can't believe I just met Luke Craven from Night Shifts Black!"

She squeals again, and unfortunately now we have the attention of everyone else in the café. Even Stan's expression has softened from irritation to curiosity. Ailee the hostess looks like she's going to be sick. She didn't know she'd been tormenting Luke Craven from Night Shifts Black.

"Do you want to go?" I ask, ignoring them all.

He shakes his head and stares back at his coffee. "I can't yet. I will in a second."

"You can't?"

I don't understand. I start to glance around at everyone else for clues, but then remember I'll probably learn more from watching him. He's studying them, too, discreetly, maybe

judging their own interest. Apart from the one table of admir-
ers, the general demographic of the café is older at this time of
the morning, and it all finally starts to come together. Stan is
not a fan of Night Shifts Black. It's doubtful the old lady in the
wheelchair or today's Hope Retirement Home Bridge Club are
fans either. Luke has nothing to fear from them. He's just
making sure, and needs to play it cool or will invite even more
attention.

"So Night Shifts Black, huh? You said you were a musician.
You aren't just a musician."

"Yes, I am."

My pulse starts to pound, and I hope it's because I find him
more interesting due to something other than what I just
learned. I don't want to be Linny and her sister.

"Right. That's like saying Abe Lincoln was just a
politician."

"He was."

I smile and shake my head.

"Perfect. So now I suppose you want an autograph, too?"

"Only if it's on the check for my tea."

This time I get the real smile, and manage to find my way
back to the Luke I was just starting to know. The Luke who
was fascinating before he was a superstar. The Luke who was
ancient, shattered, and completely obsessed with a chair.

"I hate to admit it, but I'm actually starting to remember
that whole scandal now. You left the band right after you won a
bunch of awards for your last album. Didn't you write a hit
song for that motorcycle biopic or something? It blew everyone's mind. No one could understand why you'd walk away
right as you were taking off."

Luke doesn't respond. He's heard this question a million
times. From people a lot more important than I am.

"I'm sorry. It's none of my business."

"No, it's not."

I glance at the chair then, I can't help it, and he does, too. This time he doesn't shutdown, but seems almost guilty, and his eyes barely brush the surface of it before turning back to me.

"You haven't learned anything new, Callie. Don't think for a second that this information tells you anything about me you didn't know before."

His words hit me hard.

I quiet as I absorb them, trying to decipher the painful depth of that complex statement. There are so many layers, I'm not sure which one to respond to. I play it safe instead.

"I'm sorry, but I have to disagree. I now know that you have little reverence for carwash flyers."

His eyes meet mine and it takes a moment for him to process my joke. Once he does, his grin is totally worth every agonizing second.

"I've signed worse," he returns.

"I believe you."

I pause and lean forward. "Examples?"

He laughs. "You don't want to know."

"Oh, I do. And now, even more so."

He suddenly looks shy, and I can't understand why. There's no way the former frontman for Night Shifts Black could be shy, for any reason. Then, I realize my confusion is because I'm doing exactly what he told me not to: assuming I actually know anything about him.

"I think I made it sound more interesting than it is. Just the normal clichés. You know, bras, panties, things like that."

"Ok, but worse than that?"

He gives me a mischievous look and shrugs.

"Fine. I have a jury summons in my purse, would you sign that?"

He laughs again and holds up his hands. "No way. That puts me in prison."

"What? No. A fine maybe, but not prison. I do understand your fear, though. Prison is no place for a pretty boy like you."

His eyes widen for the fight. "A pretty boy? Really." He leans back and crosses his arms. "You don't actually know our music do you."

"I don't have to. Teenage girls love you and want to marry you. That's all I need to know."

His eyes still hold the rare amusement that makes me willing to do anything to keep it there. I wish I had the courage to pat his hand, now resting on the table. It could pass as playful with my teasing, but I'm not good at that sort of thing and don't trust myself to pull it off.

"Teenage girls love and want to marry anyone they see on TV. You were a teenage girl once."

"I was."

"And?"

"And I would have been happy to settle down with any one of seven different celebrities."

"None of which was me? Undeniably sexy frontman for Night Shifts Black? How's that possible?"

I include an apologetic look with my headshake. "Sorry. I was more into moviestars than rockstars."

"Really? That surprises me."

He's not joking now, and it catches me off guard.

"Why's that?"

"I don't know. You take me as someone who charges off the beaten path, that's all. Hollywood crushes seem too cliché for you."

"Now who's judging a book by its cover?"

"What? You're offended that I think you're interesting?"

I can't even begin to respond to that. He's got me all kinds of flustered. Stupid words. Stupid, traitorous words. I'm about to say something horrifying like "you think I'm interesting?"

Thankfully, I manage to stop it.

"No comment, huh?"

His self-satisfied smirk makes me want to smack him. And kiss him. I almost blush.

"I'll have the perfect comeback in about three hours when I'm back at my apartment cleaning out my closet, don't you worry."

His smirk spreads into another genuine grin, and I can't help but return it.

"Fair enough. Make sure you write it down so you can tell me tomorrow."

He tosses a few bills on the table and grabs his jacket.

I'm disappointed until I notice he's still smiling on his way to the door for the first time since we met.

6

DAY SIX: PART I

I don't even make it through the door before Shauna is shoving me back into the cool April-morning air.

"You're here! I thought you'd never get here," she says.

I'm not nearly as pleased to see her. This can't be good.

I try to peek past her through the door, but I can't see anything.

"What's going on? Is everything ok?"

She bites her lip and glances behind her. "Not really, no." She leans toward me. "He's here and he's not good today."

"Who's here? Luke?"

I know the answer, of course I do; I just need more time to process it.

She nods. "If Ailee didn't know he was Luke Craven of Night Shifts Black, he'd probably be dealing with the cops right now."

"Really? Is he causing a disturbance? He's bothering people?"

"Um...no, not like that. But he's been sitting there for, like, a half hour."

"He's freaking people out because he's been sitting for a half hour?"

"He's..." she stops and seems frustrated that she can't explain. The thing is, she doesn't have to. I get it, and I wouldn't know how to explain it either. I realize it's better if I just spare her the attempt and agree to take over from here.

"I'll go see if I can talk to him."

"Really?" She is clearly relieved. "Thank you! We're all worried about him, you know."

I nod to be polite, but their concern doesn't mean much to me. They weren't worried until they learned who he was.

I go inside slowly, as if I'd startle him with a normal entrance. I know it's silly. My guess is he won't even notice me. He's probably not noticing anything right now.

I know exactly where to look after I'm inside, and when I see him, I completely understand Shauna's hesitation. I'm not sure how you'd describe the scene to make it sound as disturbing to the ear as it is to the eye.

It's about the chair again.

This time though, he's in it, seated casually, like he's enjoying a relaxing meal with a companion. The problem is, he's removed it from the table and placed it in the middle of the aisle. There is no companion. No meal. No silverware, napkins, or table. Just Luke in a chair, in an aisle, sharing a silent conversation with a pretend person. It is disturbing, incredibly disturbing, especially for someone who's begun to care about this person.

He doesn't acknowledge me as I move toward him. I don't know if it's because he doesn't see me or just doesn't care that I'm here. I was so sure I had to help a moment ago, but now, faced with the actual problem, I don't really know what to do. I sense speaking isn't the right approach and will just turn a strange situation into a volatile one. Instead, I decide to simply join his world like I'd done many times now, and figure out how to navigate it once I'm inside.

I take a chair from the neighboring table and position it across from him in the aisle. I can feel the gazes of the other café patrons, but I don't care about them right now. My fear quickly bleeds into sadness as his eyes meet mine. He's not crazy. He's not far away in some alternate universe. He knows exactly what he's doing, where he is. He's just broken and lost and doesn't care if he's bending the rules about how to behave in a restaurant.

"Did Shauna call you?" he says finally.

I shake my head. "She doesn't have my number. I came on my own."

He nods and leans forward, resting his head in his hands. I think he might be crying, but he's not making any sounds so I can't be sure.

I move my chair closer to him. "Hey, you hungry?" I ask gently. It's a pointless question, but it's sound and it's safe.

He shakes his head.

I still can't see his face, and now I know it's time. I can't hold back anymore and have to take the risk. Friends take risks for each other, and goodness knows I've played it so safe up to this point that we still aren't friends. I lean forward and easily cover the remaining space between us. When I touch his hands they are warm, like I thought, and so are mine. I expect him to recoil, maybe even snap at me, but he doesn't. He lets me peel his fingers away from his face and grip them. I can feel the ring against my palm and squeeze harder. He looks at me then, searching my eyes, and I catch my breath at my own glimpse into his soul. There's so much depth, so much pain, I'm paralyzed for a moment.

I don't know which one of us pulls away first. It's probably him, but I react fast enough that it can be construed as mutual.

He rubs his face and closes his eyes. I know I'm watching him recover from something, putting himself back together, so I just wait for the process to complete. Finally, he sighs and leans back.

"We should order something, huh," he says.

"It would be the polite thing to do," I agree.

"Probably at a table though?"

"Well, it would be a lot easier."

He smiles, and I return it.

"You must think I'm insane."

"I definitely don't think you're worried about restaurant etiquette."

This time he laughs, and I can almost feel the entire café collectively sigh with relief. Crisis averted.

I signal Shauna and point to our usual table. "Is this ok?"

7

DAY SIX: PART II

"You know they were ready to call the authorities on you," I whisper.

"I was a rockstar for seven years. You think I haven't been acquainted with 'the authorities?'"

"Oh right. Street cred and all. You get that ink in prison?"

He smiles before he leans back and closes his eyes. I don't know what kind of silence this is, just that he needs it, and commit myself to respecting his retreat for a while. We have returned the chair to its table, and this time I'm pretty confident Ailee will leave it unoccupied during the duration of our visit. Unlike many of her customers, she is probably a Night Shifts Black fan. At the very least, she is a fan of famous, rich people.

I glance around and notice there are more guests than usual. I would have expected the opposite, given Luke's behavior a few minutes ago, and now, I can't help but fear word is beginning to spread about his presence in our city, at this café. I don't want them to know about the chair. I don't want his suffering on display and wish I could figure out a way to explain that to him. I'm suddenly wrapped in a sense of urgency to solve this chair problem before it destroys him.

"You know how sometimes you feel like your life isn't yours," he muses out loud. "Like you go through the moment, but it could be happening to anyone, not you?"

I do know that feeling. I nod, but don't speak.

"That's been the last year for me. Every second of every day. I could recite any detail you want, but I can't tell you a single thing that's actually transformed me or made an impact. It's like this is all happening to someone else and I'm really in a whole other place right now."

I'm quiet for a moment. He's not looking at me, and I know exactly what he means. Not just because I can relate, but also because I'd had the same terrible suspicion about him since our first conversation. He's here, but he's always somewhere else, too. The rare magical moments are the ones where I actually have all of him for a brief second.

"Is it the same reason you lost your music?"

He's staring at the door now, and I wonder if he's going to answer my question or flee again.

"Yes."

"Your wife?"

He glances at the ring. I do, too. He touches it. I want to touch it, too, but don't have the courage.

"I shouldn't have asked that. I'm sorry."

When I look at him, I suspect he is also. He's not a bad person. At least, he isn't now.

"Nothing personal, right?" he replies with a weak smile.

I return it and nod. "Right."

It's quiet again, and I think I've lost him. He's gazing out the window now, past our table, the aisle, the chair. It's almost like he's looking for something, maybe someone, but it's the same haunted expression he has when he gazes at the chair. It has to be the same ghost, and I want to help him find it more than ever.

"I didn't used to be this way," he continues, still staring past the present. I'm not sure what he's referring to, nor am I sure he's even talking to me. His tone is somewhere between an apologetic confession and personal criticism. I can't begin to respond, so I wait.

"I used to be the life of the party. Heart on my sleeve. I used to be silly."

I can't imagine him being silly. I'm not even sure what he means by that. "We all change. Life changes us."

"Yeah?"

"I like to believe that anyway."

"Ok, that's fair." He's being polite again. He doesn't agree with me.

He's right of course. We don't all change. Life doesn't force it equally. We don't accept it equally either. I was just trying to throw something out there to reassure him, and now realize how pointless that was. He's too perceptive to be reassured by statements that don't mean anything.

"What about you? Has life changed you?" he asks.

"Yes."

"The insurance settlement?"

I can't look at him. It wasn't exactly an insurance settle-ment. I wonder if he knows that as well somehow. He can't possibly, but then, I've underestimated him since the moment we met.

"Kind of."

He nods, but doesn't push for more. He guards his secrets and he's not a hypocrite.

"So where do we go from here?" he asks.

"We, as in 'the human race?' Or we, as in 'our friendship?'"

He smiles, and I finally have him back. "You must think I'm a lot more introspective than I am."

"What? You're offended that I find you interesting?"

This time I get the real smile at my teasing. "Not offended, but concerned you'll be disappointed by the truth about me at some point."

"Which truth? That you used to be the life of the party and silly? It's already out."

He shakes his head, the grin still in place. "True."

"Fortunately for me and my morning breakfasts at Jemma's, I don't think you're as shallow as you think you are."

"I used to be shallow."

"Maybe. Or maybe you used to pretend you were shallow."

"I wasn't pretending."

"Then maybe we have different definitions of shallow."

"Obsessed with celebrity and all that comes with it?"

It's my turn to smile. "Ok, maybe we do have the same definition of shallow."

He returns it. "It's hard not to be shallow when you're a celebrity and drowning in all that comes with it."

Another piece falls into place. It's the way he says it. The way his eyes change. The way the circle just completed itself. Drowning. He didn't have to use that word. I start to understand what the media and masses could not. He had to walk away from them because he couldn't be a celebrity anymore. He didn't want all that came with it. I just need to find out why.

"I should probably go. I have a long day ahead," Luke says, and I regret letting the conversation die.

"Anything interesting planned?"

"Nothing that isn't personal."

"Sorry."

But he's smiling, so he's not really upset. "Don't be." He tosses some bills on the table and pauses. "It's mostly legal stuff."

I nod like I understand what that means.

I don't.

8

DAY SEVEN

"You're late today," I observe.

"Am I?"

Luke takes off his jacket and slings it over the back of the chair.

"I thought we make our own hours," he argues.

He's got a point.

"I thought you like to beat the admiring horde traffic."

I have one, too.

"Fair enough. I had a late night."

"Anything interesting?"

I was joking, but he's not, and looks away. "No. Couldn't sleep."

"I'm sorry."

He shrugs and stares back at the menu like he hasn't practically memorized it by now. I know I have. We need something to study when we don't want to look at each other or the chair. I like the "Breakfast All Day" insert. He seems to prefer the senior specials. I have no idea why. Then it occurs to me that when he buries himself in the menu he doesn't actually read it like I do. I wonder if he even notices his gaze tends to linger on the senior specials. I decide to find out.

"You know, you have to be over 55 to order from that page."

He clears his throat, and I can actually see the moment when his eyes change from vacant to focused.

"I'm sure they'd let me, I just wouldn't get the discounted pricing."

"That's true. And to be honest, I bet Ailee would overlook the age restriction and still give you the discount."

"Ailee?"

I motion toward the hostess station. She's not watching us. At least, not at this second. But she was before we looked because there is no other way to explain the awkward way she leans against the counter in the opposite direction she should be facing.

"I don't think I've ever seen a person do such a complete 180 before. You were a thorn in her side a few days ago."

"I still am, probably."

"Yeah, sure. A thorn from a beautiful fragrant rose she will dip in gold and hang above her bed."

"That's disturbing on so many levels."

"Maybe. But am I wrong?"

He glances over at her discreetly and smiles.

"I bet she saves your receipts," I continue.

"She wouldn't be the first."

"It's memories and an autograph all in one."

"Nah, just memories. I pay in cash."

"To avoid leaving an autograph?"

"To avoid having my credit card stolen."

"True. Yours would probably be more tempting than mine."

He smiles again. A crafty one this time. I haven't seen that one before. "Yeah, maybe, but they'd be disappointed."

"Why's that?"

"I only have a thousand dollar limit on the card I use for this type of stuff."

"That's smart."

"I said I was silly, not stupid."

"Yeah, about that. Does silly mean the same thing in South Africa that it means here?"

"Frivolous."

"Ok, fine. Although, for the record, it can also kind of mean stupid."

"I was making a point."

"I know, sorry. I just struggle to see you as silly. Either definition."

"You wouldn't have a year ago."

"When you were the life of the party."

"When everything was a joke and I refused to take life seriously."

"A lot of people are like that."

"Silly people."

"Scared people."

He quiets. I struck something.

"You sound like a psychiatrist."

"I'm sensing that. And how does that make you feel?"

His grin is genuine this time, and I relax. Nothing personal. I keep forgetting that.

"So just to be clear, you're paying for the coffee today, right?" he asks.

"I don't know if I can risk it. I have more than a thousand dollar credit limit on my card."

He glances at Ailee. "I think you're good."

9

DAY EIGHT

Luke isn't alone today. At first I'm disappointed and wish I could disappear into the floor. I begin to anticipate the embarrassment when he will pause on his way by, apologize, and strand me at our table by myself.

I brace myself as he approaches, my mind trying to formulate a response that can help preserve my dignity by some impossible miracle. I can almost feel our morning audience's curiosity about how the drama will unfold.

"Callie."

"Luke."

"This is Casey."

"Hi. I'm Casey."

Luke rolls his eyes and pulls out his chair. My breath returns when I realize I haven't been rejected, I've been included.

I have trouble tearing my eyes away from Luke, like always, but I also realize there's a limited window to evaluate Casey while he's distracted with his own chair. He's dressed like Luke. Same styled hair that's meant to look like it's not. Monochrome tattoos, jeans from some high-end store I don't have access to. An air of confidence bred by more than unjustified ego. Casey has to be a band-mate.

Ailee is probably hyperventilating right now.

"Do you always get up this early?" Casey asks, a little teasing and a lot serious.

Luke shrugs. "If you come later you don't get to eat. You know how it is once you're spotted."

Casey seems to understand, but I get the sense he's not as bothered by the intrusive attention as Luke. Casey didn't walk away from celebrity. Casey might still be silly. Casey doesn't have a ghost chair.

"Welcome to our breakfast club," I say, mostly because if I don't say something soon I will lose my status in the group. I don't want to be downgraded to Luke's diner sidekick.

"Yeah, Luke was telling me about your little breakfast club. Pretty crazy story."

It is, but I don't want to discuss it. I don't know Casey yet. "Then I'm sure he also told you about how incredibly witty and smart I am. I'm great company."

Casey grins and casts a look at Luke that I don't miss. "He's told me some things," he responds cryptically.

Surprised, I watch Luke, figuring I'll get more information out of his response. Sure enough he doesn't look happy about his friend's confession. And of course, now I have to wonder what "things" Casey was told.

"How about you not be a jerk for twenty seconds," Luke mutters, and Casey's grin only widens. Our guest turns to me.

"Don't let his puppy dog eyes and sob-story fool you. This man is no boy scout."

"Casey, not now."

"What? I know you, dude. You get lost in your head and shut down."

Now, Luke is very upset. "Will you stop? It's not your business. Not now!"

We're starting to get more attention, and Casey's smile falters. "I'm just looking out for you. You have to move on. You can't keep doing this to yourself. You screwed up. We all do. That doesn't mean everything that happens from that point on is your fault."

Luke's eyes narrow, and I think they might bore a hole through his friend's brain.

"You agree with me, right?" Casey continues, drawing me into this for some reason. "He needs to stop punishing himself. It's been a year. He can't torture himself forever."

"Casey!"

"What? I'm just..."

"She doesn't know," Luke hisses.

Casey looks startled. "What?"

"She doesn't know, ok?" Luke repeats, and now we all feel miserable.

An awkward silence follows.

Casey figures out there's a menu he can pretend to read, but isn't good at that yet. He turns the pages too fast and doesn't move his eyes enough. Luke abandons decorum altogether and glares through the restaurant, seemingly irate at some offense of the coatrack. For my part, I'm both haunted and fascinated by the new clues into Luke's story and almost forget about my companions as I try to piece them together with the old ones.

Casey gives up on the menu. "Hey, man, I'm sorry. I just thought, I don't know, after everything you said about her. I thought you were closer."

Luke gives him a sharp look, and I catch my breath. I'm not sure what to do with that. Luke's not either, and Casey finally catches on that he's trying to tame a fire with gasoline.

"Um...ok, I'm gonna shut up now."

"That would be a good idea."

I need to intervene or this is going to be a disaster and I can't afford for that to happen. I can't be part of a circle that doesn't exist.

"So, Casey. Are you in Night Shifts Black, too?"

Casey seems surprised at first, then the grin returns. Even Luke cracks a smile so I know I'm hilarious, but I don't get the joke.

"What? What did I say?"

Luke shakes his head. "Nothing. You're fine. It's just a funny question."

"Why's it funny?"

Luke shrugs. "I don't know. It's not, I mean, it's just that we're not used to hearing stuff like that except from old people trying to be nice at charity events."

"Remember the Morning Star Senior's Ball?" Casey laughs.

Luke's eyes ignite. "Don't!"

Casey ignores him. "So there's this lady with a, what was that thing again? I don't know, some huge hat and boa thing. Anyway..."

"Case!" Luke turns to me. "She had good intentions."

"She thought he was the one benefiting from the charity because of the 'dreadful condition of his clothing!'"

"I was wearing three-hundred-dollar jeans and a Julian Salitoni jacket."

Casey smacks the table as his laughter hits a new decibel. "Oh man, I just about died when that happened. Dude, she was ready to take you home and give you a hot shower and cot in her living room."

I squint over at Luke and do an appraisal of my own. "I don't know. I kind of see it. I mean, there's the messy hair, and the jeans may be $300 but they look like they're one wash away from disintegrating. Your t-shirt could definitely use a bit of mending. I'd slip you a twenty as long as you promised not to buy booze with it."

Luke grins, and there's a strange dynamic heat that pulses through me. "I never would have promised that."

I sit back and give them a wry look. "Ok, fine, so I'm guessing what I'm supposed to take away from this little tale is that it's not often you encounter people under seventy-five who don't know who you are."

"Only because we don't have time to come in contact with those people." Casey realizes his mistake too late. I'm one of those people. "Well, you do, apparently," he says to Luke, and I'm not sure how that fixes anything.

Luke doesn't seem bothered by the comment, which surprises me.

I jump in anyway. "Alright, fine, so I get it. You're a super famous rockstar in Night Shifts Black. Then can I ask what you play? Or should I already know that, too?"

"Now, I get why you like her. She knows nothing about us, does she?"

Luke's grin returns. "Nope."

I don't know if I'm blushing, but still manage to give them a stern look. "So, what, I'm supposed to grovel at your feet because you're big rock gods? Sorry if I was the only person on this planet who didn't know that."

"No, but now that you know, you should be groveling," Casey teases.

"Oh boy," Luke mutters.

I raise my eyebrows. "Really? What if I'm an undercover royal princess? Maybe you should be groveling at my feet."

"If you're really an undercover royal princess, I will. You'd have to prove it, though."

"Prove you're in Night Shifts Black."

Casey turns to Luke. "Am I in Night Shifts Black?"

Luke holds up his hands. "I'm not getting involved in this one. You're on your own."

"You're not involved. You're just verifying a fact."

Luke looks to me.

"It's ok. He's right. You can answer his question."

He sighs. "Fine. Yes, Casey plays drums in Night Shifts Black."

Casey leans back and crosses his arms, a satisfied smirk on this face. "Ok, there you go. Now, it's your turn, princess."

I clear my throat and turn to Luke. "Am I an undercover royal princess?"

This time I get Luke's real laugh, and my own grin breaks.

"Yes, she is," he replies, clearly amused.

I turn to Casey and shrug. "There you have it."

"Why do I feel like I've been conned?"

"You haven't been conned, just out-voted," I return.

"Ha, fine. This is all breakfast club politics. I get it."

"There are no politics involved until you order. We only judge based on food selections here."

Luke signals Darryn. The servers at Jemma's have learned not to bother us until we're ready. We pretend we're being respectful of their time, but really they don't want to confront Luke before they get the all clear that he's not nuts that day.

"Coffee, please," Luke says, and Darryn nods.

"What about you?" Darryn asks Casey.

"Yeah, coffee's good."

"Tea for you?" he asks me.

"Yes, please."

"You guys eating today?"

I notice Darryn asks Luke, not me.

"Probably. Can we have a couple minutes, though?"

"Of course. I'll be back with your drinks."

We thank him.

"He knows you," Casey observes.

"He's a breakfast club regular," I explain.

Casey smiles. "If I'd known about breakfast club, I would have visited sooner."

"Yeah, right," Luke grunts. "You don't have time to visit. I still can't believe you showed up last night. Don't you have to be in Richmond tonight? I thought you guys were playing the Calisto Festival."

Casey almost looks hurt, and I'm surprised. "I would have stopped by as much as I could if you'd let me. You just didn't want me around. I didn't even know where you were until TJ called a few days ago. I got here the first second I could."

I can tell Luke doesn't want to have this conversation. I think it's more the subject itself than the fact that I'm present, however. I can't see him ever being comfortable with it.

"One of us needs to try the French toast," I say before we return to the uncomfortable silence.

"Why's that?" Casey asks.

"We've never ordered it, and I think it's time to diversify breakfast club. What do you think?" I ask Luke who shrugs. He hasn't recovered yet, and I turn back to Casey.

"So tell me more about being famous rockstars. I want to hear about the groveling."

Casey smiles, but the humor is gone. "Well, it hasn't been the same without your friend here, that's for sure. Luke was Night Shifts Black. Without him we're basically just a sad cover band."

I realize this conversation isn't going to help Luke's current state, but I'm too fascinated to give it up at the moment.

"At least you're still touring though, right?"

"Yeah, kind of. But we don't headline much anymore. We can't sell out a stadium without Luke Craven."

"Sweeny does fine," Luke mumbles.

"Yeah, sure," Casey smirks. "They're your songs, bro. No one will ever be able to handle them like you do."

Luke shuts down again, and I notice Casey's reaction this time. The other man legitimately cares about his friend. He's worried about him. He knows why Luke left and stuck them with Sweeny. He knows something about the ghost chair. I want to know now, more than ever, and wonder if Casey would tell me. He probably wouldn't, but I probably wouldn't have the heart to betray Luke and ask anyway.

Darryn returns with our drinks, and I'm afraid he notices the sudden unrest around his table. He might make us prepay for our food.

"Did you decide on your orders?" Darryn asks, but he's not optimistic.

We're quiet for a moment. Casey and I both look at Luke who is staring at the chair. Darryn shifts his weight and seems just a fraction below annoyed. I'm about to speak up and put us out of our misery when Luke suddenly orders French toast.

We all stare at him, and Darryn seems flustered. I quickly rescue the moment by doing the same.

Darryn hesitates before scribbling on his notepad and looking to Casey.

"What the hell, why not?" Casey adds, handing over his menu.

Darryn clears his throat. "Ok, three French toasts it is. Anything else?"

We shake our heads.

"No bacon? Fruit? Home fries?"

"Nope."

"Um, ok. Thanks."

"Do you think he has to go to counseling now because of us?" I ask after he disappears.

"He's at least insisted on a raise," Luke responds, and I grin. We're back.

"So has my boy here told you about his other passion?" Casey asks.

"You mean, besides music?"

Casey nods, and Luke rolls his eyes.

"It's not a passion."

"You have eight of them."

"I like them."

"Exactly. It's a passion."

"And *it* is what?" I grunt, interrupting their argument.

"Bikes," Casey explains.

"Bikes? Like bike bikes, or motorbikes?"

Casey laughs. "Motorbikes? I love this girl. Where did you find her? She's like my grandma in the body of a cute college chick."

I give him a mock glare. "I'm sorry, but maybe if you used more adjectives I wouldn't have to ask so many stupid questions."

"Adjectives? Sorry, hon, the writing part was his thing, not mine."

"That's obvious," I tease.

"Luke is awesome with adjectives," Casey continues.

"He is. One of the best."

Luke smiles and shakes his head. "Wow, thanks, guys," he says dryly.

"He also sucks at taking compliments," Casey adds.

"How's that possible? Isn't a love of being worshipped part of the superstar thing?"

"It's supposed to be."

"Just let me know if you need me to weigh in on anything

about myself," Luke interjects, and I smile over at him. He returns it, igniting another flutter inside me at the private connection. "Actually, I'll make it even easier for you to talk about me, and hit the restrooms. I'll be back."

He pushes away from the table, and we quiet as he takes off in the direction of the corridor to the bathrooms.

We watch him go.

"He's not good, is he?" Casey asks, the mood instantly settling. His tone is so subdued that I'm not sure he's even talking to me.

I don't answer at first and my gaze instinctively shifts to the chair. "No, he's not," I say finally.

Casey shakes his head and sighs, lost in thought. "You know, I've barely seen or spoken to him in months. Last night, today, it's the first time I've really spent time with him in a while. He's not the person I knew. Not even close."

"And I can't even imagine him being the person you knew."

"We both know two completely different people."

He's right, and I'm surprised by his insight. Despite his easy smile and playful demeanor, he's no idiot either. I'm not surprised they were close in another life.

"It appears so."

He quiets for a moment and picks at his napkin. "He wasn't a good person, Callie. It wasn't all his fault, he had a lot going against him, but he wasn't."

I swallow, not sure how to respond. I don't like hearing that, but I'm not surprised for some reason. I look up and notice Casey watching me. He wants good news.

"I think he might be now."

Casey nods and seems to relax a little. "I think he might be, too. I really do...If he recovers."

I'm disturbed by his qualification. It's probably all over my face.

"If?"

"He's not good, Callie. Luke's been like a brother for over ten years, and I'm telling you, he's not good."

His words tear at me, grinding at my heart. Maybe it's because I thought I was making a bigger difference than I am. Maybe my naiveté turned breakfast club into more than it is. Maybe I care about him way more than I should. Whatever the reason, I'm suddenly overwhelmed by the weight of the chair and the hidden monstrosity I can't begin to fight. How can I help him recover if I don't even know what's killing him?

"People are drawn to him. They always have been. It's hard to stay grounded when you're adored. It was harder for him than most because I don't think he's wired to be adored. He didn't know how to deal with it, and it all happened so fast for us once it hit."

I'm watching the shadow of the corridor now, absorbing Casey's words as best I can, which isn't very well.

"Is that why he left? He couldn't handle it anymore?"

Casey doesn't respond at first, and I know that's not why. But he's not going to give away any more of his friend's secrets. I actually respect him a lot for that.

"You seem like a cool person and it's obvious you care about him. All I'm saying is don't fall for him. Please." Casey is actually pleading with me now.

"Are you worried about me or him?" I ask.

"Both. He can't be worshipped right now. He needs an anchor not a dreamer."

His statement hits me hard. I want to be an anchor, but I'm suddenly terrified that I'm not. What if I'm a dreamer?

"I understand," I reply. I wish I could say more, he's expecting a promise, but I don't want to be a liar on top of everything else.

Luke is on his way back now. He doesn't look nearly as

broken as we just made him out to be. In fact, he looks so normal rounding the corner, rubbing his hands on his jeans to clear those last drops of water the paper towel always misses. For a brief moment, I wonder if we've misread him.

We quiet as he approaches, but I'm not sure how to pretend we weren't talking about him when I'm still reeling from the conversation. He seems to sense our tension, despite our weak attempts to hide it with fake smiles. He's too perceptive to believe fake smiles.

"So did I miss anything good?" he asks. We're being tested, but I have no idea how to pass.

"Nope. In fact we learned you know a lot more about your-self than we do, apparently."

I'm rewarded with a slight smile, but I don't think I did as well as I'd hoped.

"Well, since we're sharing, I learned the third sink in the men's room doesn't work."

The arrival of our food prevents what was poised to be a very boring, and awkward, conversation. I eye my French toast in anticipation, giving it way more credit than it deserves out of gratitude for saving this encounter.

"I like the powdered sugar. Nice touch," Casey comments.

I nod. "It's not too much, but just enough to add a hint of sweetness."

"Exactly. With the syrup, it would have been too sweet if they used any more."

"It's incredible, huh, that powdered sugar. They must have invested a lot of hours perfecting this particular application. Do you think they commissioned a full research study or just went with the classic focus group?" Luke asks, and then I catch the amusement seeping into his expression. He's mocking us, glancing back and forth between Casey's forced admiration and my forced enthusiasm.

I can't help but smile in return.

"You were talking about me, weren't you," he reasons. "Of course you were."

"We care about you," Casey responds.

"What did he tell you?" Luke asks me.

I can't tell if he's defensive, curious, angry, or intending to elaborate.

"C'mon, man. Nothing," Casey interjects.

I nod. "Seriously, Luke. Nothing. You have a good friend here."

"Right..."

We all quiet again and pretend our French toast is a fascinating mystery.

"You know, just once it would be nice if people stopped treating me like a mental patient," Luke spits suddenly.

Casey grunts. "Then maybe you should stop acting like one," he mutters.

I glance at him, startled, as Luke's eyes narrow.

"Yeah? Well, I don't remember asking you to stop in and check up on me. I don't want you guys dropping in on me because I don't need a nurse."

Now, Casey is getting riled. "Check up on you? I'm not checking up on you! You're my best friend, my brother! And I thought I was yours. Sorry if I'm supposed to be ok with you just disappearing from my life, but I'm not!"

"You know what? This was obviously a mistake."

"What? Becoming human again for five minutes?" Casey hisses. He leans forward with a fire I can feel across the table. "Look, I get it. You had a rough road. But it's time to get back up and move on. You think you're the only one who's suffering? You think yours was the only life ruined? You know that's not fair, and if anyone can understand this, it's me.

"And anyway, what about the other guys, huh? What about

your band, your *friends*? What about our dreams and lives that got all messed up when you walked away and left us with a shell of what we could've been? Do you ever think about that? You think we want to be playing nightclubs and opening for singing competition winners when we were booking stadiums a year ago? The Calisto Festival? God, what a joke." He draws in a breath and tosses his napkin on the table. "At some point suffering gets old and is just selfish. Call me when you're ready to be friends again."

With that, Casey pushes his chair back and storms from the table. I don't watch his exit because I'm too worried about Luke. He's staring again, the blank look on his face that tells me he's far away from this place. I'm not sure if I should say something to try to draw him out of it, or if returning him to the present will only make things worse.

"It's hard to argue that, isn't it?" he asks suddenly, surprising me. I glance over, expecting a vacant monologue, but he's watching me. I'm not sure what the right answer is. I don't even understand the question.

"What's hard to argue?"

"That I ruined everything."

"You mean the band? Their careers?"

"No, I mean everything."

He pushes back from the table and slaps some bills down on the table. Actually, he slaps a lot of bills on the table.

"That's what I do, Callie. I ruin things."

Now, I really don't know what to say. I don't know how to counter something I know nothing about.

"Luke..."

"I should go. Good luck."

I want to stop him as he leaves, suddenly terrified his strange ending was a final goodbye. Of course I need to stop him. It can't end like this. But I don't. By the time I know what I need to do, it's too late.

I bite my lip instead and stare at the table of French toast and assorted cash. I gather the bills into a neat little pile and realize they aren't all from this country. After pulling out the foreign ones, I signal Darryn who quietly hands over the check and spares me the embarrassment of a comment. I don't even cry until after I'm safely on the sidewalk.

I DON'T GO BACK the next day. Somehow I know Luke won't be there, and I don't want to subject myself to the disappointment. I think about him constantly, however. Picturing his face, his jacket, his expressive eyes. Wishing I was important enough for him to include me in his life instead of me secretly including him in mine.

I debate skipping the following day as well, but decide I'd never forgive myself if I missed him. I'm happy Shauna is on duty when I arrive. She seems to be the most understanding of the staff, but she hasn't seen him. I wait outside for a few moments, studying the crooked streams of pedestrians for any sign of Luke. Finally, I come to terms with my futile mission and slip Shauna a note with my phone number. She promises to send me a message if she sees Luke.

I don't hear from her for three days.

I push through the door in anticipation, my eyes scanning the café for signs of Shauna or Luke. I don't see him, but I catch a glimpse of Shauna's blond hair pulled back in a twist held loosely with a clip. I ignore Ailee and the chair and my table, and practically jump into Shauna's line of sight. Her eyes change when she sees me and she excuses herself from her customers.

"He was here this morning," she begins in a low voice.

I nod, concerned, waiting for the report.

"Didn't stay or anything, just came in and gave me this."

She pulls a small envelope from the pocket of her uniform and hands it to me. Shocked, I stare down at the artistic hand-writing, beautiful from a distance, but actually hard to read when I look closely. It's clearly my name, however, and sparks of nerves begin to flare through me.

"I texted you as soon as I could. It was only a little over an hour ago that he was here."

I smile and thank her, wanting to be polite but eager to escape with my treasure. She only shrugs, and it occurs to me that, as crazy as this whole drama seems to me, it's probably not the strangest thing she's had to deal with as a restaurant server in this city. I determine to give her a very generous tip if I ever eat here again.

For now, I nearly run from the restaurant and drop to a bench outside, not even able to wait until I return to my apartment to read the note. I pull the paper from the sealed envelope and am surprised by the indentation of the script pressing through the backside of the folded paper. There doesn't seem to be enough text hidden underneath to be worth the effort of this exchange, and I'm almost disappointed. Until I open it.

Shocked, I stare at the address for a moment, completely numb. It's a hotel, one of the top ones in the city, complete with a room number and the word, "anytime."

I stare at it in silence, trying to interpret this surprising turn and not explode from anticipation. Somehow, I instinctively know this isn't about sex. This isn't an invitation from a lonely rockstar to a desperate fangirl. This is a broken man reaching out to the only person he thinks might be willing to understand.

I move to the curb and flag a cab. Walking would be cheaper, but much longer, and right now time is more important than money. It's not a far drive, and I tip the driver more than necessary so I don't have to wait for change.

I've never been in this hotel before. Seen it, of course, with its massive columns and intricate stonework. Its handsome valets stationed at the entrance, greeting the wealthy, famous guests who don't blink at the ridiculous suite rates.

It's incredibly obvious to all of us that I don't belong, and it takes a moment for me to collect the courage to ignore the doormen's indignant stares as they're forced to open the vault for someone who clearly has no business going inside.

Once I'm beyond the gatekeepers, I forget all about their snobbery as I take in the majesty of this royal dreamland. Gold, tapestries, rich woods, velvet, art, flowers, statues, wealth. Everywhere wealth, status, celebrity.

I'm almost surprised Luke would choose this place, given his desire to escape everything it stands for, until I realize, it's not about that. He's a flashing neon sign in Jemma's Café but practically anonymous here, surrounded by the subjects of the other magazine pages and gossip websites.

I sense the disdain around me, mostly from the hotel employees, not the guests themselves who don't even notice me, but try not to let it get to me.

I've just spotted the elevator and started moving toward the welcomed escape route, when my path is blocked by a woman in a stunning tweed business suit.

"Excuse me, ma'am. May I help you?" she asks in a tone that indicates her "help" will most likely involve guiding me back to the exit.

I force a smile. "I'm here to meet a friend. Room 403."

Her look doesn't remotely hide her skepticism. "I see. Well, please wait here for a moment. I will call ahead and make sure your friend is available. I'd hate for you to waste your time."

I struggle to hold in my glare, but am impatient to see Luke and don't want to jeopardize my journey any more than necessary.

"Of course, thank you. You can tell Luke it's Callie."

It seems to surprise her that I have a name. That I use it so freely. That I speak his with such confidence.

She nods and thanks me. I wait awkwardly as she crosses to the main desk and directs the polished hostess to make the call. The girl looks over at me as well, and I almost would have preferred their blatant disrespect to this fake deference.

She picks up the phone and dials. Business Suit Woman waits beside her, watching me carefully, as if afraid I'll run into the elevator and contaminate the fourth floor with my poorness.

After a few seconds, someone must pick up on the other end because the girl starts talking. She looks surprised. She glances back at me and then at the other woman. She hangs up the phone and says something to the other woman who purses her lips and forces a tight smile. She heads back toward me, and I suck in my breath as I await the verdict.

"Thank you for your patience. Mr. Craven is waiting for you. Please let me know if I can be of further assistance."

I want to laugh at her, but manage to reduce my penalty to a polite thank you instead. Forcing that sentence from her mouth was punishment enough. Besides, all I can think about is Luke, waiting for me, wanting me here. Finally, inviting me into his life.

The elevator seems to take forever. I think maybe it's because it's old, but then realize it's probably just me and my impatience. I wish I'd taken the stairs when I notice the other guests tipping the uniformed boy who saved them from the gross inconvenience of having to push a button. I nearly grunt when I hand him a bill as well, and step onto the thick, soft carpet of floor Four.

I begin scanning the plaques on the doors to determine the numbering pattern and am surprised when I realize I only have three choices. These aren't rooms; they're bigger than my apartment.

Luke's suite is the furthest from the elevator, and I stand before his door for a moment, still in disbelief that I'm here. This moment doesn't seem real, and I think back to his comment once about feeling like you're living someone else's life. Maybe this is what he meant. Finally, my hand rises and knocks, my stomach fluttering and heart pounding in my ears. I try to remember it's only Luke. Rye toast, orange marmalade, Luke.

I hear scraping at the door and force myself to breathe. Then, it all falls away. It really is just Luke.

Our eyes meet and his smile brings me right back to pancakes at Jemma's.

"You came," he says, and I have no idea why he's surprised by that.

"Of course I did. Is that an invitation to come in?"

He shakes his head, almost embarrassed. "Yeah, yeah. Of course." He steps aside so I can enter, and I notice his relaxed look is incredibly sexy today. I hate that such a thought pollutes the moment. It's not fair to him.

"I came right from the café. I've been worried about you."

He nods and moves some papers aside so I can sit on the couch in the living area. The suite is as impressive from the inside as it is from the outside, but I don't spend much time on that fact. Instead, it occurs to me that even though he lives here, it doesn't look like he does. Other than the newly formed pile on the coffee table, I don't see any immediate evidence that this room is occupied.

"Can I get you anything? You want a drink or something?"

He's asking me, but I think I'm just an excuse for him to fill his own glass. I nod to let him complete his journey to the bar. He removes an expensive crystal glass from a tray and grabs a bottle.

"Whiskey, ok? I can send for wine or something if that's better."

I shake my head. I've actually never sipped whiskey before, but I'm not here to drink and don't want to waste time on alcohol procurement.

"Whiskey is great, thanks."

I wonder if he'll pull out cigars next, but my smile fades when I notice how much empty space is in the bottle. His glass is already full, and he takes a swig from it as he walks toward me to hand me mine. I had wondered since the day we met what he did with the other twenty-three hours, and I think I just found out. My heart breaks.

"I'm sorry for all of this, but I'm not ready to go back there."

"To Jemma's?"

He nods. "Casey was right. I don't belong there."

I'm not sure what he means by that, but I'm also not sure how to ask for clarification.

He laughs bitterly to himself. "You must think I'm a nut job."

I watch him closely before I respond, trying to understand the expression on his face. It's a mix between wry humor and self-hatred.

"It wasn't an insurance settlement," I blurt suddenly.

He looks at me. Most people would ask a question then. "What wasn't?" "What do you mean?" but Luke doesn't. He knows what I'm talking about. He has secrets so he remembers mine.

I study the dark liquid in my glass. I surprise myself by taking a giant swallow. It burns as it goes down, and I almost gasp and cough. I force it away, not wanting Luke to think I'm not like him, because I am in more ways than he can imagine.

I bite my lip and let the alcohol settle, rumbling in my empty stomach, still burning. I suddenly realize that we have hard liquor in our hands at ten in the morning. He still hasn't said a word, and when I glance at his face, I see that he doesn't intend to. I have the floor if I want it. Only *if*.

I stare back at my drink. "The reason I'm here, my money, it wasn't insurance. It was a different kind of settlement."

I meet his eyes. They're deep again, probing into me this time. "I was one of three employees assaulted by the owner of the grocery store where I worked." I look away. I'm still not sure it's ok to admit this part. "We didn't have enough evidence to prove it beyond a reasonable doubt, but we had enough to make his life miserable with a lawsuit, so he settled."

I feel the burn of tears somewhere deep inside of me, rising up into the open wound that I thought had scabbed over.

"My father was the one who pushed for me to take the money. He said it's the best girls like me can hope for." I laugh bitterly. "Of course, his daughter the 'victim' became his daughter the 'slut' when he realized I was of legal age so the money would go to me, not him." I glance at Luke. "So here I am. Living off a rich guy's money like a prostitute."

It was supposed to be a joke, but he doesn't think it's funny. I don't either; I just don't know how else to tell this story. He still doesn't speak. In fact, I'm starting to get concerned. I see his mind working, his eyes telling the story of his complex thoughts, but I can't interpret them. I wait, barely breathing, until he suddenly closes the distance between us and removes the glass from my hand.

My pulse pounds as the war rages in my head, conscience screaming, body pleading, but my brain already lost the second I'd decided to enter his room. I remember Casey's plea, echoing in my head like an alarm I'm too tired to acknowledge.

Luke takes my hand and traces the lines in my palm, igniting a longing that swells up and fills me with an addictive ache that's turning my willpower into a joke. I don't care anymore. If I don't touch him back, I will probably explode. I shift and lean into him. His arms tighten around me, and I suddenly feel safe, calm even. It's a strange contrast to the burning tension a moment ago. I wonder what it would be like to sit here forever, perfectly tucked in his arms, listening to the rhythm of his heart. Its rapid pace begins to accelerate which sends my own blood racing again.

"I really did miss talking you," he says quietly. "I wasn't sure you'd come."

"There was no way I wouldn't," I reply. He knows what I mean, and pulls me tighter.

"I know. I'm glad you did."

I want to say I am, too. I know he's waiting to hear it, but the words don't come out. I'm still not sure I am. I know my heart hadn't really given me a choice, but that doesn't mean my brain isn't going to torture me for giving in. What if Casey is right? What if I'm just filling the female role of the daily escape that includes drinking and sex? He certainly hasn't made any promises otherwise. Am I right where dozens, hundreds, of other women have been before me?

I settle into him, suddenly afraid to pull away. A hug is safe and buys us time, but we both know this encounter is not going to end in a hug. If I pull away... It doesn't matter. He does.

He doesn't fully let go, and his hands remain around my waist. Our faces are inches from each other, close enough that the next step isn't optional. Our eyes meet and my body ignites. I stare at him, knowing he's going to kiss me. Knowing once we start there's no way I will stop him. I've wanted it for a while now, dreamt about it, maybe even fantasized those long hours alone in my room, wondering where he was, wondering about that chair. There'd be no stopping it. I'm still not ready, but I don't know how to deny myself at this point. No one is that strong.

He moves toward me and draws me in. Gentle at first, testing my reaction, and I immediately sense his comfort with this situation. He's done this before. Many times. There's a huge gap in experience and now a new fear sets in.

"What's wrong?" he asks, concern all over his face.

I look away, slightly flustered. This isn't the first time the thought of his accomplished past has crossed my mind, but I hadn't realized it would be so obvious that I was out of my league.

"Nothing, it's just..." I'm not sure how to say something like that. I don't want to insult him, but suddenly I'm terrified of embarrassing myself more than anything else. I have no clue what he's expecting, but I doubt it's what he's about to get. "Look, I'm not good at this. I mean..."

"Not good at what?"

I lean back and wave my hands. "This. All of this."

"Kissing? Meeting up in hotel rooms? What?"

I shake my head. This is going terribly. Maybe that's good. Maybe he'll change his mind about the whole thing and I won't have to be the strong one anymore. His grin isn't promising.

"You worry way too much," he laughs.

I bite my lip. "I just thought you should know. I don't want you to be disappointed."

"Disappointed?"

"It's just..."

I don't get to complete my sentence. This time the kiss isn't gentle. It's the one I've wanted. The one I've been waiting for, dreaming about. The kind that takes your breath away, explodes brain cells. His hands are in my hair, guiding me, preventing any kind of instinctive hesitation. Not that I would have been able to stop myself at this point, anyway. I'm not entirely sure what to do with my own hands, and find myself gripping his t-shirt. I want it off him, to feel the heat of his body against mine, but I'm not confident enough for that. I'm still not sure about any of this. It doesn't feel right. I'm here with him, but I'm not entirely sure he's here with me.

We move to the couch, and I start to get more comfortable once I stop thinking. It's my head, that sprinting brain that revels in its ability to shoot itself in ten directions at once, considering every fear, consequence, and insecurity, paralyzing me in a constant daze of anxious numbness. It's that brain I finally manage to turn off, and I suspect Luke has had that effect on a lot of women in his life. The thought should sober me, but instead I find the ache returning, inciting an urgency that suddenly makes his t-shirt a barrier I can't stand anymore. I grab the hem, and he helps me pull it over his head.

Without his shirt, I can now feel his body against me. Firm, solid, he's stronger than I'd thought. I'm not sure why I'm surprised. The tattoos run along his shoulders and down his chest as well. If there had been any doubt about his past, there was none now. He is beautiful. A tragic work-of-art.

I like this even more and reciprocate by grasping the edge of my own sweater. He pauses, and I can feel his eyes, sense his anticipation. He's been waiting, too. Imagining what I look like under the layers that have always separated us. I'm nervous again but know I've invited this.

His fingers slide along the contours of my waist, leaving a searing trail of heat under my skin. I wait, not wanting to rush him, but nervous that the longer he waits, the longer he'll have to remember I'm not the supermodels he's accustomed to. It's not fair, petty even, but my brain stopped playing fair a long time ago. After another moment, I finally take his hands and lock them behind my back, closing the gap between us. My lips find his again, and this time there's no hesitation. I want every inch of him, mind, body, and soul. He understands, and I fall back on the cushions, pulling him with me.

His lips are on my neck now, and I close my eyes, gasping as the fire ripping through me tears apart the little that's left of any hesitation. He locks his fingers with mine and pushes my hands along the fabric, anchoring them above my head. This time it's his lips tracing my body, taking my breath away with each perfectly executed kiss. He lets go to focus his grip else-where, and I run my hands along his back, loving the way his muscles tense at every movement, and hint at the explosive power that will be mine in a minute.

Our contact is desperate now. A fervent magnetism that drives us into each other, connecting us in a uniform motion, a single resolution. We aren't able to get close enough.

"Are you ok? You're sure?" he asks. It's a silly question, but I love that he asks. The way his eyes search mine as he waits for the answer he already knows. I respond by kissing him again, reaching for his jeans.

"Ellie," he whispers.

I freeze. "Ellie?"

He does, too, and we stare at each other. Our breathing is heavy. The silence is like a massive curtain settling over us, pressing us into the couch, and suddenly his weight is more than I can bear. He understands and moves away, his head buried in his hands. It's then that I hear it, the sobs. I know now he's probably drunk, but realize it's the tears causing the drinking, not the other way around.

I close the distance between us as my heart shatters and wrap my arms around him. He leans into my shoulder, crying like the neighborhood bully after another beating from his abusive father. They're hard tears, unfamiliar, but completely wild as they push through the fortress protecting his battered soul.

We sit like that for a long time. The tears eventually subside into an embarrassed swat at his face, and he rubs hard, as if punishing his eyes for putting on such a display. I refuse to let him be embarrassed.

Instead of pulling away, I loop my arm through his and lean against him, gripping his hand in mine. I'm not looking at him anymore, instead staring at our reflections in the giant screen hanging on the wall across from us. I'm not letting him go. I'm not letting him face Ellie's ghost alone.

After another long pause, I can feel him start to relax. I run my fingers along his arm, partly out of my own fascination, but mostly to remind him I'm here, and he's alive. I don't need to see his face to know he's left me to go to that other place again.

"Her name was Elena," he says finally, his voice still trembling a bit as it cuts through the silence.

I don't respond. It's my turn to listen. But it quickly becomes clear that name is all I'm going to get. Ellie is Elena. End of story.

I'm not surprised by the stingy gift, just disappointed. I want more than anything to be his anchor, but he doesn't seem prepared to come into shore yet. I wonder if he'll ever be.

"That's a beautiful name."

"She was a beautiful person."

I nod. "I'm sorry, Luke. Really." I'm completely sincere but I can tell by his expression that my words don't mean anything to him. In fact, I suddenly sense that I understand even less about his story than I thought.

"I am, too," he says quietly. He shakes his head. "But nothing personal, right?" he snickers, pulling away and pushing himself up from the couch. I understand his joke, a ridiculous comment to make while we are both half-naked in a hotel room. He doesn't elaborate and moves back to the bar, draining his glass and refilling it. I instinctively want to stop him, knowing he's doing himself no favors by hiding in expensive liquor, but it's not my place. I will accomplish nothing by turning myself into the enemy. I have no choice but to accept him as he is at this moment.

I reach for my sweater and pull it back over my head. He watches me quietly, and I wonder about the darkness I see suddenly seep into his features. I hold my breath when he looks away.

"Callie, about what just happened, I'm sorry. About all of it. I shouldn't have asked you to come here. I shouldn't have...I just..." he doesn't finish.

"No one can do life completely alone. We're not supposed to."

He looks at me then. I'm close, I can tell.

I get up and join him at the bar. It's my turn to remove the glass from his hand. I place it firmly on the table and drop the remote in his hand instead.

"I'm free the rest of the day. Let's watch a movie."

The light returns to his eyes as a slow smile spreads over his lips.

"Really? You're sure?"

I nod. "One hundred percent."

"Comedy, ok?"

I almost laugh. "Definitely."

11

DAY TEN - FIFTEEN

Room 403 becomes our new Jemma's Café, and breakfast club becomes more of a brunch room service. Luke is careful to keep his distance when I visit, and we both understand more and more about what happened when I first came to his room. How the vacuum created by two empty souls sucked them into each other in a moment of mutual weakness. We don't regret the connection, just understand what it was and that it doesn't have an impact on the present.

We spend our days as friends now. Watching movies, chatting about safe topics, and drinking. Lots of drinking. Well, by Luke anyway. I try not to say anything as I watch him fill his glass over and over again. I'm actually amazed he functions as well as he does, given the amount of alcohol that's probably in his bloodstream at any given moment. I know it will be my business at some point in our friendship, but we need each other right now, and I can't bring myself to alienate him quite yet.

"Here," he says after about a week of my visits. "You might

as well just have this. It's not like I have anything here worth stealing anyway," he adds with a smile.

I roll my eyes, but my heart nearly stops when I peak inside the small, card-shaped envelope to see a key to his room. I stare up at him in shock.

"Are you serious?"

He shrugs. "I feel bad that you had to wait so long yesterday before I heard you knocking. Now I don't have to roll out of bed to let you in."

I laugh. "I see. So this isn't so much a statement about our friendship, but about your laziness."

He grins. "Basically."

"Business Suit Lady would lose her mind if she knew you did this."

"Business Suit Lady?"

"Yeah, the Guardian of the Lobby who gives me a death stare every time I soil these grounds with my commonness."

Luke laughs and drops beside me on the couch.

"You're talking about Mara Jacobson. Yeah, she's a piece-of-work."

"She's something alright."

I pull my legs up under me and lean back against the armrest to face him. "Really, though. Thank you. I promise I won't abuse the privilege. You tell me when you don't want me to come and I won't."

Luke waves his hand. "Nah, you'd be invited to all my wild parties anyway."

"Oh? What about the ones I want to host here?"

"Will there be pancakes and toast?"

"Absolutely. And all the orange marmalade you can handle."

"Whoa. Let's not get crazy now."

I laugh and study him for a moment. "Luke, tell me what it's like being a rockstar."

He glances at me before laughing. I think maybe it's an uncomfortable laugh, but he doesn't seem overly surprised by the question.

"What do you want to know?"

"I don't know. Anything. It's not every day a girl gets to hang out with one on his couch."

"Ah, I see," he replies, suspiciously. "So I was right all along. This whole thing was an elaborate ploy of a psychotic fangirl."

It's my turn to laugh. "Yeah right. A fangirl who had no clue who you were."

He grins, but studies me with that intensity that makes me want to climb inside his head.

"It's different than what people think, I guess."

"Different how?"

He shrugs. "They think it's all glamour and supermodels and drugs."

"It's not?"

He stretches and closes his eyes for a moment before staring at the far wall again. "Maybe it is at the end, I don't know. Not in the beginning."

"You mean when you were first starting out."

He nods. "Then it's all late nights, smelly vans, cheap hotels, and constant fear that your gear will get stolen."

"So no supermodels is what you're saying."

He lets out a snort. "No. You aim for the hot bartender, if you're lucky."

"And were you?"

He shrugs. "Sometimes."

He quiets, and I can tell I'm getting into dangerous territory again. He's determined not to let me, so he continues. "It's not an easy life. I've seen more people give it up than stick it out. You have no roots, no home, just night after night of setup and teardown. Lukewarm catered food, pizza, and cheap beer."

"Did you ever have your gear stolen?"

He grunts. "Yeah. We were parked at this cheap motel outside of Austin. We took the van to get something to eat, but left our trailer. It was locked but they still got in and took two guitars, a pedal board, and pretty much all of Casey's stuff. Thankfully, they left the in-ear system and most of the rest of the equipment. They obviously only took the stuff they recognized. Amateur thieves, I guess."

I laugh. "You lucked out then."

"Yeah. We could barely afford our gas at the time, let alone replacing all our equipment. Believe it or not, I was more upset about losing my pedal board than the guitars. I had my best one in my room. Those were backups I'd tune to different keys when we played 'Sanctimonious' and 'Argyle.'"

"Argyle? Like the sweater?"

"Like the only thing a kid sees as his father is beating him."

I swallow. "Oh."

He grins at my expression. "Still think we're a boy band?"

I shrug. "I don't know. The old ladies really love you."

"No, the old ladies want to make me vegetable soup and teach me Pinochle to keep me off the streets."

"Well, it's no wonder with your ripped jeans and frayed t-shirts!"

He instinctively glances at his shirt. "It's not frayed. It's worn. There's a big difference."

"Wow. I'm surprised in a place like this they can't afford better laundry service."

He laughs and shrugs. "You're very critical of my wardrobe. You would prefer me in polo shirts and khakis, I guess?"

I scrunch my nose, almost horrified at the thought. I can't

think of a more ill-suited look for him. "I see your point. Although, I'm dying to know what your tattoos would look like with a pink polo shirt."

"Pink, even? Wow. You have the strangest fantasies."

"What, fantasies about rockstars in pink polo shirts? You've never encountered worse? Come on."

He grins and shrugs with a mischievous expression. "Not until I got famous," he comments cryptically.

"That's not fair! Come on, Luke! Give me something!" I cry, instinctively leaning toward him in my earnestness.

He laughs.

"At least tell me the weirdest gifts you've gotten from fans. That has to be safe, right?"

He squints and bites his lip, as if deep in thought. "Weirdest gifts, huh? Let's see." I wait, not about to interrupt him. "Ok, once a fan gave me a calendar she made of shirtless pictures of myself."

I burst out laughing, and he returns my amusement. "Of yourself? Why in the world would you ever want that?"

He shakes his head in disbelief. "I have no idea. The guys just about died when she presented it to me at the autograph table. She waited in line for over two hours for that."

"Wow. That's devotion right there. I'm going to guess it didn't have the intended effect on your heart."

"Unless she was trying to get me to double my security for the rest of the night, no." He gave me a sly look. "What about you?"

I glance back, startled. "What about me what?"

"What's the worst gift you ever got?"

I laugh. "I can't top that, believe me."

"That's ok. You must have gotten something you hated at some point in your life."

I think about his question and wonder if my face resembles

his a moment ago. "Hmm...well, one time I got a stuffed cabbage."

His brows knit in confusion. "A stuffed cabbage? You mean a stuffed toy shaped like a cabbage or an actual cabbage."

I chuckle. "Does it really matter, given those options?"

He laughs. "I suppose not. Still, I have to know now."

I grin. "An actual cabbage. Well, cabbage leaves stuffed with some kind of meat."

"Was it good?"

"I didn't eat it!" I laugh.

"Why not? Maybe it was good."

"I had no idea where it came from or who made it. It was a door prize at some school event."

"They gave away a stuffed cabbage?"

I shrug. "Yes. Apparently."

He lets out his breath. "What kind of school did you go to? You weren't kidding about Sheltertown, were you."

"Shelteron."

"Whatever."

I shake my head in amusement and lean back against the cushions. After a long silence, I finally glance at him again. "You don't happen to still have the calendar do you?" I ask.

He glances at me in exasperation, and I laugh.

12

DAY SIXTEEN

I give Luke's door a gentle courtesy knock, but when he doesn't answer after two attempts, I let myself in. The room is dark, except for a small lamp on an end table, so I assume he is still in bed. Not wanting to disturb him, I grab the remote and plop on the couch, turning the volume low.

There isn't much on network TV that interests me so I try the movie channels. I find it strange that despite the six hundred options at my fingertips, there's not one thing I feel like sitting through. Maybe not so strange when I consider that I'm only here for Luke and he's absent.

Shortly after noon, it suddenly occurs to me that he may not even be in his room. I mute the TV and begin my self-tour of his suite. I'd never explored his accommodations apart from the main area, and figure now is as good of a time as any to satisfy my curiosity about how an ex-rockstar lives.

I figured the place had to be large. After all, basic math skills illustrate that, given the huge structural dimensions of this hotel and the tiny number of doors on this floor, each door has to be hiding a massive space. I was always good at math, but I'm still not prepared for what I find as I venture from the enormous open room of the main living area. I don't understand why a hotel room needs a corridor, but it has one. Two, actually, I learn, as I reach the end of the first and realize another juts to the right. I count one bedroom in my journey, which contains an unexpected custom stall shower along one wall of the room. The random bedroom-shower throws me for a loop, and I stand staring at the floor-to-ceiling glass, intricate stonework, and multiple jets. I spend a long time wondering why one would want to shower in their bedroom rather than the attached bathroom, how many people it was intended to accommodate at one time, and what I'd have to do to convince Luke to let me test it out. I notice the bench and controls, and suddenly realize it's a sauna, as well as, a shower. I'm even more impressed, if not confused, about the floor plan. I see no sign of human occupation, however, so quickly determine this is a spare room, not Luke's. Clearly, a guest of a guest would need a private wall shower.

The next room is an office. Not the particleboard desk with a lamp and hospital waiting room chair I'm used to, but an actual office. I see a giant oak wall unit with matching hutch, a solid hand-carved workstation that would make a lawyer jealous, and an actual, honest-to-goodness, coordinating filing cabinet. Because every rockstar needs a filing cabinet when they travel. I smirk, imagining Luke sifting through three-tab folders and hanging files with his ratty tee, ripped jeans, and glass of whiskey in hand. I'm not surprised that it appears I'm the first to even open the door to this room.

The next room is just another bathroom. There's a powder room off the main space for visitors, but this must be for those who get lost touring the suite and can't find their way back without a break. It's decorated in the same rustic stone style as the other bathing amenities I've seen, so I don't waste much time here.

Only one door remains, so I'm certain it must be the master suite. I hesitate as I approach the open doorway. It's dark inside, which leads me to believe it's probably vacant as well, but I'm still not totally comfortable about invading his space. The other rooms were easy. They didn't seem like his, for some reason, as though they still belonged to the hotel and he couldn't care less what happened to them. This room though...

My curiosity wins out, and I move toward the darkness.

The stench of alcohol assaults me when I enter, and I almost cough. Despite everything I've witnessed so far, I'm still surprised by this. Luke seems so together most of the time. He laughs and jokes and makes his way around the city. I'm very familiar with the bar in the main space, but the idea that the bulk of his drinking occurs back here hits me harder than I expect.

"Oh, Luke," I mutter to myself, shaking my head.

"What?"

I freeze. "I...I'm sorry...I was worried."

By now my eyes have adjusted to the darkness enough that I can make out the lump on the massive king-sized bed centered against the wall.

The lump doesn't respond, and neither do I, not sure if I should apologize again and leave in shame or call an ambulance.

"I'm fine," he lies. I know he's lying. I can hear it in his voice.

"It's after noon."

"So?"

"So, you're still in bed. Have you eaten today? I'll order something for you."

"I'm not hungry."

"Are you sick?"

"No. Just tired. I don't want company today. Sorry."

"Luke..."

"Callie, I don't want to be a jerk, but I need you to leave me alone right now, ok?"

It's not ok. His voice is trembling. I know now he wasn't sleeping.

"Luke, please. Let me..."

"Just go!" he shouts, and the lump transforms into a half-man as the comforter reveals a head and torso.

I know I should, but I can't.

I pause, my mind racing furiously, and yet in no clear direction at all. I get the heavy sense that I'm standing at a crossroads, although I suspect it's not just one on my journey.

I choose a path and sit on the edge of the bed. I don't look at him because I know I won't like the anger and accusation in his eyes, so I face the wall instead, staring in silence, daring him to physically remove me from his presence. I am fairly confident he won't because I know where he is right now and it's a place that rarely has the energy for such things.

"It's a curtain," I say quietly.

He doesn't respond, but I know he's listening. I turn and glance at him briefly so he knows it, and has to accept the fact that I'm not leaving until I've finished my speech.

"Depression, that is," I continue. "People who've never experienced it think it's a mask, but it's not. It's a curtain. And when it falls, it shuts you off from your life, plunging you into complete darkness. There you stand, arms flailing around you, reaching for anything to find your way back. But after exhausting yourself, grasping at only more darkness, you give up and drop to the floor in resignation.

"And so you sit. You and the blackness. You and the accusations. You and the self-hatred, the lies that become truth, the failure and pain and hopelessness and black thoughts that twist through you, impaling you to the floor. There you bleed, alone in your black hole, convinced the audience on the other side of the curtain has given up and gone home. The show is over.

"Before you know it, you realize the curtain has turned into a cement wall, and you couldn't escape the darkness even if you wanted to, but by now you don't care anymore. What's the point? There's nothing waiting for you on the other side, and even if there was, you're such a useless waste of space that you wouldn't dare to contaminate the world outside with your cancer anyway."

I stop, my eyes burning, my voice heavy in my throat.

"You feel like crying all the time but you rarely do. Depression isn't sadness; it's numbness. You don't have the energy for sadness. You can't sleep. You don't eat. You have no desire for the things you used to love, but it doesn't matter because you can't love anyway. You feel nothing, just a dull, heavy ache that makes it hard to breathe sometimes, let alone get up to start the search again. You fantasize about disappearing, just erasing your pointless existence and sparing the Earth from your toxic presence. By now you're so exhausted just from the effort of living that there's nothing left to live it."

I wipe my face now, the tears dripping down my cheeks. I had almost forgotten about Luke. I'd stopped talking to him somewhere along the way, lost again in the caverns of my own backstage nightmare. But when I remember, I don't give him a choice. Too many people had let me choose.

I lie down on the bed beside him and take his hand. I can tell the action has startled him, but he doesn't pull away. I squeeze, holding tight, warning him that he's crazy if he thinks I'm letting him do this alone. I don't expect him to respond. In fact, I hope he doesn't. I hear the soft sound of his breathing as he stares at the ceiling, my words disrupting the void around us.

"It's Depression, Luke," I whisper into the darkness. "And it's lying to you."

———————

"DID you ever try to kill yourself?" Luke asks finally, after a long silence. I had begun to wonder if he'd fallen asleep.

I consider his question for a moment. It's a simple question with a very complex answer.

"Consciously?" I ask, even though I know the answer.

"Yes. Did you knowingly try to kill yourself?"

"No," I answer honestly. "No, not on purpose."

My answer has an effect. "By accident then," he concludes, and I squeeze his hand again. I hadn't let go and I don't plan to.

"No, it wasn't an accident either. Somewhere in between."

"Meaning?"

"Meaning I made destructive choices to escape without caring where I was escaping to."

"You didn't try to kill yourself, but you didn't care if you did."

"Something like that."

"Drugs?"

"I picked fights."

"Picked fights?"

"With my dad, my boyfriend, strangers, whoever got near me. I wanted them to hurt me. I wanted them to hate me as much as I hated myself. I wanted them to punish me for existing."

"And did they."

"Sometimes."

"Your boss at the grocery store?"

I quiet. "No. That was something else."

"I'm sorry. You don't have to talk about it."

"I know. I will one day, but not now."

It's his hand applying the pressure this time, and I'm relieved for a variety of reasons. I turn toward him and wrap my arm around his chest, pulling him close to me. "I know Depression, Luke, and I know you want to be alone, but I'm not going to let you. I can't make you let me in, but you're going to have to get used to the fact that I'll be here when you're ready."

He still hasn't moved, and I can see his eyebrows knit together in the dim light as he continues staring at the ceiling.

"I'm not who you think I am, Callie," he says after another pause. "If I let you in, you'd know I deserve my prison."

13

DAY SEVENTEEN: PART I

I get the frantic call early in the morning, before I'm showered, dressed, or sufficiently roused by my cup of black tea. Definitely before I'm equipped for drama. It's Shauna, and if I don't get over to the café in the next five minutes, the cops will be involved.

My heart stops long before she confirms the disruption involves Luke, and I have my jeans and sneakers on by the time we end the call.

I can hear the yelling as I approach Jemma's. Evacuated patrons and random bystanders are huddled on the sidewalk, attempting to peer through the door, the windows, each other, with looks of fear and curiosity.

"Excuse me! Please! Let me through!" I cry, pushing past them.

I hear some curses, but also warnings as I plow forward. There's a crazy homeless guy in there. No, he's not homeless, just a café regular who's lost his mind. He's trying to rob the place.

I glance back in surprise at that one, I can't help myself.

Still, I don't need more speculation, I need the truth, so I don't ask and continue my journey.

By the time I get through the crowd and into the café, there are only a few brave patrons left, mostly the regulars who have come to expect such erratic behavior from the weird chair guy who turned out to be someone important. The rest of the witnesses are staff members. Both Darryn and Shauna are on today. Lucky them.

"Why can't I have it? You have a hundred of them!" Luke cries. The Chair is firm in his grip. A table is overturned, a shocked audience curved around the scene. The manager has her hands up in surrender, using her managerial crisis training to try to calm the crazed guest. The problem is, he's not crazy.

"Luke!" I call, rushing toward the front of the circle.

His desperate eyes turn on me, rooting me several feet away.

"What are you doing?" I ask, forcing myself to take a step forward. He moves back. "They're going to call the police. They'll arrest you," I reason.

He shakes his head, eyes dark. "So what? They should."

I soften and cover more of the distance between us.

"You don't want that," I say.

"You know I do," he replies, the pain starting to replace the anger.

It hits me harder than I expect, the transformation, the bitter consequence of my attempt to reach him yesterday. My speech was supposed to be a cautionary tale, not an instruction manual.

"Luke..."

"Leave me alone, Callie!"

I shake my head. "No!"

"I said, leave!" he cries, swinging the chair in my direction. I duck away, surprised by the outburst, but not prepared to give up. His aim was too bad for him to have had any intention of hurting me. The others don't realize that, they don't know him well enough, and gasp at the new violence. I can see Ailee dialing the phone.

"Luke, please! This won't help you escape! You want to hide? How will you hide with the cameras and reporters? You really want another mugshot for the tabloids?"

That argument has an affect, and I can tell what I said means even more to him than I'd thought.

He glances around the room again, suddenly seeming startled, and drops the chair with a curse. Another string of expletives slips from his mouth as he locks his hands on his head in distress.

"We're sorry. So sorry!" I explain to the manager who's look is somewhere between fear and fury. "It won't happen again. You won't see him back here."

"I better not!" she hisses. "We will call the cops the second he touches the door."

I nod, completely understanding her position, and turn back to Luke. He's broken again. No longer a threat, just a terrified stranger staring at a chair.

"I need it, Callie," he whispers as I approach. His eyes search mine, willing me to understand, to help him. "Please, just explain it to them."

"I know, Luke. But it's not going to help you. It's not," I reply softly, taking his arm.

He shakes his head, angry tears in his eyes. "Please. Please!" he repeats, one last desperate appeal to the manager.

She glares at him, but waves her hand with a curse. "Fine, take the damn chair. Just get out of my restaurant and never come back!"

I'm still not sure it's a good idea for him to permanently

possess the haunted object, but at the moment, it keeps him out of jail so I have no choice but to accept it.

He sighs with relief, and I see the visible change as a weight seems to lift from his shoulders. He picks up the chair and heads toward the door. I apologize profusely to every face I can't avoid and do my best to clear an awkward path.

WE WALK BACK to his hotel. Him with his chair, me with my apologies to those we displace on the sidewalk as we march past. I don't know what to say to Luke, so I remain silent, focusing instead on making sure we arrive safely at our destination, still afraid the manager called the cops after all, and they'll be showing up any minute to take the crazy rockstar into custody. I'm sure he's legally drunk, so the media would be merciless with that report. As it is, I'm almost certain bystander photos and recordings of his outburst are going to explode into the pop culture conversation anyway, fueling the thirst for celebrity blood with another tragic train wreck.

The Chair will be famous now, too.

I don't think Luke understands that yet. What he's done, the firestorm he's just exposed himself to hasn't registered, but it will soon, and I suck in my breath at what he'll face. The ghost chair will now be legend, encased in speculation, investigated with a rabid persistence that will scrape old wounds raw.

I glance back at his face, and am surprised at the stern concentration. Maybe reality is starting to settle in his mind as well, or maybe he's simply trying not to trip with his heavy burden, but either way I have hope that once we're safely home we can reason through this. The present. The future.

The doormen give us a strange look as we approach, eyeing the chair with their characteristic skepticism, but it's in the hands of Luke Craven of Night Shifts Black, so they respond by opening the door a little wider than usual. I'm sure my reception would have been less accommodating.

"Mr. Craven! A new purchase? Please let us help you with that!" Mara Jacobson cries, rushing toward us as we enter.

"Thanks, Mara. I got it."

She glances at me, her expression more veiled than usual, and I give her a stiff smile.

"Thanks, Mara. We got it," I repeat just to watch her squirm.

She does, but has no choice except to nod in defeat. "Well, of course if you change your mind, let us know," she says, and Luke barely acknowledges her as he continues toward the elevator.

I follow him in, shifting to allow him enough room for his chair, and he finally lowers his burden to the floor. He shakes out his arms and stretches as the elevator boy pushes the buttons. Despite everything, I can't stop the slight grin of amusement as I watch the poor teenager try not to react to the strange scene. Luke seems to notice too, and when his eyes catch mine, my grin breaks. He returns it, and I suddenly feel safe again.

"Thanks, Aiden," Luke says, slipping him a bill larger than anything I'd ever tipped a server at a restaurant. Aiden will not be talking about the chair, that's for sure. I give him a smile as well as I exit onto Luke's floor and follow him to his door.

I can see him struggling with the chair and push past him.

"Here, I got it," I say, producing my own key and sliding it into the slot.

He gives me a grateful smile, and I hold the door for him as he shuffles past me.

I'm about to speak when I realize he's lost in his head again.

This time it's not sadness, but the same concentration I saw on the sidewalk journey.

He stands at the top of the step leading into the giant, open living area, surveying the space with an intensity I've rarely seen before. I don't dream of interrupting, and watch him from a distance, curious about the latest glimpse into his confusing mind.

First he moves an end table against the wall and places the chair in the empty space beside the couch. He studies it for a moment, but isn't happy, and moves the end table back. Next, he tries the space under the bar. He's even less satisfied with that.

"The office," I suggest gently.

His head shoots up in alarm, and I suspect he'd forgotten I was here.

"I have an office?" he asks, and only the serious expression on his face keeps me from laughing. I figured as much.

"Second door on the left. After the extra bedroom."

He hesitates, staring at the chair.

"It's yours, Luke. No one else should have access to it."

He nods and removes it from the bar.

I follow him down the hall, completing our strange parade, and watch as he tests the doors to each room. How long has he lived here and he never even bothered with them?

"Wow, you're right," he observes, moving inside and turning on the light. "I should do more paperwork," he jokes, and I almost laugh that I'd had the same thought.

"There's a nice filing cabinet, too, for you to keep it organized."

He gives a wry smile, and I return it. Then, he focuses back on the chair. He moves a fake plant in the corner and puts the chair in its place. He steps back to admire his work and nods in satisfaction.

"Perfect," he says. "Good call." Then he turns to me with a quizzical look. "You know my suite well."

I shrug. "I'm a poor girl. This place was worth exploring."

He nods, but doesn't chastise me. I don't know if he forgives me or just doesn't care. Maybe both.

"Anything else I should know about?"

I grin. "Actually..." I take his hand and pull him from the room. We move back to the first door, and I push him into the guest room.

"Can you please explain that?"

He laughs, and I love that life has finally returned to his eyes. "I wish I could, but I have to admit that this monstrosity threw me for a loop as well."

I sigh with mock disappointment. "You're supposed to be my guide into all things ostentatious and ridiculous."

He gives me a sheepish grin. "Sorry. If I had to guess, this suite was custom built for someone who is no longer here."

"Someone who felt the need to offer their guests multiple showering options," I observe.

I continue to stare, still fascinated by the absurd luxury, and can feel his amusement. I blush when my gaze catches his.

"You're dying to try it aren't you," he teases, and I swallow.

"What? And you're not?"

He laughs again and moves into the room. "The shower or sauna?"

"Both?"

He grins and opens the glass door, inspecting the many buttons and knobs. He triggers two of them and the steam unit buzzes to life. He closes the door and steps back as bursts of hot air begin filling the sealed glass case.

"Not now!" I cry, laughing at his crooked grin.

"Why not?"

"I don't have clothes or anything!"

"Here."

He moves to the closet and removes a luscious robe that's more enticing than any blanket or comforter I've ever touched. "I'm sure there's shampoo and whatever else you need in the real bathroom right through there."

"You're not serious," I breathe. "You are serious!"

He shrugs, tosses me the robe, and closes the door before I can respond.

LUKE IS LOUNGING on the couch when I emerge from the guest room, wet and relaxed, wrapped in my cozy robe.

"Thoughts?" he asks with a knowing grin.

I return it and drop on another section of the massive sofa. "Surprisingly effective as a shower. Verdict is still out as a wall of a bedroom."

He laughs and motions toward the bar.

"You want something?"

I shake my head. "No thanks."

He shrugs and finishes off his glass before relegating it to the end table beside him.

"You know, I was thinking, you can keep some stuff in the guest room if you want. For the next time you feel the need for a shower in the middle of the day."

I stare at him for a moment. He's not looking at me and already seems to be worrying more about working up the energy to refill his glass than anything to do with me. I have no idea what to make of the shocking offer he's already seemed to forget.

"Sure, maybe at least a change of clothes," I manage as casually as possible.

He nods, and finally pushes himself up from the couch.

Will he even remember he made the offer later? I try to guess how drunk he is, but it's almost impossible to tell with him.

"I'm having some people over tonight," he continues as if he hadn't just dropped the bombshell that's left me reeling.

"Ok," I say, somewhat disappointed. "When do you need me out of here?"

He glances over at me in surprise. "You're not staying?"

It's my turn to be surprised. "You want me to stay?"

He looks at me like I'm stupid and shakes his head. "Why wouldn't I? You think I'd offer you a room in my suite and then kick you out for a party?"

I swallow. Offer me a room. But somehow I sense that this "giving me a drawer" thing doesn't mean the same thing for the two of us as it does for most people. I have no idea what it means, only that I'm not about to refuse it.

"Well, I know I'm not really part of your other world."

He lets out a bitter laugh and removes the lid from the decanter. "My world." He spits the words like it's some cruel joke. "No one is part of that world, sweetheart," he mutters, taking a swig. "It's not even real."

He must sense me staring at him, waiting for more, but instead only waves his hand with a dismissive laugh this time. "I'm drunk," he explains in the most obvious statement of all time.

It's my turn to laugh. "Yeah. You are. You sure you're up for having people over?" I ask, concerned. I study him closely. Today was a hard day. I would have questioned his intention to fill the void with his old life even if he hadn't spent most of it drinking and acting like a crazy person.

He glares at me, and I know I've pushed the overprotective-ness too far.

"How about you just get ready? You may want to change into something less...Sheltertown."

"Shelteron," I correct, matching his annoyed eye roll.

"Whatever."

"And what's that supposed to mean, anyway?"

He shrugs. "I don't know. Nothing. Wear what you want." But I hate the way his eyes scan me this time. It's the first time I've seen him evaluate me as anything except his friend Callie.

"You know what, I should probably just go back to my place. Maybe we could use some time apart. I wouldn't want to embarrass you with my Shelteron-ness," I mutter, rising from the couch.

"Callie..."

I ignore him and make my way toward the guest room and my clothes.

"Callie, wait!"

I hear him call after me, but there's no point in answering. He's right. I have no business with his "people" and their "less Shelteron" attire.

I've already slipped on my underwear beneath the robe when the door opens after a brief knock. I spin around with indignation at the invasion of privacy, but my protest freezes on my tongue at the look on his face.

"Callie, I'm sorry. You know I didn't mean anything by that. You're my only friend right now. My only real one, I just..." he stops, and I can tell he's sincerely trying to explain. "I'm not worried about me, but about you. I want you here tonight, but I know these people, and I don't want you to feel underdressed. I don't want you to be uncomfortable and want to leave. That's all I meant. Really."

"And you think I'd feel underdressed in your bathrobe?"

He seems startled at first, then grins when I do. "Maybe less so than the dirty jeans and hoodie you had on when you rescued me this morning."

I sigh. "I know, Luke, but that's what I'm trying to explain to you. A nice dress isn't going to change the fact that your people are not my people. I'm not going to be comfortable no matter what I wear."

He looks away, and I know I've hurt him somehow but I don't understand how.

"Ok, sure, yeah," he says finally with a weak smile.

Then, I get it. He's still torn between two worlds, the one where he belongs and the one where he wants to be. His past and his present. I've been so consumed by my role in his present that I'd given very little thought to what it must be like to have such a powerful past constantly pulling you back.

"Here," he says, pulling out his wallet. "There are shops on the second floor, by the spa. Go get yourself something. You won't even have to go all the way back to your place."

I almost laugh at the absurd thought, but manage to hold it in. He doesn't mean anything by it. He's not trying to offend me. Money means nothing to him. The ridiculous offer was just a simple solution to a current problem. I'm actually touched that he cares so much.

"Thanks, but I'll just go home and change. It's a ten minute cab ride, not a big deal."

"You sure? You don't have to go."

I almost change my mind when I suddenly realize it's not about me at all. He doesn't want me to go. He doesn't want me to leave him alone with today. With his poor choices, his guilt, his thoughts about reality. His upcoming battle to survive a night with "his people."

But I have limits, too.

"It's fine. Really. I'll go home and change and be back in a couple hours, ok?"

He forces a quick smile, awkward almost, and shakes his head. "Yeah, of course. Yeah. Sorry. See you later, then." He backs toward the door.

"Luke, hey," I call after him, grabbing his arm. He stops, and I squeeze. "I'll be back soon, ok?"

He laughs, but there's no humor in his eyes. "Yeah, of course. I have some things to take care of anyway."

He pulls away and moves in the direction of his own room. I sigh and finish pulling on my clothes.

FOR SOME REASON, I don't want to rush back. I'm not sure what to make of the awkward end to our day. I pull out my best cocktail dress, sexy, but not slutty, and spend more time than I ever have before on hair and makeup. My goal is to completely disguise myself from Lobby Queen Mara Jacobson. Not because I care what she thinks, but because I'm amused by the challenge.

I slip on a pair of earrings and devastating heels, and stare at my reflection in the floor-length mirror on my closet door. I stare for a long time, scrunching my nose, surprised, maybe slightly disappointed, at what I see. It's still me.

Sure, it's a glamorized, polished version of me, but my eyes are the same color, my face the same shape. I'm taller and thinner from the heels, and my curves are more pronounced, but it's definitely me. A girl from Shelteron pretending to be a girl from Hollywood. I'm almost angry with myself, embarrassed as it occurs to me that I'd actually thought I could somehow be one of "them" just because I tried to be. That deep down I had liked the idea of proving it was just fancy clothing and makeup that separated us. That I could fit into Luke's world if I wanted to, I was just too good for that. I didn't fit because I didn't care, not because I couldn't. But as I sense the unexpected disappointment creeping in, I realize my disdain isn't for them, like I'd thought. Maybe for one night I actually did want to be one of them. Maybe there is something more complex separating his world from mine, something I didn't understand as well as I'd thought.

Maybe he'd been right to ask me to go home and change into something less...Shelteron.

I glance at the clock and realize it's later than I'd thought. I don't know what time an event called "having some people over" starts, but I plan to be the first. I want access to Luke before anyone else, and yes, that includes having his undivided attention as he observes the startling truth that even girls from Shelteron, Pennsylvania own makeup and killer shoes. Then, my eyes fall on my laptop.

As the days have passed, it's been getting harder and harder to resist the urge to open it. To search on the vast stores of truth and lies out there about the man I've come to care about deeply. Luke fills me with so many questions, and I know some of the answers could be at my fingertips, but I've been terrified of letting what we have be tainted by other people's interpretations of his past. I care about him too much to let my opinion of who he is be corrupted by who he was. Casey had only cemented my fear that day at Jemma's, warning me about a Luke I didn't know and can't imagine. The Luke that everyone knows but me.

I swallow as I realize that if I go tonight, if I truly enter his world, I might meet that Luke. I might meet the man I've been afraid of, and I shouldn't do it blindly. I sigh and drop to my bed, pulling the laptop off the nightstand and firing it up, even as every ember of my conscience screams against it. Still, it's time. I'm not going to be naïve, and it's not like I'm going to learn anything everyone else doesn't already know. He can't expect me to remain completely ignorant in a world that's left him totally exposed.

It turns out to be a simple search. So simple. He's everywhere. Pictures, articles, websites, everything I could possibly want to know about Luke Craven of Night Shifts Black is right in front of me. Well, everything except what I actually know. And yes, maybe everything that's actually important.

I close my eyes, my fingers hovering, stuck between temptation and loyalty. He had asked me once, practically begged me, not to let these pages impact who I thought he was. I'd held out for so long, but I can't do it anymore. Why should I have to? I shut off my conscience. I can't deal with that right now.

Opening my eyes, I jump in.

I start with the images. There are hundreds. No, maybe thousands. I don't know how you can even tell, but I skim through them, stopping longer at the ones that catch my attention. Luke's face and body is all over my screen. Many of the photos are clearly professional. Staged shots for album covers, magazine shoots, promotional materials for the band and sponsors. He's rarely fully-clothed in these images, and I'm not surprised as I study them intently, trying to convince myself it's only research. It's only because I care. But the truth is plastered all over my screen, bare and visceral. If I were his manager, and my client could market sex the way he does, I'd never let him wear clothes in front of a camera. Never.

I blink as my blood starts to pound, the images doing exactly what I feared they would, exactly what they're intended to do, market Luke Craven as a commodity. A commodity my young, female body desperately wants to possess.

I suck in a deep breath and force myself to keep going.

There are many other pictures also. Some are harmless. Red carpet shots, live performance photos, fan pics, but my gaze starts getting stuck on the less innocent ones. These come with headlines. Rumors. Drugs. Disturbances. Disputes. Arrests. I skim some of the articles themselves, but they don't seem real for some reason. It's his name, sure, but the person they're describing isn't the man who offered me a drawer in his guest room. The man who loses sleep over a chair.

It's time. I've delayed long enough, and I add the name "Elena" to my query.

I slam my laptop shut.

I saw it. It was too big, on too many links. I couldn't escape it in time. I knew I shouldn't have done this. I close my eyes and clench my fists, wanting to run to him and hide from him at the same time. I shouldn't have given in, but I did, and now I've sentenced myself to the truth. One word. One clue that changes everything. And now it belongs to me, too.

Suicide.

14

DAY SEVENTEEN: PART II

I can hear the music blasting from Luke's suite as soon as I step off the elevator. Aidan, the elevator boy, and I exchange a look as he holds the door for me. I know he recognizes me, even if he's as surprised as I am that I've tried so hard to not look like me.

"You look great," he offers, and I can't tell if he means it or if he's just fishing for a bigger tip. I give him the same amount as always, but he doesn't seem upset. Maybe he actually meant it.

I don't bother knocking on Luke's door. Luke and I had done away with that formality a while ago, but I doubt this is the kind of party where anyone would answer a door anyway. These aren't people who knock.

I'm not sure what to expect as I open it, but it's certainly not what I find. "Some people" means something very different to Luke Craven than it does to me. Music blares, the lights are dimmed to an uncomfortably low level, and voices swell around me. Laughing, talking, shouting, beautiful people pressed together everywhere. And sex. Lots and lots of sex. Not the shocking kind from Roman orgy documentaries, but the

obscure kind, the subtle kind oozing from every flirtatious interaction and scantily clad body. The kind I'd just seen saturating
every professional image of Luke. The kind that doesn't define
sex as an act but as a lifestyle. It's everywhere and nowhere at
the same time.

I'm about to turn and leave when I feel a hand on my arm. I
spin toward it, expecting Luke, and fear I don't cover my disappointment enough when Casey leans close.

"Breakfast club girl!" he shouts toward my ear.

I force a smile. "Rock god!" I return, and he laughs. He's
clearly already well on his way to a great time, and I make the
decision right then to stop fearing and resenting Luke's world.
How can I even start to understand him if I don't try to understand what created him?

"Where's Luke?" I ask, and Casey points toward the main
living area.

"Come on! I'll get you a drink."

I can feel him looking at me as I pass, and I realize, in yet
another self-shaming moment, that I don't hate the attention. In
fact, it feels good to be admired. To be wanted. Even if deep
down I know I would do anything to have Luke look at me the
way Casey is. I also find it hilarious that he's trying to guide me
through a room in which I spend more time than my own apartment. It's a valiant maneuver, however, so I allow him to show
me around.

A tour guide turns out to be more helpful than I'd thought.
I do my best to take in the lights and sound, but the peaceful
oasis in which Luke and I have spent hours in escape has been
transformed into a club-like atmosphere I barely recognize.
Women who must be famous for being beautiful sway and
move to the music, cocktails in hand, smiles suggesting they're
waiting for something. I'm not sure what, so I quickly move on,
still concerned that I don't see Luke.

"Here!" a voice interrupts behind me, and I turn to meet Casey again. He hands me an empty champagne glass and holds up a sealed bottle with a mischievous glint.

"I can tell you're cautious. You don't trust us wild rockers!" he calls, opening the seal on the bottle. He pops the cork and fills my glass. He's not wrong, and I smile in-spite of myself. I would not have accepted a drink from him, or anyone. Not unless I'd watched him pour it himself. I'm actually kind of impressed that he thought of it, but then can't help but wonder why he'd thought of it. Some answers are more flattering than others, but there's something about him that's always seemed genuine, so I go with the flattering ones.

"To Luke," he says, holding up his own glass.

I stare at the bubbly liquid and nod. Fair enough.

"To Luke."

I take a tentative sip and am afraid I don't cover my reaction fast enough. Casey laughs at my expression.

"Undercover princess, my ass!" he cries. "You've never even had good champagne before!"

I shrug with a grin and empty the glass. "A girl could get used to this," I agree. He refills my glass, then his own, before placing the bottle on a table and pulling me toward the music.

"Where are we going?" I cry.

"To dance!" he returns.

"What? No way!"

He rolls his eyes and clearly has no intention of accepting a refusal. It's my turn to laugh, and I let him lead me to the tight pack of swaying bodies.

"Hey, darling!" a gorgeous brunette purrs as we work our way through the crowd.

Casey accepts her embrace and kiss on the cheek, but I don't miss the brief shadow that washes across his face. Her arm remains tightly around his neck as they exchange more words, and I find myself getting slightly jealous. Ridiculous, since I barely even know Casey, let alone care who touches him. It's probably just my insane fear that if he abandons me for this woman, I will have no idea what to do with myself next.

The interaction doesn't last long, and the other woman eyes me with a mix of suspicion and disdain as he pulls away. She gives him another kiss, this one less polite and more determined, but he only smiles and ducks away with a very satisfying awkwardness.

"Sorry about that," he says to me when I finally get him back. "Ex-girlfriend."

"Ex? Does she know that?" I ask, and he shrugs with a smile.

"Sometimes the lines get blurred," he explains. "Ok, enough stalling. Let's dance!"

I manage to forget all about my discomfort, and even Luke, as Casey pulls me close. I know this means nothing to him, that this is yet another night in the life of a rockstar, that I'm yet another decent-looking girl in a tight dress he can impress for a bit, but for me, every sound, smell, second, is like a dream I'm trying to absorb before reality dumps me back in my one-bedroom aimless existence.

Casey reminds me a lot of Luke, at least, according to the champagne, and as it works its way through my system, I start to find him extremely attractive. His hair is darker than Luke's, almost black, and his eyes hold a constant amusement that's the opposite of Luke's saturated depth. I suspect that Casey would make me laugh if I let him. Humor without the constant eggshells. Right now, that's exactly what I need, someone I can't break, and when he pulls me against him, I suddenly remember the photos I'd just seen of him as well. Apparently, not wearing clothing is a popular pose for rockstars, drummers included, even though at the time I had skimmed over Casey's images in search of Luke. Now, I wish I hadn't. I suck in my breath at the annoying thought, knowing it's not real, this sudden attraction. Casey isn't Luke, and part of me is just grateful to him for taking me under his wing and showing me a good time. But as the moment pounds on, I find it harder and harder to care what my brain thinks.

Our bodies are close now, moving together with the music, pulsating in the sensual wave of light and heat surrounding us. Couples on all sides are touching each other, lips coming together, exploring, laughing, drinking. I glance up at Casey and am startled to meet his expression, very different than what I'd expected, what it was just a moment ago. I almost feel hurt as his constant smile fades and he puts some distance between us. He gives me a quick, almost apologetic, twist of the lips.

"I'm thirsty. Let's go get a drink," he shouts, taking my hand and leading me away from the group.

Surprised, and yes, disappointed, I nod and follow him toward the kitchen island which has been transformed into a full-service bar. Instead of more champagne, however, he asks for water, and the bartender pours a glass for each of us. Then Casey pulls out a stool for me, and drops to the one beside it.

"Whew. It's hot in here, huh?" he says, holding the glass up to his forehead. I know he's just trying to explain away the sudden retreat, but I'm not buying it.

"Is everything ok? Is it your ex-girlfriend?" I ask.

He looks confused, then laughs. "Jana? No."

"Oh, I see. So it's me. I'm just a terrible dancer."

He grins again. "Yes, that's it." Then grows serious when I refuse to let him off the hook.

"You don't want to sleep with me, Callie," he states bluntly.

I almost choke on my water. "What?"

He shrugs. "Am I wrong? Is that where you wanted that to go?"

"We can't dance without sleeping together?"

He shrugs. "You tell me. Would you have let me kiss you out there?"

I look away, starting to understand. "Probably."

"You would have. And you would have loved it," he adds with a glint that somehow makes the boast sweet instead of obnoxious. His smile fades as he shakes his head. "Anyway, this isn't your scene. I'm trying to remember that. The normal rules don't apply."

I swallow and look away. There it is. I'm filled with some strange mix of embarrassment, anger, gratitude, and admiration. I certainly hadn't expected Casey Barrett of Night Shifts Black to play the gentleman, and I don't know how to thank him without admitting he's right, I don't belong here. I certainly don't belong with him.

Then, my eyes catch a glimpse of Luke, and I forget all about the awkward moment. Casey senses my shift and follows my gaze across the room. Distracted, I miss his reaction as my stomach turns at the sight of Luke surrounded by three women, all clearly from a magazine cover. Their hands run over his body as they move in sync with the music. Even in the dim light, I can see that he's wasted. The women may be dancing, but he's just trying to stay upright. I notice they're practically supporting him, his other hand braced against the wall. One of the models pulls his shirt over his head, tossing it aside, and he laughs for a second before her mouth covers his. They all move in, shoving him into the wall. I can barely see him anymore.

Tears burn my eyes as I stare in shocked horror. I don't know what to do. He's so out of it, he can't possibly be making this choice. And yet, I know somehow he made this choice the second he decided to "have some people over." This is his world. Like he said. This is what he meant. This is what he wanted. This is today's escape from the emotional scars. My efforts aren't enough anymore.

"He doesn't care about them," Casey says gently. "I doubt he even knows them."

I nod, completely numb. That doesn't make me feel any better as I'm torn between running over to either rescue him or smack him.

"He's completely wasted. He can barely stand."

Casey nods. "Yeah. Believe me, they wouldn't have a shot otherwise. He doesn't fool around like that anymore."

My gaze shoots to him in alarm. "Wait, what are you saying?"

He shrugs, but doesn't seem nearly as distressed as I am. "Huh? I'm not saying anything."

"Shouldn't we do something?" I cry.

Now, he's totally confused. "Do what?"

I glance back at the small circle and observe with concern that it's moving away from the crowd. I can't breathe. They're going back to his room.

"Casey! This isn't him! We can't just let him do this!"

"Do what? What are you so upset about?" Casey is clearly annoyed.

"That! They're taking him back to his room!"

"Taking him? You act like he doesn't want to be alone with three models. He's a big boy, Callie. He can handle himself."

Casey pops another bottle of champagne as if to prove how ridiculous I'm being. "Here, have another drink."

I shake my head in disbelief. "No, this isn't like him. Something's wrong!"

Casey laughs, and I glare at him. "This is exactly like him, sweetheart. That's what I tried to tell you at breakfast. You don't actually know him. The guy you know is very different than the real Luke Craven."

He softens when he sees my expression and sighs. "Look, you're a very sweet girl. I totally understand why Luke wants you in his life, and I'm sure you're really good for him, but he's not good for you."

"What's that supposed to mean?"

He shrugs. "Luke is a force. He's my brother and I love him, but you're lying to yourself if you think you're going to fix him before he destroys you."

I stare at him in shock, in anger. "You really think so little of your 'brother?'" I mock.

He raises his eyebrows before letting out an irritated laugh. "Whatever, hon. Good luck with that," he smirks, grabbing his bottle and leaving me to my craziness.

I glare after him, annoyed with myself more than anyone for not hating Casey as he retreats. He's not a bad guy, I can see that, he's just not used to fighting hard battles he doesn't have to. In his own way, he was just trying to help me, and I hurt his ego by refusing to let him.

I glance back down the hallway toward the bedrooms, but Luke and his models are long gone. Then, suddenly, I don't care anymore. I don't need to fit in here. I don't have to impress Casey Barrett, or that man with the fake glasses by the door, or the woman with the thousand dollar shoes. I'm not here for them.

I jump up from my stool and march down the hallway toward Luke's room. I can hear the sounds as I approach, the giggling, the purring, and it makes me sick, angry. I don't knock, I don't care if Luke's mad at me, and push through the door.

Three shocked faces greet me, then convert to a scowl.

"Occupied," one of them spits.

I ignore her and try to peer past them to the body beneath them. Luke is still conscious, but the look in his eyes is not one I recognize. In fact, I'm not sure he recognizes anything.

"He's obviously out of it. I think you're done here," I hiss.

"Really? I think you should mind your own business, hon," another woman barks.

"Hon? I'm not the one climbing all over a guy who's practically unconscious. What, he wouldn't touch you sober?"

She looks ready to explode, but clearly has no interest in wasting her highly valuable time fighting with a nobody like me.

"Who are you anyway?"

"I'm his cousin," I lie.

And they laugh. I expected as much, but I don't care. This isn't about me.

"Right. So are we."

I cross my arms, making it clear I'm not leaving. They can stand here and waste their night arguing, or go have fun with someone else. They glare at me as they climb off the bed and begin gathering their garments from around the room. Finally, they're dressed enough to return to the party and start filing out, each one shredding me with her eyes as she passes.

"He invited us back here. It was his idea," the last one mutters.

"I'm sure he did. Have a nice time. Enjoy the hors d-oeuvres," I reply evenly with mock politeness.

I close the door behind them and approach Luke slowly. He's completely naked, and has tried to push himself up on the bed with little success. He falls back to the sheets, eyes closed.

"Where..." There's some question in the string of sounds that follows, but I have no idea what it is.

"Do you even know their names, Luke?" I ask, more to myself than him, since I doubt he could answer me even if he did.

I don't think I can handle the intimate act of dressing him at the moment, so I simply pull the blanket up to his waist. He's sweating, and I can see he's already too warm to completely cover him. I move to his bathroom and return with a wet rag, placing it on his forehead. He flinches and his face contorts into a brief grimace before he fades completely from consciousness. Concerned, I lean close, but hear his steady breathing. My stomach starts to constrict when I wonder what his "guests" would have done at this point if I hadn't followed them. I think about what Casey had said. How could this really be what Luke wanted?

I study his face, so beautiful, so serene without the fear and grief in his eyes. Without the lines of ancient pain that make him look much older than he is. His body, marked with tattoos, perfectly sculpted for the consumption of the masses, now still against the silk sheets, held captive in its shell by a sickness no one will ever understand. A sickness no one wants to understand, I think, as I recall Casey's disappointing show of concern for his friend's state.

He's Luke Craven. A force. A god. He's not real. Just a fantasy outside the grasp of our own realities. A face. A body. A cover. A story. A goal for aspiring models.

I swipe at the hot liquid in my eyes and take his hand, tracing his palm with the other, wondering what it would be like to live in parallel with everyone around you. To know that they only see you for what they think you are. To not be able to truly connect with your own existence.

A knock at the door startles me, and I glance up to meet Casey's concerned look peeking through the crack. I'm suddenly flooded with warmth and swallow the odd sensation. He enters and closes the door.

"Is he ok?" he asks, eyeing Luke's motionless form.

I glance down at the patient as well. "I don't know. What are the different stages of substance abuse unconsciousness?"

He covers the distance between us and kneels beside his

friend. I watch quietly, a new sensation coursing through me as I observe Casey's gentle evaluation. He's done this before, many times, and I'm amazed his expression doesn't hold an ounce of disdain or disgust. Just sadness. I start to regret my harsh critique of him a minute ago.

"He'll be ok. We need to try to wake him up in a bit and get some water in him. Has he thrown up, yet?"

I shake my head. "Not that I've seen."

Casey nods, concerned. "Ok. We'll have to do that, too. Let me get some water. Hang on."

He pushes himself to his feet and disappears into Luke's bathroom. I wonder why until he returns with a basin.

"It's for soaking feet, but in case you need this before I get back," he explains with an apologetic smile. "I'll be right back with the water as soon as I can."

He closes the door quietly, and I'm not sure my opinion of someone has ever changed so abruptly.

CASEY RETURNS AS PROMISED, and I find a strange sense of relief settle over me as he moves through the door. His arms are full, and I notice he's brought more than just water for Luke.

"Gonna be a long night," he explains with another smile. He hands me a bottle of water, as well as, a plate full of snacks. "Sorry they didn't have French toast."

I laugh, grateful for his joke as much as the food. I shift on the bed so Casey can take a seat beside me. He does, and leans against the headboard like I am.

"I'm sorry about how I acted out there," he begins. "It hurts you know? Seeing him like this. Sometimes I'm not strong enough to deal with it the way I should. I try to pretend he's the same person now that he was then, but he's not."

"Messing around with supermodels?"

He offers a weak smile, and I can see the guilt in his eyes. "That wouldn't have been a cause for concern a year ago. But you were right to be worried. It doesn't mean now what it meant then. It's just..." He quiets and looks away, and something about his sad expression touches me. "I want to help him, I do, I just don't know how. At some point..." He meets my eyes again, almost pleading. "How can I help him if he won't even let me? You remember what happened at breakfast. He doesn't want to be helped. I'd be here every day if he let me."

I surprise both of us by taking his hand. I don't know why I do it, it just seems natural at that moment. He accepts the gesture and runs his thumb over mine. It's the best we can do to share our mutual struggle.

"What about you?" I ask after a long silence.

"What about me?"

I smile over at him to prove I'm changing the tone of the conversation. "What's your story?"

He laughs. "You're not some undercover investigative reporter or something, are you?"

I shrug. "Would that change your answer?" I tease, and I love his return grin.

"I guess not." He leans his head against the bed again and studies the opposite wall. We can see our reflections in the mirror there. I would have thought it'd be awkward, but I actually like watching Casey's thoughts flash across his face. He's not nearly as guarded as Luke.

"I was one of ten," he announces, and I stare at him in shock.

"Ten? As in ten siblings?"

He grins and nods. "Yes. Lucky number seven actually."

I let out my breath and rest back against the headboard, trying to imagine life with nine other siblings.

"Wow. I'm surprised you ended up with Luke and Night Shifts Black, then. Shouldn't you be committed to some cheesy family band? Geez, with ten of you, you could have the whole road crew, too."

He laughs. "Oh, believe me, my parents tried. Three of my siblings actually still play together."

"Really?" I ask.

He nods. "Yep. They've even put some albums out. I could never get into the country thing, though. The black sheep, I guess," he jokes, and I grin.

"Seriously. When you made a left, you made a hard left, huh. Well, it seemed to work out for you anyway."

He shrugs. "What about you?"

I give him a quick smile. "No bands. Not even country ones."

He rolls his eyes. "You know what I mean. Luke said you're a writer."

It's my turn to shrug. "I guess."

"You guess?" he asks with a smirk. "What does that mean?"

I smile over at him. "It means that saying 'I'm a writer' implies I'm actually making a living at it."

He seems skeptical. "Really? I thought it meant you spend lots of time writing things."

I like his response and find myself shy for some reason. "I guess it can mean that, too. Would you still consider yourself a musician if no one paid you to play?"

"Of course." He smiles. "Let's hope that doesn't happen for a long time, though."

I laugh. "How much do you make for a show anyway?" I can feel his surprise, and immediately stiffen. "I'm sorry! I don't know where that came from! Don't answer that." But he only seems amused.

"Not as much as you'd think. Well not anymore, anyway. We used to get three to four hundred in guarantees. Now, it's more like one or two. Less when we're not headlining."

My eyes widen. "Two hundred? Like two hundred dollars? That's it?"

He laughs and shakes his head. "Oh my god, I love you! Ha! No. Two hundred thousand, hon."

I stare at him in disbelief. "Wait, per show? And that's not much?"

He studies me again, and I can see his expression change, but I can't read it. "I mean, it's fine, I guess, but it's not where the real money is. We make most of it through writing and performance royalties." He glances over at our sleeping friend. "This guy here hasn't touched a guitar in a year and is still making a fortune passed out on his ass, believe it or not."

"Ok, Luke I get, but I thought you didn't write. You said at breakfast Luke was the writer. You weren't good with adjectives."

He shakes his head in exasperation. "Seriously? Do you remember everything?"

I shrug with a grin. "Am I wrong?"

He laughs again. "I guess not. I did say that. But to answer your question, I was just messing around. My name's in the credits, too. It's true, Luke tends to bring the magic to the lyrics, but I'm the music guy. That hook in 'Better Get Back' that they use for all those hockey ads? All me."

"The hockey song is from one of your songs?" I ask in surprise.

He nods. "Yeah. It's not one of our bigger ones. Well, it wasn't when they negotiated the rights to it."

"I'd say it is now," I mumble. I instinctively start humming the line, and Casey rolls his eyes.

"Yep, that's it."

"Wow, I had no idea. I actually really like that song."

He shakes his head with a smile. "You sound so shocked."

I grin. "Sorry. I guess...I don't know. I try not to think too much about Luke the Superstar, so I haven't made much of a connection between him and his music. You know, staying out of the whole pop culture bubble thing so I can see him for who he really is. I guess I did the same for you by association."

He nods, and I can tell he understands. "I like that. He needs someone in his life who's real, but you should still pick up our stuff sometime. If you truly want to understand your new friend here, you need to listen to his music. I think it might surprise you." He pauses and studies him. "Or maybe it won't."

"'Step back, fast, I'm coming for you. Step back, you can't handle what I've got.'"

I recite the words absently, imagining the hockey players slamming up against the boards in a series of vicious checks.

Casey smiles and nods. "That's it." He quiets, and I can see from his reflection in the mirror that there's a lot more to this. A lot more to him.

"People think it's an aggressive song. A challenge to someone, and the hockey link certainly doesn't help," he muses. I glance over at him in surprise.

"It's not?"

Casey shakes his head. "No. That's not what Luke's saying at all. It's actually saturated with self-loathing."

"Saturated with self-loathing?" I repeat in amusement. "What do you mean you're not good with adjectives?"

He shrugs with a shy grin. "I've been known to string a few together. Anyway, the part you know is just the hook. The chorus is, '*I'm the anchor drowning you. I'm your infection, better get back. I'm the hurricane, angel, shred those wings. Step back, better get back.'"*

We're quiet for a moment as the lyrics settle around us. I glance over at Luke who hasn't moved.

"And that was even before Elena's suicide?" I ask, realizing I've only begun to scratch the surface of this enigma.

Casey seems surprised by my comment at first, then relieved that the topic is finally out.

He sighs. "Yes. Elena was..." He stops, and I can tell this subject is difficult for him as well. "She was a beautiful person, inside and out. Deep down he never thought he deserved her." He quiets again. "I think that's why he did the things he did."

"What things?" I ask, unable to stop the question.

He stares ahead again, but only ends up meeting my eyes in the mirror. "You know, things. There are a lot of temptations out there. On the road. For us."

"He cheated on her?"

"A lot," Casey admits quietly. "He never should have married her and he knew it. For her sake. He couldn't be the person she deserved. Not with the way things were for us. He couldn't forgive himself before, but especially after. God, you want to see a person who hates himself?"

We both stare over at Luke.

"And what am I supposed to do? Huh?" he continues in a haunted voice. "What do you say to a monster you love who's finally figured out what he is?"

I swallow hard. I feel something burning deep inside me again, but I don't know what to do with it. There's so much going on in my head, in my heart, my soul, at that moment, I don't even know where to begin.

I have a lot to think about, and the sudden silence comes at a good time. I can tell Casey's mind is racing as well, and I wonder what he's thinking. I want to ask, but I'm not ready for that yet. I'm starting to care way too much about what's going on in this surprisingly deep and compassionate drummer's head for it to be a safe topic.

"I should go check on the party and see if I can wind it down," he states abruptly. "When I get back we'll try to get some alcohol out and water in."

I give him a grateful smile, which he returns. He squeezes my hand before rising from the bed, and I blush a little. I hadn't even realized we were still holding hands.

CASEY RETURNS SHORTLY, and the purging procedure proves to be unpleasant at best. I know without Casey, I never would have had the strength to complete it. Luke struggles violently against his friend as Casey drags him to the bathroom, forcing him against the toilet until he vomits, repeatedly.

I stand watch at the door, my heart breaking at the sight, but somehow finding peace in Casey's calm strength. He speaks to Luke in a tone mixed with comfort and confrontation, refusing to send the message that what's happening is ok, even as he pours every ounce of himself into nursing his friend. It's a fascinating thing to watch, this strange combination of compassion and criticism, something that I'm sure can only be born from a genuine love of someone who cares deeply.

"Can you grab the towel there?" Casey calls over to me, and I pull a hand towel from the shelf below the sink. "Thanks. Oh, hey, can you wet it? Yeah, thanks."

He takes the towel and uses it to wipe Luke's face. Luke is still only half-conscious, but awake enough to control a string of every curse word he knows. Casey only rolls his eyes at his friend's impotent tirade and drags him back to his feet. I jump in to help, and between the two of us, we manage to get Luke back in bed.

"Here, drink this," Casey commands, holding a water bottle to Luke's lips.

"I don't want it!" Luke slurs, trying to wave it away.

"Drink it, you idiot!" Casey continues, turning the bottle up. Luke curses him as water spills down his chin and onto his bare chest.

"Can you find a pair of boxers or something in his drawer?" he asks me.

I nod, relieved that Casey is willing to take on that challenge as well. I find an acceptable option, and by the time I return to the scene, Casey has managed to get Luke to drain a bottle of water on his own. I hand him the shorts and move toward the bathroom.

"I'll clean up in here."

"Thanks," Casey calls after me.

I'm not surprised there are no cleaning supplies, after all who would need them in a place where maid service is a phone call away, so I do my best with water and more towels. Casey's nursing skill quickly becomes apparent, however, when I realize there's not much to clean up. I wonder how many times they've been through this routine. Still, I make sure to give them enough time to finish their own mission before returning to the bedroom.

Luke is already tucked in and sleeping when I get back.

"He'll be ok. We'll get more water in him a little later," Casey assures me.

"Casey..."

He glances up at me, waiting, but I'm not sure how to continue. I want him to know what I'm feeling, how much I admire what I just saw, how grateful I am for him, but it all gets stuck on my tongue.

"Um...you can go enjoy your friends if you'd like. I'll stay with him."

He gives me a silly grin as he straightens to his feet and stretches.

"Are you kicking me out and telling me to go play with my friends?"

I blush but relax when I can tell he's amused, not annoyed.

"No, that's not what I meant, I just...if you want to...I like your company."

He smiles and shakes his head. "Well, they're not my friends, anyway. I don't even know most of them. I'm not even sure Luke does either." He pauses and glances down at his clothes. "I could use a shower, though. You never really get used to puke."

A laugh escapes me, and I nod. "Not a bad idea. There's a nice one in the extra room, but what about all the guests?"

Casey glances over at the clock. "I think it's late enough that we can wind this down without damaging Luke's reputation."

I stifle my grin, not sure if he's joking or not, and watch as he moves toward the door.

"Be back in a minute," he whispers with a conspiratorial glint.

I lower myself beside Luke again and close my eyes. In all the drama, I hadn't realized how tired I was. Or how hungry. I lean over and grab the plate from the nightstand to pick through some of the snacks. Even though they'd been sitting for a while now, the food is still more delicious than any "party food" I'm accustomed to. I wonder how Luke had managed to pull this event together so fast, catering included. Had this been planned for a while and he only warned me about it today? Or do rockstars just have a team of party planners and vendors on call should they decide they're in the mood to "have some people over."

Casey interrupts my meditations by popping his head back in to let me know the guests should be disbanding soon and he found the shower I'd told him about. I was right, it looks fantastic, so he'll be back in a few minutes.

I find myself grinning long after he disappears again and realize what a strange effect he has on me. I wonder if Luke used to be that way. After all, he'd said he'd used to be silly, but I quickly decide Casey's easy smile warms me in its authenticity, not it's silliness. Casey isn't silly, just genuine.

"Callie?"

The voice almost startles me, and I glance down to see Luke squinting up at me. I place the plate back on the nightstand, so I can focus on him and be ready for whatever he needs.

"I'm here. How are you feeling?"

"I don't know yet."

I nod. "Casey took really good care of you."

He looks away, but I'm not sure if any of it registers.

"Where is he?"

"He's just cleaning up in the other guest room. He'll be back soon."

Luke's expression changes again, but I'm not sure what to make of it. "He's a good friend. He shouldn't be, but he is," he mutters.

"He is."

"I'm not."

"Luke..."

"What? You know it's true."

"Just get some rest. We'll talk tomorrow, ok?"

"Laurie?"

"Who?"

"Um...no. Laura. Uh...Laurel..."

"Luke, seriously, just get some rest."

He nods and closes his eyes again, and I find myself relieved to be released from more confusing conversation with him. It's a strange contrast to the fact that I miss Casey and look forward to his return. I get my wish soon enough when he bursts through the door, a relaxed smile on his face.

My relief quickly transforms into something entirely different when he comes into view.

"Man, you weren't kidding!" he exclaims, moving into the room. His hair is wet, messy, and he has a towel secured around his waist. I swallow and try not to stare, but fail miserably as he roots through Luke's drawers for a change of clothes.

"Have you tried it? The wall one? Completely ridiculous."

I force a smile. "This morning, actually. Well, I guess, technically, it was yesterday, at this point."

He shakes his head and pulls on a pair of jeans. He applies the newly freed towel to his hair again and leans against the dresser.

"Who the hell needs a wall shower? What's that about?"

I shrug in response as he hovers half-naked a few feet away, and I consider closing my eyes. I have to. I don't know how else to avoid gaping at him like a spellbound teenager. How did I miss this before? But of course I can't close my eyes. I'd look like a crazy person. I feel like a crazy person. I must be more tired than I'd thought because I'm pretty sure I'm not drunk. I clear my throat and hop off the bed.

"Where are you going?" he asks.

"Nowhere. Just thought I'd take a break from this room for a while. Luke is doing fine. He woke up a second ago and mumbled some stuff that made no sense, but at least proves he's starting to work his way back to our world. Is it safe yet?"

"Out there?" Casey asks, motioning toward the door.

"Yeah, is everyone gone?"

Casey shrugs. "Got me. Probably. I cut off bar service, so I doubt anyone will stick around much longer."

"I'll go check."

He seems concerned by my strange behavior, and I don't blame him. I'm concerned, too.

"You got weird all of a sudden. You ok?"

My mouth goes dry as his dark eyes search mine, and I force a smile. I don't know how to explain why I'm not.

"Fine, yeah, just need a change of scenery for a bit, that's all."

Casey nods. "Ok, sure. Let me finish up here and I'll meet you out front."

I smile and suck in my breath as I'm forced to move past him. Dammit, he smells as good as he looks right now.

THE GUESTS ARE STILL THERE. Not as many as before, sure, but enough that I'm positive the scowl is evident on my face. I toss my shoes in the corner and consider taking Casey's lead by borrowing some of Luke's clothes. I suddenly feel completely restricted in this tiny dress that has no business on me anymore. I'm done with that and ready for this room to be mine again.

I turn on the hi-hats to a chorus of groans and curses, mostly from the few presumptuous guests who errantly thought they'd be crashing here tonight.

"Does anyone need a cab?" I call out, relishing how freeing it is not to care if any of these people hate me. Heck, not even knowing who they are or why I should care.

No one takes me up on my offer, but their glares indicate they're getting the hint. Several of them begin collecting their belongings and making the exodus toward the door. It briefly occurs to me how strange it is that they're following my orders, and I wonder if Luke will be mad that I was rude to all of his friends. Oh well, he should have thought of that before he passed out and left me to my villainy.

"Thanks, everyone. Thanks for coming. Actually, if you ask for Mara Jacobson in the lobby, I'm sure she'll be happy to book a room for you. Thank you. Oops, your purse...yes, there....thank you.... Thank you... Thanks. Ok, you ok? Ok good, thanks."

I sense someone watching me and shoot my gaze toward the hallway to meet Casey's ever-present grin. He found himself a t-shirt, and now leans against the wall, observing my efforts with an amused expression. He waves me on with an encouraging gesture, and I roll my eyes. I know he's a second away from laughing.

I turn back to my task, and notice with surprise and relief that it's basically been completed. With the exception of one guy still asleep on the couch.

"You missed one," Casey teases, drawing up beside me and staring down at the body.

I give him a mock glare before leaning down and shaking the guest. The man doesn't even stir, loud snores rumbling from his face.

"What do we do?" I ask.

Casey shrugs. "That's Orin Cantea."

"Who?"

"Orin Cantea? Rhinehearst Media?"

I continue to stare at him. "Does that mean he freeloads on other people's couches?"

"Freeloads?" Casey laughs. "The guy is a gazillionaire."

"Good. So he has people that can come get him."

Casey shakes his head in disbelief. "Nothing fazes you does it. Or is it, no one?"

It's my turn to shrug. "Probably both. I'm beat, but not ready to sleep. Want to watch a movie or are you ready to crash?"

Casey considers my offer and stares down at our "guest."

"What about him?"

I grunt and scan the living room. "Think we can move him over there so we can have the good couch?"

He nods. "Probably. You get his feet. I'll get the top half."

15

DAY EIGHTEEN

I'm not sure what time it is when I wake up, but I don't remember anything about the movie last night, which means I lasted all of five seconds once Casey and I got comfortable. I feel warm, though, and am surprised by the blanket tucked around me. I blink and instinctively glance toward the other end of the couch where Casey is still passed out.

Rising from the couch, I grab the blanket and return the favor, tucking it around him as best I can without disturbing him. Then I scan the room in disgust. It's a complete disaster. There's no way I'm leaving this mess in its entirety for housekeeping, although I'm still way too groggy to start the cleanup process. I shuffle toward the guest room and notice as I pass that our new friend Orin Cantea is gone. That comes as a relief.

A grimace covers my face as I stare into the mirror in the guest bathroom. My makeup has smudged under my eyes and my hair is a mess. I need a shower badly and am grateful I'd thought to bring supplies this time. I remember leaving my bag by the door where Casey accosted me, and retrieve it as quietly as possible. I almost laugh at my instinctive relief that it's still there. As if any of the guests at last night's party would have been interested in the belongings of a poor girl from Shelteron, PA. Still, not my smartest move.

I return to the guest room and this time opt for a shower in the real bathroom, curious how it compares to the ostentatious display on the other side of the wall. The warm water works wonders on my tired body and mind as I close my eyes and let it wrap me in a comforting embrace. A barrage of thoughts and memories keep trying to break through my serenity, but I manage to block most of them. I don't want to think right now. I don't want to worry about Luke, or try to process this strange and abrupt shift in my attitude toward Casey. I don't want to think about people like Orin Cantea or entitled supermodels. I don't even want to consider the pleasure of good champagne and fancy appetizers. For a few brief moments, I just want to be warm and calm.

I enjoy the peace for as long as I can, but after a while the heat from the water starts to transform from soothing to uncomfortable. I know it's time to get out and face the confusion waiting for me beyond this stall, and turn off the water. I stand still for a moment, enjoying the chill on my wet body after the hot shower. It energizes me, and I reluctantly reach for a towel.

Casey is awake when I emerge from the guest room, and I hate how he can look exactly like he did last night with no effort whatsoever. Men have no idea how easy they have it.

"Morning. I had some food sent up if you're hungry," he says, motioning to the spread in front of him on the island counter. Last night's bar is this morning's breakfast table. Rockstar living at its best.

I join him and take the stool beside him.

"You sleep ok?" he asks through a mouthful of something.

I smile, still not sure I'm ready to confront him yet. Will my confusing feelings still linger this morning without the aid of alcohol and crisis? He definitely looks more like a normal guy, and less like a superhero, this morning with his messy hair, scrambled eggs, and lack of heroic feats. But the playful light is still in his eyes, and that damn goofy grin is still a second away from making me smile whether I'm in the mood or not. He also got us food.

"I think so. You?"

He shrugs and swallows some of his coffee. "I guess. What'd you think of the movie?" he teases, and I roll my eyes.

"Have you checked on Luke yet?" I ask, suddenly feeling guilty for not doing that myself.

"Yeah. He's fine. He's awake, actually. Working up the energy for a shower."

I nod. "Good. Thanks. I should have done that before my own. Sorry."

Casey shrugs again and turns back to his eggs. "You're not his mother or his nurse. Your life doesn't have to revolve around taking care of him."

"Says the guy who literally had to wash his puke off last night."

He gives me a wry look. "You know what I mean. I think it's great that you're looking out for him, but you can't be consumed by it. You can't let it define you or you'll start to internalize his issues and judge yourself for things you can't control."

He quiets, and I study him carefully. The way his eyes shift as he focuses back on his breakfast, the distracted movement of his fork over the plate.

"You've been there," I guess, and he glances at me sharply.

"There's only so much you can do, Callie. You can't force someone to heal no matter how much you care about them. Not if they don't want to."

I swallow and look away, struck by his words. Casey and I

have even more in common than I'd thought, and I'm suddenly able to understand his protectiveness. He's already been down the path I'm going. Maybe he'd stayed away for so long because he'd finally accepted reality, the hard truth that Luke's pain could not be his or it would destroy him, too. Then a new thought strikes me as I consider last night, Casey's compassion, his presence here even now. Did I draw him back in? Is he here to protect Luke or me?

The thought warms and concerns me at the same time. It's crazy. It has to be. There's no way this famous celebrity who could have everything and everyone he wants would give a damn about some random nobody from Smalltown, USA trying to help his friend. No way.

"Hey, so hear me out. We wrapped up our tour last week and I was thinking of crashing here for a while and seeing what we can do about Luke. Maybe between the two of us we can make some progress?"

I stare at him, speechless. He can't possibly know what had just been going through my head, but it gives me chills. I'm even more unsettled about how much I want that, how relieved I feel at the thought of having him around. A strange thought, considering I'd been jealous of anyone else in Luke's life a week ago. How quickly things change.

I try to stay casual. "Yeah, I mean, if he's up for it. I guess it would be fine to have you around more."

He laughs. "Thanks?" and I'm afraid I'm blushing again. I don't know how he manages to make me so relaxed and nervous at the same time.

"Sorry, I didn't mean...I meant..." I grunt in frustration.

"You meant, 'why Casey Barrett, I am simply tickled at the thought of seeing your sunshine-lemonade face every day!'"

"Hey!" I cry, giving him a mock glare. "I do *not* talk like that!"

"True. Except when we're on our motorbikes," he smirks, and I reach over for a good smack on the arm.

He laughs and cowers. "Ok, ok. Sorry."

"And anyway, so what if every other thing out of my mouth isn't about 'effing the establishment.'"

His eyes widen in shocked amusement, and I can't stop the grin that escapes my lips.

"'Effing the establishment?' Oh my god, you can't even curse in your mock quotes!"

"What? So that's a thing? Making fun of someone for their lack of cursing?"

He laughs and shakes his head. "Please, please do me one favor, though. Call it 'foul language,' not cursing. I just need to hear it once!"

I hit him again. "And also, I like that you were more concerned that I didn't use the word 'fuck' than the fact that I basically called you a stereotypical anarchist rocker."

"You just said it," he snickers.

"Said what?"

"Fuck."

I stare at him in exasperation. "Seriously? What, are you eight-years-old, all of a sudden?"

He laughs and shrugs. "I'm just pointing out that the universe didn't explode. I doubt any old ladies even died from it."

I roll my eyes and grunt. "So that's twice now," I return with a smug look.

"Twice what?"

"Twice that you've skipped over the part about raging against 'The Man.' Is that your thing or what?"

He grins. "I don't know. Maybe it is. Maybe not. How much will it bug you if I don't respond?"

"Alright, that's it," I cry, jumping off my chair.

"What are you doing?" he asks in surprise.

"I want to hear your music."

"What? Like, right now?"

"Yes, right now." I pick up my phone and start searching. It's not hard to find, as I was sure it wouldn't be. "What should I start with? Oh wait, I know. I remember one of them from Luke."

I type in "Argyle" and "Night Shifts Black." Apparently, this is a much older song, which makes sense based on the story that went with it, but must still be pretty popular because I find several versions of it.

"What are you looking for?"

I give him a mischievous look, but pull away so he can't see what I'm doing. I click the link and set the phone on the counter.

As soon as the song starts, Casey glances at me in shock, the amusement fading from his eyes. My own mood shifts at the change, and I regret it, although I'm not sure how I would have known.

"That's the one song Luke talked about?" he asks. He doesn't seem angry, just surprised, maybe concerned.

I shrug. "In passing. It wasn't in reference to the song itself, but something about guitars and tuning? It just happened to be the only one I remembered."

Casey seems to relax, and it's my turn to be surprised. He forces a smile. "Yeah, the guys like to tune down half a step so they can play it open."

I have no idea what that means, but I don't want to remind him his whole world is a mystery to me.

"Who wrote this one?" I ask, and for some reason I'm prepared for his look this time. It only lasts a second before he glances away.

"All of us, like everything," he replies cryptically.

"Ok, then who had the original idea for it?"

Now I have his attention and meet his gaze with a steady look, daring him to brush me off again. I know it's not fair. I never would have forced a response from Luke and would have backtracked the second I realized I'd approached a controversial topic. Actually, no, I wouldn't have even asked the question in the first place. But somehow I know Casey is different. He can handle hard questions, even if he doesn't want to.

"What do you think of it?" he asks, deflecting again anyway.

I sigh and let him off the hook. "Honestly, it kind of sucks," I say. "I'm more of a country girl."

His face falls for a second, and then the grin breaks when mine does.

"Liar," he replies, and I laugh.

"Yeah. I'm kidding. Actually, I like it a lot. Not what I was expecting."

"Really? What were you expecting?"

I shrug. "I don't know, the way you guys talk, I thought it would just be lots of incoherent screaming and banging."

He laughs. "There's some of that."

I nod with a smile. "Yeah, but it's beautiful, too, in a way. I love the strings in the chorus. Right there! That part you can hear under Luke's voice." I quiet. "Wow. He's really good. Like, really, really good."

Casey seems amused again. "Shocking, huh? Bands generally prefer frontmen who can sing."

I roll my eyes. "That's not what I mean. I just never heard him doing his thing before, that's all. Well, that I recognized anyway. I never truly listened. It's like learning something new about him."

"Yeah, this is a pretty old one, too. That's why I was surprised Luke brought it up."

"He was talking about the time your gear got stolen from the motel parking lot."

Casey grunts and sits back. "Oh yeah. That sucked big time. We were all broke to begin with, and of course, those bastards took off with most of my stuff."

"Luke said they took the stuff they recognized."

Casey nods. "Yes, and apparently drums and cymbals are pretty obvious even in their cases."

"Well, thankfully you've recovered."

"Interesting choice."

Casey and I are both startled by the new voice, and turn to see Luke shuffling toward us, disheveled but alert.

"You couldn't at least play our good stuff for her?"

"She picked it," Casey defends.

"I like it," I say. "Besides we were actually reminiscing about your gear getting stolen."

"Please tell me your reminiscing includes coffee," Luke mumbles.

"Here, dude," Casey says, passing him the carafe. "There's food, too."

Luke grimaces and pours a cup. "Let's go with coffee first."

We're quiet for a moment and the song finishes, forcing the silence even louder. None of us knows how to begin. Especially, since we're not sure which Luke we have with us at the moment.

"You know, Casey wrote most of that one," Luke announces, and I'm not surprised based on our earlier interaction.

Casey just shrugs. "Black sheep, right?" he says with a quick smile of explanation. I have mercy on him and return it. I remember what Luke had said about the meaning of the song, and realize Casey must have a story I'll need to hear one day, too.

"It's basically what got us signed," Luke continues.

"Well, that and our devastating good looks," Casey jokes, not even acknowledging Luke's praise. I roll my eyes, and he grins, although he's probably not far from the truth. It certainly wouldn't have hurt.

"She thinks it's pretty," Casey continues, and a knowing smile flashes across Luke's face.

"Pretty? 'Argyle?' She would."

"I would? What's that supposed to mean?" I counter.

Luke shrugs lightly. "Nothing, I'm just not surprised, that's all."

I blush a little, not sure what he means by that. "Well, excuse me if I'm not dark and depressing enough for you edgy rockers."

Luke and Casey exchange another grin, and I cross my arms. "What? What did I do now?"

"Nothing," Luke replies.

I glance to Casey, but he just shrugs and looks like he's stifling a laugh.

I glare at them both. "Fine. I should probably get going anyway," I retort.

"Callie..." Casey grabs my arm as I pass. "We didn't..."

I pull away and continue on.

"Callie!"

I know I'm being childish as I hide in the extra room, but deep down I'm also smarting from the nerve they struck. The truth is, I really am self-conscious about the fact that I don't fit in. I act like I'm confident and don't care, and maybe a lot of the time that's true, but sometimes, moments like today when I'm tired and coming off a string of trials, I'm too exhausted to be the ambassador. Sometimes I just want them to try to come into my world for once.

A knock interrupts my thoughts, and I glare at the door. I

don't respond, but it doesn't matter, and I'm surprised when it's Luke who pokes his head in. He gives me an apologetic look and completes the journey into the room. I still don't say anything, but shift a bit so he can sit beside me.

"You know we fought over who would come in here," he begins, and I'm not sure how that helps.

"You lost, I guess?"

He looks surprised and laughs. "No, I won!" he cries in exasperation. "God, Callie, don't you get it? We don't want you to be like us! We want you to think our music is pretty and tell us when we're being assholes. You have to stop thinking that the gap that separates us is because of a shortcoming on your part. Did you ever think that it might be on ours?"

I swallow, floored by his words for so many reasons.

He lets out his breath, staring at the floor. "I can be a major pain-in-the-ass. I know that. Last night..." He shakes his head, and I'm not about to correct him. "Anyway, my point is, I'm sorry. I'm sorry for last night. I'm sorry for this morning. I have a ton of issues, but I never want you to think you're one of them, ok?"

I finally allow myself to glance over at him, and all the fear, and longing, and pain, and confusion come rushing back into me at once. I don't know what to do with it as my eyes fill and I lean into him. Luke wraps his arms around me in return, and I hold on, terrified that I will lose him one day.

"I was so scared last night," I whisper into his shirt. I pull back slightly, and look up into his face. "I didn't know...I mean, you...I hated seeing you like that."

He looks away, and I catch a glimpse of all the agony that led to last night before he tucks it out of view. I let him go, and he squeezes my hand gently before retreating into himself and facing the wall again.

"That used to be normal."

"I know."

He glances at me sharply. "Casey told you."

"Casey loves you and is probably the best friend you have."

Luke seems skeptical, and I shake my head. "No. You need to listen to me, Luke. Last night it was Casey who took care of you, not me. It was Casey who wiped the puke off your face and nursed you back to health." I pause. "You need to let him back into your life."

Luke's expression hardens. "I can't."

As does mine. "You have to."

"You don't understand."

I shrug. "Ok, then explain it to me. We're past the 'no personal stuff.'"

Luke shakes his head and won't look at me.

"He's a good person, Luke. And after what I saw last night, I'd venture to say, better than both of us."

Luke shakes his head again, looking like he wants to speak but can't. Or won't.

"What? I don't know if maybe you've had a falling out in the past, but he wants to make it right again. He wants to be a part of your life."

Luke glares at me, and it's then that I see the self-loathing Casey was talking about. It's so vivid I almost gasp.

"He can't be part of my life. I'm not doing that to him again," he hisses. Then rises from the bed.

I watch him leave in stunned silence.

———

CASEY IS oblivious when I emerge from the room, still seated at the island, studying his phone. He glances up at my entrance, but his smile fades when he sees my face.

"You're still mad. I'm sorry, we didn't..."

I cut him off with a hug. He doesn't speak, even though I know he's confused as my arms tighten around him. He reciprocates, and I feel his chin resting on my head. He adjusts so we can be closer.

"What is it? What's wrong?" he asks, allowing me to settle into him.

I want to say something, to explain, but I don't know how. Nothing's wrong and everything's wrong. And some things are right, but maybe not enough things.

"I want you to stay," I whisper. "No matter what happens, what he says or does, you need to stay. Please?" I ask, pulling back so I can search his face.

His eyes fill with concern, and I realize how beautiful they are. I'd thought there could be nothing more consuming than the painful depth of Luke's gaze until I got lost in the compassionate abyss of Casey's.

He just nods. I know he knows there's more to this, that he's going to regret his promise as much as be glad for it, but he makes it, silently, and I rest against him again, holding on.

"I can't help him alone, Casey. I know that now. He needs you. I need you, too."

"I'm not going anywhere," he responds softly.

"Promise?" I ask, looking up at him again.

He nods. "Promise."

I force an awkward smile that he returns, suddenly feeling safe again. It's funny how Luke stirs me up but Casey seems to calm me down.

"He told you he wanted me gone, didn't he," Casey guesses after a long pause.

I don't respond at first. It does us no good to lie.

"Yes, but not for the reasons you'd think. I actually think it's because he believes he's bad for you. I think he's afraid he'll drag you down with him. He said 'again.' What does that mean?"

Casey looks away, conflicted, and sighs.

"Please, Casey, I'm tired of being involved in your lives and yet not knowing anything. I don't know how to help, how to even act, when I'm around you two."

He nods and glances down the hall, probably to make sure we're alone, before leading me to the couch. We sit facing each other, and I wait as he gathers his thoughts.

"If you think things are bad now, you should have seen what happened after Elena," he begins quietly. "Luke completely imploded. I doubt he even remembers the first month. The band took a hiatus, everyone understood, and the publicity actually helped us. You know how tragedy goes...well, as long as it's not your fault." He stops and looks away. "And it wasn't, and the media had a field day with it. Our Label didn't help matters and sucked every last dollar and headline they could out of Luke's devastation."

He takes a deep breath. "The problem is, it kind of was his fault. Not in an obvious way, a criminal way," he adds quickly. "But the kind of way that tears you apart inside and turns compassion into poison." He quiets again. "Everyone said he just needed time...and space. Even the other guys let him go. They wouldn't have known what to do with him anyway, but I couldn't. I stuck by him." He looks up again, and I can see how painful this story is, and yet, how relieved he is to finally release some of it.

He lets out a bitter laugh. "Oh, he hated me for it, believe me, and made nothing easy, but he was my brother, and I couldn't just abandon him and take advantage of his pain like everyone else."

He sits back and shakes his head at another memory.

"You know, at one point the Label almost cut me because I

refused to be part of some major cable 'special' about the whole thing. I don't know why Sweeny and Eli did it, but they did. I guess the Label realized Night Shifts Black couldn't afford to lose both Luke and me, so they agreed to let me sit out the interview if I agreed to participate in another tour. We had canceled the rest of the current one after what happened."

"And Luke blames himself for almost getting you kicked out of the band?" I guess, studying him carefully.

He shakes his head. "No, Luke blames himself for almost getting me killed," he says quietly. He draws in a deep breath. "I'm not an expert at grief, and I certainly wasn't then. I didn't know what to do with Luke, how to take care of him. I was full of my own pain, too. All I knew was that I wasn't going to abandon him like everyone else. But I'll admit, in the beginning, I made the mistake of thinking 'being there for him' meant 'joining him.'"

He looks away again, and I find myself instinctively taking his hand. My instinct reacts surprisingly open with him for some reason.

"I tried to be the responsible one, but failed more times than not. One night..." He shudders. "Anyway, we both ended up in the hospital, along with a ton of headlines the Label was not happy about. Unfortunately, since I'm not Luke Craven, I didn't get the grace Luke did. They basically gave me a choice at that point, distance myself from Luke and rejoin the band, or they'd drop me. So I had to make a choice. Career or friend."

"And you chose career."

Casey laughs. "No, of course not. I chose Luke, but he wouldn't let me. We fought about it for days, and then suddenly, he just disappeared. Abandoned his house, his accounts, everything, and stopped answering his phone. No one knew where he went, including me." He sighs. "To this day, I don't know if he ran for my sake or his, but the result was the same. I had no other choice at that point. If I couldn't help him, I had to go back. So I did. Cleaned myself up, got back on track, and was thrilled when our manager called to say that he'd finally heard from Luke. That he was here. I came as soon as I could which was during our quick break before the Calisto Festival."

"The day you came to breakfast club," I recall, and he nods.

"Believe me, I was in shock he not only let me in when I showed up, but let me stay the night. It was a short honeymoon, as you saw, but at least we started talking again." He shrugs. "He invited me to his party, right?"

"He loves you," I say, squeezing his hand. "He does, he just hates himself too much to let anyone love him back."

He grunts. "I know. I mean, most of the time I know. It's hard to believe that sometimes, but I try to keep hoping he'll let me back in at some point. I don't know how to help him if he doesn't."

Casey's phone starts buzzing, completely startling us, and he glances at the screen. He curses and gives me an apologetic look.

"I should take this. Sorry, give me a minute?" he asks, and I offer him my most forgiving smile. I have plenty to absorb anyway.

I watch his face as he answers and gets to his feet.

"Yeah. Wait, what? Why would you do that?" Casey cries, clearly exasperated, and rubs his hand over his face. "No, I know. I just...yeah...Yes, I know where he is. I'm with him now. No, it's not...Because he's not ready!...I don't know, I'll figure something out...Dammit, TJ, I told you I know! I'm working on it! ...Ok, yeah...Ok...just don't...no...I know...ok, just don't call him again, ok? Call me if you need anything. Me, not him!... ok...yeah, ok. You, too."

Casey hangs up with a curse and shakes his head. "What an idiot," he mutters.

He gives me another apologetic look. "Sorry about that." He takes a deep breath. "You know, sometimes I think I wish my life was more shallow, but then I talk to TJ. He always snaps me out of it."

"TJ?"

"Our Manager."

"Oh."

"Yeah...He's awesome at what he does it's just unfortunately all he does. He tried to call Luke."

My eyes widen. "Oh..."

"Yeah."

He glances toward the hall as if expecting Luke to come marching down in a fury. He sighs.

"We have four months before our next tour and they want at least three new tracks. We should be releasing an entire album and building the tour around that, but they know that's not going to happen. They're ok releasing the album next year if we can have some new material now."

"But without Luke..."

Casey shakes his head. "I don't know, Callie. I honestly don't. I mean, I've got some ideas, but..."

"Maybe I can help."

"What?"

I cringe. I don't even know what I'm saying. It's that darn instinct again. "I mean, I've never written a song before, but I write a ton of poetry. Is it a lot different?"

I can tell he's trying not to laugh. Especially, after our blow up earlier over their teasing, but his skepticism is all over his face. It hurts, but I can't really blame him. It would be like a med student offering to do open-heart surgery on the President.

"Well, it's not that I don't appreciate the offer, it's just, I mean, it's not that easy. There's a lot of politics to songwriting. The band, the Label, legal stuff..."

"Ok, so we don't write for Night Shifts Black. We just write to have something to do while we hang out and try to find you some inspiration."

His face changes. "Really? You'd do that?"

I shrug. "Of course. I mean, it's not like I do anything else with my writing. No one's ever even read it."

He seems shocked by that. "Wait, what? You've never shared your stuff?"

I shrug again. "I never really thought about it. I write because it's part of me, but I could never actually be a real writer."

"Why?"

His question is almost funny to me.

"Why? I don't know, because that's not realistic. You don't just get to 'be a writer' because you like to write."

I can tell he's confused, and I'm starting to get irritated. Of course he doesn't understand. He's a superstar. He got his dream and lives in a world where he can do whatever he wants because of who he is. That's not reality for the rest of us.

"Don't get mad, I'm just not understanding what you're saying," he defends, and I hadn't realized my thoughts were so transparent. "You like to write, so write. Why do you have to put labels and expectations on it?"

I swallow. It's an excellent point. I'm not sure how to counter it.

"Show me something," he says, not giving me the chance to continue the debate.

"What?"

"I want to see something you've written. I saw you come with a bag yesterday. You have to have something in there."

"Oh, you know writers so well?"

He laughs. "I *am* a writer."

He jumps up and disappears down the hall, returning a few seconds later with his own bag. "I kept my stuff in the office," he explains. He fishes through the main section and pulls out a notebook. "I do all my serious stuff on the computer, but carry this for any spurts of unexpected inspiration."

I swallow. I do the same thing.

He hands the book to me, and I accept it with a shocked sense of reverence. Am I really holding a portal into the mind of a world-class musician and celebrity? I can't believe he's willing to show me this, and I realize how much he must trust me. I doubt this happens often.

I start paging through the priceless notes, gazing at line after line of words and scribbles. I don't recognize a lot of them and assume it's some kind of musical shorthand.

"I know. It's kind of a mess. I hear the music in my head but it's hard to get it down exactly right without my guitar or piano, so I just make notes to myself for later."

"I thought you played drums."

He laughs. "I do. I also play guitar, keyboard, and violin. Well, with any skill, anyway. I dabble in a bunch of others, but those are my main ones."

"Then you probably sing, too," I muse. Actually, he probably rescues puppies and climbs mountains and discovers new atomic elements also, but we can save that for another conversation.

He shrugs. "Yeah, a little. We back Luke up at the live shows."

"What's this one?" I ask, turning the page so he can see.

"Oh, that's actually the rough outline for 'Fourth Chair.'"

"Wait, I think I know that one! It's about an orchestra or something."

He snickers. "It's about realizing your dreams don't always

match reality and accepting what is. That the world owes you nothing and will kick you in the face if you live like you think it does."

I nod, impressed, and trace over the sloppy letters, numbers, and drawings on the page.

"*You're nothing but a fourth chair, baby. Forget the lights, your day ain't coming. Roses are red but they're not for you, just remember they die for the first chair too.*"

I grin, and glance up at him with a new admiration. "I thought Luke was the lyric king."

He returns it and seems almost shy. "He is. I just happen to have the orchestra background," he jokes.

"I guess. But apparently, you weren't very good," I tease, and he grins.

"At organized accompaniment? No. Not at all. My parents withdrew me from orchestra after a couple years, but I'm pretty sure the conductor didn't give them a choice. No matter how good you are, you eventually have to fall in line. I guess I just didn't always agree with the musical decisions of Strauss and Mozart."

I laugh, totally believing that. "So you switched to drums and became a rocker."

"Well, it wasn't that easy of a transition, believe me, but ultimately, yes. My parents were not on board. I can assure you of that. I was kid number seven, so according to the plan I was supposed to be a concert violinist."

I raise my eyebrows. "Really? Then who was supposed to be the drummer in a disgustingly successful rock band?"

He grins and shrugs.

"Ok, your turn," he commands, taking his book back.

I suck in my breath. I'd expected the request, just not so soon.

"What? I showed you mine."

"I know but..."

"Callie."

I grunt in exasperation. "Fine. Give me a minute."

I get up from the couch and move to the guest room. Casey's right. I do carry a notebook with me. Just like he does. Just like him, the complete works are on my computer, but I feel naked without my little notepad to capture my thoughts whenever, wherever, whatever they are.

I grab the worn book from my bag and stare at the cover, suddenly paralyzed. Am I really going to do this? Expose myself so openly to a relative stranger? Can I even choose not to at this point? He just risked a lot more than I am by showing me his own music diary.

And if I'm truly honest with myself, I opened myself up to Casey Barrett long before this moment. If I don't dive in and take a risk at this point, then there is no point. Maybe I'm just a fourth chair, but I'm nothing if I don't accept that. Casey's song hits home a lot harder than it ever had when I'd heard it on the radio. I finally get it.

I steel myself and clasp the notebook tightly to my chest. I'm going to do this. I have to do this. I move from the room with a resolved look on my face.

"Ok, but you have to promise not to laugh..." I call as I move down the hall.

I stop abruptly when I see Luke seated next to Casey.

"Promise not to laugh at what?"

I swallow, completely frozen.

"Um, nothing..." I mutter, spinning back around.

"Callie!" Casey calls. "Where are you going? It's fine! Come back!"

I freeze again, having no idea what to do. I'm shocked that I was prepared to open my soul to Casey whom I've known for a day, and yet, stalled by Luke who's been the center of my life for weeks. I can't possibly open up to both of them together, can I? No, absolutely not. Being ridiculed by one is bad enough. Maybe that's it. I can take Casey's rejection, but not Luke's. No, that's not it either. I care a lot about what Casey thinks. Too much.

I lean against the wall out of sight and can hear them speaking in low voices.

"She was going to show me some of her stuff."

"Yeah, she writes poetry. I see you got the bible out. You let her see it?"

"I was hoping if I showed her, she'd open up."

"I bet it's good."

"I bet it is, too."

"Guess I'm not her favorite anymore. She never wanted to show me anything."

I draw in a deep breath and push away from the wall.

"Sorry, guys! Just realized I had grabbed the wrong book. Got it now," I lie, and cover the distance to the couch. "You're back," I add to Luke.

He gives me one of his real smiles, and I relax a bit. "You know me. Just have to pout for a while, then I'm good. So Casey says you're finally going to let us see some of this mysterious poetry. Gotta say I'm jealous that I couldn't get a look after a month, and this loser got in after a day, but whatever. Let's see it."

I swallow and open the book, suddenly regretting every-thing about this moment. I should have at least told them I'd show them some of the finished versions later. The polished and pretty ones on my computer. These sketches are mainly nothing but stream of consciousness thoughts. Word vomit on the days I was feeling particularly depressed or inspired.

"I told Casey this is my private book. Ideas mainly. I clean them up and do the actual writing on my computer."

Neither of them seems fazed by that, and I realize I'm starting to sound like a diva with all my hesitating. I'm not showing them the next classic novel here, just some rough musings of an introspective drifter.

Then, I remember I actually did complete one of the verses in here. Well, kind of. It was on the bus ride from Shelteron that first time I made my way to the city. My battery had died on my laptop so I worked on it the old-fashioned way. Pen to paper. I never truly finished it, but it was the most complete of anything I had with me.

They're too far apart to read it together, so I hand the book to Casey first since he's the reason I'm in this mess in the first place. I'm still not entirely convinced Luke even cares.

I watch Casey's face as he reads, suddenly horribly embarrassed by it all and re-regretting every second of this encounter. I never should have done this. I never should have let them in. They...

"Holy shit," he mutters, and my heart drops. He shakes his head and glances up at me briefly, then over at Luke. "Listen to this:

> "Mirror mirror, what do you see, when you look
>   at me
> Mirror mirror, what are you thinking, I see
>   those eyes staring
> Mirror mirror, what are you saying, it's always
>   something I believe
> Mirror mirror, you're a liar, so why do you
>   own me
>
> Hello hello greetings from the inside
> Hello hello framed in all your lies
> Hello hello how you love to see me cry

Hello hello always so unkind

Mirror mirror, why the tears, you made me
Mirror mirror, who do you think you are
I made you!

Hello hello greetings from the inside
Hello hello framed in all your lies
Hello hello how you love to see me cry
Hello hello it's time to say goodbye"

"What else do you have?" Casey asks, paging through the notebook with interest.

"What? Nothing..."

"What else? I want to see the rest."

I grab the book from him and shake my head. "There is no more. I mean, not here, not finished."

"It doesn't have to be finished. Please, Callie?" he asks, and I sigh. "What's the last thing you wrote?"

I look away. "I don't really write much anymore."

"Why not?"

I shrug. "I don't know. I guess... Maybe there's no point? Like I said, I'm not really a writer. Well, not a real one."

Casey almost seems annoyed. "Will you stop with that? That's bull."

"It's not! I just...I don't know."

He softens. "Look, I don't want to pressure you, I just really want to see it."

"But it's not even finished!"

"So what? I know how the process works."

"Dude, she says she doesn't want to show you. Let it go," Luke chimes in, and the spell breaks.

I feel badly then. I don't know why except that somehow

I've betrayed Casey. His faith in me. I'm being everything I hate about Luke.

"No, it's fine. Sorry. Here," I jump in. "But like I said, don't expect too much."

I hand him the book back, and he starts going through it again like I've just given him the secret to eternal life.

"I think he likes it," Luke teases, and I give him a look.

"Hell yeah, I like it."

He skims over a few more pages, then lands back on my mirror poem.

"Dude, where's your guitar?" Casey asks, and Luke's face falls. Casey only grunts. "Come on, man, not now."

Luke glares at him. "You know I don't play anymore."

"Yeah, and I also know you don't go anywhere without that piece of junk. Just get it for me and then you can sulk all you want."

Luke smirks. "It needs new strings. I haven't touched it in forever."

"You think I care about that right now? I'm not gonna play a show in the lobby, I just want to try something. Come on! Don't be a dick for once. Please!"

It's Luke's turn to grunt as he rises from his seat and saunters off down the hall. I glance at Casey but see he's pretty much forgotten about me at this point. I can see his mind working furiously on something, scanning the page over and over again. I decide not to interrupt, I'm not sure what to say anyway, and am relieved when Luke finally appears, an acoustic guitar in hand. Casey looks about to explode if he doesn't get whatever this is, out.

The instrument is a beaten mess, which surprises me. I'd expected a star of his caliber to require newer, flashier equipment, but apparently the instrument that "goes with him everywhere" has gone with him for many, many years to many, many places.

Casey barely even acknowledges him as he rips the guitar from his hands and starts tuning. Luke doesn't seem upset, however, and appears amused more than anything. I wonder if they're simply accustomed to this kind of rabid exploration of an idea from each other.

"Well, you kids have fun. I'm gonna go back to my room and lie down. Way too much excitement for one day."

I doubt Casey even hears him.

I watch Luke until he disappears, then turn back to Casey who finally seems satisfied with his tuning. He closes his eyes and nods his head as if counting to himself, and I'm fascinated at the glimpse of his own genius at work.

His fingers wrap around the neck of the guitar with a familiar comfort that makes it obvious he spends a lot of time in this position. He starts strumming, his eyes still scanning my notebook, pausing, strumming again, picking out some individual notes, pausing and returning. I gaze in silence, completely captivated.

Finally, he seems satisfied with something that makes sense in his head, but I have yet to hear beyond it.

I don't even get an intro or explanation before he starts playing an actual song, my words connecting in a rhythm and flow I'd never thought of, but find incredibly beautiful. They come to life, transforming from thoughts into action.

Casey has a good voice. Not as unique as Luke's, but good enough that any lesser band would probably be happy to have him as their own frontman. I doubt he'd agree with me, but I'm surprised by his confidence. I guess I shouldn't be. I'm witnessing a superstar doing what made him a superstar.

He stops and takes in a deep breath before meeting my gaze with an uncertain expression, the confidence suddenly gone.

I'm startled by it, the open vulnerability of someone who should be invincible.

"That was amazing. I never thought my words could sound like that," I breathe, stuck in all kinds of awe at the moment. Of Casey. Of me. Of what we just created together.

I thought I'd gotten used to Casey's grins. He shares them often enough, but this is a new one. He seems almost transcended as he nods and opens his own notebook. He scribbles for several minutes. Stopping, thinking, scribbling again. Every so often he'll play through some chords, humming to himself, muttering something, then return to the notebook.

I wonder again if he even remembers I'm here. He hasn't acknowledged me in a long time, when suddenly, he stops and gives me a direct stare, almost startled.

"You need to go back to your place, wherever that is, and get your laptop."

This time I know what he's thinking. I'm not even going to bother with the familiar line of insecure questioning.

"Are you sure?" I ask, still concerned this can't possibly be happening.

He nods. "Positive. Get it now." I continue to hesitate. "Go!"

And I rise with a grin of my own.

BY THE TIME I return to the suite, Casey and Luke are seated at the table, containers of food half-empty, and a clean plate at the open spot. They look up when I approach, and Luke waves me over.

"Thai," he explains.

"With your hangover?" I ask in disbelief.

He just shrugs with a grin. "Burns away the alcohol?"

"What, so she has a key now?" Casey asks, interrupting our greeting.

"She's here all the time anyway. I gave her the guest room."

Casey studies us for a moment, and I swear I can see his expression fall. I don't know what it means, but my pulse starts to pound as it occurs to me he might be jealous. Could that even be possible? No, of course not. He just thinks it means something different than it does and is mad that I broke my promise not to fall in love with Luke. I can't exactly explain that to him at the moment, however, so I just drop my bag and take my seat.

"It's more convenient, that's all," I offer quickly.

I can feel his gaze, but I'm not ready to meet it and start filling my plate with food.

"Did you bring your laptop?" he asks, changing the subject, but his voice is different now. Some of the magic is gone, and I finally dare a glance in his direction. His eyes...I look away again.

"Got it."

"Ok, good."

"Heard you working on something," Luke comments. "Sounded pretty good."

Casey nods, but doesn't seem as pleased as I would have thought. "Yeah. Got a call from TJ today..." His voice trails off, and they exchange a knowing look.

"I'm surprised they weren't on your case sooner," Luke says.

"They've been bugging me, but this was the first 'do or die' call."

"What do they want?"

Casey studies him for a moment, and I wonder if he's surprised Luke's still engaged in the discussion at this point. I know I am.

"New tour in four months with at least three new tracks."

Luke smirks. "Got tired of waiting, I guess."

"I'd love your help, man."

Luke doesn't respond and only stares at his plate. "Yeah, well, that's not my thing anymore." And there it is. The leg positioned clear of the table, the knee at attention. He's about to run.

"I know, but maybe if..."

"Alright, well, I know I'm full. What about you guys?" Luke cuts in, disappearing from his half-eaten plate before either of us can respond.

Familiar ending to any meal with Luke Craven.

Casey curses and shoves his own chair back in frustration. He doesn't move, however, and just sits in silence, lost in thought.

"You ok?" I ask, and he turns on me with a fire I haven't seen from him before.

"You're living with him? Why didn't you tell me you two hooked up? Don't you think you should have led with that?"

My eyes widen in shock. "What? Whoa, wait a second. We didn't hook up."

"No? But you moved in?"

"It's not like that! I mean, I know what it sounds like, but it's not!"

I lean forward, suddenly terrified at the thought of losing him, maybe even more than I ever was of losing Luke. I'm startled by the thought. Disturbed.

"I didn't move in, I just keep some stuff here in case it gets late. Come on, you know he's not ready for a real relationship. I know you know that better than anyone!"

He studies me, considering my testimony, and I let every ounce of my soul pour onto my face. I need him to believe me for some reason.

"He's not, you know," he states finally in a calm voice, and I'm actually able to breathe again. "I'm not sure if he'll ever be. I warned you about that from the beginning."

I lean toward him in earnest. "I know that, trust me. I'll admit in the beginning I had thoughts, but now I just care about him. I want to help him. Just like you."

He's still evaluating, I can tell, but I keep meeting his gaze, forcing him to give me a fair chance.

Finally, he sighs and shakes head. "God, I'm sorry, Callie. It's just..." He stops and tries to collect his thoughts. "They all fall for him. Every single one. How can they not? I'm not saying he does it on purpose. Maybe sometimes, but mostly he just doesn't realize the effect he has. But I know where he's at right now, and you will get hurt. I know you will."

"I know. Seriously, Casey, I know, ok? It's not like that. I don't have those kinds of feelings for him anymore."

No one is more surprised than I am that I can make that statement with confidence for the first time. I swallow, feeling free somehow. It makes me brave. Or stupid. Both?

I get up and take his hands. I'm still not sure what exactly is going on between Casey and me, but I know that brief moment when I thought I'd lost him was bad enough that the ache is still pressing on my lungs.

Then, it happens. I'm not sure which one of us moves first, but before I know it I'm falling against him, my lips connecting with his. It feels so different than the moment with Luke. This kiss is pure, considered, natural. The lack of desperation making it seem more real, like it could actually last this time. I lock him against me, loving how he does the same, and remember what he'd said at the party. He was right. I did let him kiss me and I do love it. I love it so much I want to write about it.

I pull away, and he seems concerned, then softens at the grin on my face.

"Let's write."

"What?" he laughs. "Right now?"

I nod. I give him another quick kiss and jump to my feet, reaching for his hands to pull him after me.

"What about dessert?" he asks with a sly grin. "I was enjoying it."

I groan. "Seriously? And you're a songwriter?"

He laughs again and lets me lead him back to the couch.

WE END up working mainly on the mirror song. By the time we wrap up our efforts, we're pretty comfortable with the general framework of what we put together. Casey is already talking about demos and scratch tracks and a bunch of other things that I guess mean he wants to do more with it. He clearly has a lot more of the song pieced together in his head than what he can play for me on the guitar. He tries his best to explain and demonstrate his masterpiece, but even with his makeshift couch cushion drum set, and surprisingly effective humming and hand motions, isn't able to fully translate his vision. After everything I've seen from him, I have no doubt that whatever it is, it will be spectacular.

"You hungry?" he asks as I get to my feet and stretch.

"A little. I want to go check on Luke though."

Casey nods. "Good idea. I'll go get us some food."

"You could just order room service if you don't feel like going out."

He grimaces and shakes his head. "No, I need some air. Be back in a bit."

He jumps up, grabs his jacket, which I doubt he needs, and

heads to the door. "Make sure you let me back in, though! Unlike you, I don't have a key..."

I return his smile. "Depends what you bring back."

He gives me a look, and I can't help but laugh.

"I'm kidding! Hang on, I'll get you mine. We might be in the back watching TV anyway."

He waits while I grab my key, extending a dramatic bow when I hand it to him with great ceremony.

"Don't get me in trouble," I warn.

"Who me? I would never!" he returns with a glint before disappearing through the main door.

I shake my head in amusement and head down the hall toward Luke's room. My nerves start to burn in my stomach as I move forward, however, as though I'm transporting from the sunny spark of creativity to the pain of lost identity. I'm not sure what's waiting for me at the end of the hall, but I'm terrified it will be something I'm not ready to handle again so soon.

When no one answers my knock, I peek into the room and am surprised to find it empty. I call for Luke, but there's no response, and my blood starts to pound. I enter the room, holding my breath, searching the bathroom and anywhere else he could be hiding. Nothing.

Confused and concerned, I back through the door and try the guestroom. Maybe he finally decided to take his own turn with the whacky shower. The extra room proves to be empty as well, and now I'm very worried. I'm sure he didn't leave, we would have noticed, so I try one last possibility: the office.

There's no light coming from under the closed door as I approach, so I'm skeptical. This room can't possibly be occupied, but I'm out of options and push through into the darkness anyway.

I nearly scream at the dark figure in the corner.

My heart pounds as I freeze, hand still on the door, terrified of the shadowed ghost. I force air into my lungs. It's only Luke. It has to be Luke. The dim light from the hall illuminates the figure enough that I can see the head turn toward me. I can also see that it's sitting on a chair.

"Luke?" I whisper. I turn on the light, and he squints against the bright blast. He doesn't speak, and after a brief glance in my direction, returns to staring at the floor.

I move into the office and close the door behind me. I don't know what to do, what to say, to draw him out of his nightmare, so I just do what I always do when I lose him, follow him. I pull out the desk chair and move it to the wall so I can sit near him.

And that's what I do. Sit.

For a long time I do nothing, staring at the floor, the ceiling, the wall. Every now and then casting a glance at Luke, but he's never here with me. He's forgotten about me already. The fancy clock on the wall with four different time zones ticks, no, hammers, each second into the stifling air around us. I hate time right now, how unpredictable and inconsistent it can be.

The carpet on the floor is softer here than in the other rooms, and I guess it's because this one isn't used as often. The padding probably isn't as worn. I like the way my foot squishes into it and leaves a clear impression. I make four identical ones in a row, and lean back to admire my design.

"What are you doing?"

I jump, startled by Luke's voice after the long silence.

"Making a footprint ladder."

"You can't do that somewhere else?"

"You're not somewhere else."

He quiets, and I allow myself to look at him again.

"You shouldn't be here."

"Why not?"

"I told you why. I hurt people..." He shakes his head. "No, I break people."

"Ok. Well, I was already broken long before I met you, so we're good."

His gaze shoots to mine, and I stare back. He's wrong if he thinks he has a monopoly on pain and an aimless existence.

"You don't know, Callie. You don't."

I lean my head back and stare at the opposite wall.

"I know more than you think. I know that Elena was an amazing person who killed herself, and that it was probably your fault because you treated her like crap."

I let my words settle for a moment before turning my head toward him to gauge how much I'd hurt him. He has tears in his eyes, but I'm not sure if they're new or not. He closes them and becomes perfectly still.

"Except here's the thing, Luke, it takes a lot more than someone being a jerk to you to make you kill yourself. You're giving yourself too much credit. You're not important enough to do that. She was sick. You may have been the trigger, but only on a gun that was already loaded."

He shakes his head slowly, eyes clenched, tears slipping down his cheeks.

"You don't understand, Callie," he whispers.

"Ok, so explain it to me. I'm done with this 'no personal stuff' bullshit. Explain to me how you picked up a gun and shot your wife in cold blood, because unless that's what happened, you don't belong in this prison anymore."

He shakes his head again, and I can't take it anymore. I grab his hands and jerk him awake.

"Stop! You have to stop this! You did your time! You paid for it! Now, it's time to be the person she loved, not the person she hated."

I search his eyes, refusing to let him retreat this time. Refusing to let him escape to that place where everyone is happy to abandon him. His hands start to shake in mine, I can feel the trembling, and his eyes fill again. The mounting tension burns through me as I watch the armor melt away from his face.

The tears become sobs, and soon he's in my arms, completely shattering before my eyes. He falls to the floor in a crumpled heap, and I pull him tightly against me. I hold on as his body shakes, stroking his hair, resting my head on his. I can feel my own heart aching at the horrific pain exploding into the small room that doesn't seem able to contain it. I can't hear the clock anymore. Time must have stopped.

But I hold on anyway, absorbing what I can, accepting what I can't, and just letting him shatter. We will sort through what's left when it's over, but for now everything needs to break apart. I know the place where he's trapped himself, and I know it's not real but will imprison you forever if you let it. It's that damn mirror from my poem. There's no escape from it until it disappears.

"I killed her," he sobs, pounding the floor. "I..."

I pull him tighter as he continues to melt into the carpet. I said what needed to be said. There are no more words for this. None that I know anyway.

So we wait, melded together, transported to a place where there is no time. No rules. No expectations. Just Luke and I, slowly dissolving into something else, something we don't understand yet, and can't begin to define.

He killed her. Maybe. But only in the same way he's now killing himself. Turning lies into truth. Allowing the mirror to reflect that new distorted truth and giving it the power to shine through every thread, every second, of his existence. It's a prison of the worst kind since it only shows one captor, one executioner, one victim, one criminal. One blighted life that's infecting the rest of us. Luke. Just Luke.

It showed me once. Sometimes, on the really bad days, it still does, and I'd almost guarantee it showed Elena before she decided she couldn't look anymore. It's that damn mirror, devouring souls with its lies, and I realize at that moment why I'm here. I know what I am to him, what I have to do. I'm not here to be his girl-friend, or his nurse, or his counselor, or even his friend. I'm a hammer, and I'm not leaving until that damn mirror is destroyed.

I'm not sure how much time passes like that. I can hear the distant door clatter and know Casey has returned from his errand. I'm disappointed in a way, almost fearful, as the sound forces us back from our exclusive universe. I'm not sure if my job is done, but there's Time again, mocking us by ending this round.

"You should go," Luke whispers, but I just kiss his head and hold on.

"I'm not leaving."

"But Casey..."

"Understands a lot more than you think." I force his head up, and suck in my breath when our eyes finally connect us again in reality. "He was a friend to you when you didn't deserve one. That's who Casey is."

Luke nods and pulls away. Leaning against the side of the desk, he rests his head on his knees.

"You have no idea," he breathes. "Please, Callie. I'm ok now. I'll be ok. I just need a few minutes."

I study him carefully, evaluating his mind, his heart, his soul like Casey had done with his body the night before. I want to believe him. I've hit hard with my first major strike, and decide it can be enough for now.

"I'll be right outside. If you're not out with us for dinner in ten minutes I'm coming back."

He doesn't respond other than to wrap his arms around his legs, and I finally let him go.

"I love you, Luke. And you know the kind I mean. The kind that won't be defined and won't go away."

He glances up and settles his gaze on me. I touch his cheek briefly before leaving him to his broken glass.

"YOU OK?" Casey asks when I join him in the kitchenette. "Wait, did you just come out of the office?"

He stares down the hall, obviously confused.

"Long story. What'd you find?"

Casey grins, and it's exactly what I need at the moment. I swear that smile could do anything. I wonder if he even knows the dangerous weapon he has.

"Burgers. But not just any burger. Here, try this."

I'm expecting tin foil wrapped mounds to come out of the fancy bag, but instead they're extravagant boxes of some kind. Probably high-end organic, recycled cardboard originally harvested from sustainable seaweed beds or something. That makes no sense. Whatever. It was a difficult morning. There's a simple logo on top, which is how I know this burger is more expensive than anything I've ever eaten.

I almost cringe at the thought.

"You're not going to laugh at me again because I've never tasted a burger that costs more than a pair of socks, are you?"

"A bit sensitive, I see," he snickers.

"Well, sorry, but you seem to take pleasure in exposing me to all the forbidden fruit of rockstar living."

Casey chuckles and shakes his head. "Now, you're just being dramatic."

"Am I? First the champagne, now the fancy burgers."

"I'm from a family of twelve. Trust me, I do not need to eat like this to survive." He shrugs. "I don't know. I just thought...I wanted you to try something you otherwise wouldn't. I thought you'd like it."

Touched on so many levels, I'm not sure how to respond at first. I don't understand how he can keep surprising me, but his timing is impeccable. I cover the distance between us, and he stills as I wrap my arms around him.

I can feel him laughing to himself in surprise. "What's this?"

"Nothing," I murmur, resting my head against his chest. His own arms tighten around me as he sighs.

"Will Luke be joining us?" he asks quietly, knowingly. I keep forgetting how intuitive he is.

"I'm not sure. Maybe." I pull back so I can see his face. "Something happened while you were out. I...I don't know what yet, but something. It may be what we've been waiting for."

He brushes some stray strands of hair from my face, and I think about the burgers resting two feet away. So stupid, but so important that I can feel the tears burning again. After everything, after what I just endured with Luke, it feels so good to have someone taking care of me for once, caring about me. Knowing that they want to be part of my world and follow me into my nightmares to battle my demons. Casey hasn't said as much, and maybe he never will. Maybe he will leave in a couple days to return to his other life and forget all about me, but right now, right at this moment, he is significant. He's exactly what I need, whether conscious or not, and I'm grateful.

"Thank you," I whisper, and he kisses me.

This time, I'm ready for it and let myself melt into him. I let myself get lost, starting to think maybe I can heal, too. Maybe there's hope for me somehow in this whole whirlwind of desperation and compassion. He tastes so good, so pure, which makes no sense given what he is, but I start to get it now. What he is, is not who he is. What Luke is, is not who he is. What I am, is not who I am. None of us are. It's the rest of the world that tells us what we are, regardless of who we are. Strip it away and we just are. Luke, Casey, me. We're not different, we're just burdened by different expectations.

"Wow," he says as we finally pull away. "Now, that's a proper thank you. You could have just gotten me a beer."

I laugh and hit him, loving his playful return grin.

"Yeah, well, these burgers better be worth it."

CASEY SEES him first with the better vantage point, and I'm grateful he chooses to go with his easy smile as a greeting.

He shoves the third box toward the empty seat beside me at the island, and Luke pulls out the stool.

"Adaline's?" Luke asks, his own lips cracking into the slightest of smiles.

"Thought we could all use a dose of heaven after our night of Hell."

Luke doesn't respond, but I can tell he agrees.

"Callie, here, is a convert already."

"How can I not be?" I mutter through a mouthful of perfectly grilled brioche, arugula, beef, and a bunch of other stuff I never would have thought to put on a burger because I didn't know it existed and/or was edible.

"We should take her to 49th & Finch."

Casey's eyes light up at the thought. "We totally should. Oh man, they have the best bar food."

"Bar food?" I ask, skeptically. "So basically you guys just upgraded the same stuff you ate when you first started out as a garage band ten years ago."

Casey grins. "Basically. Although to be fair, we still eat that stuff, too."

I laugh. "And you're not 500 pounds, why? Because I'm pretty sure I would be."

Casey shrugs. "I don't know, good question. Stress?"

I shake my head. "Ok, first of all, if you're going to hang with me, you're going to learn to eat a vegetable."

"What about fruit cups?" Luke asks with a snicker, and I glance over at him in surprise, then amusement.

"Yes, that's a start."

"Fruit cups?" Casey asks.

"Part of my standard balanced breakfast order at Jemma's," I explain.

"She doesn't drink coffee either."

"I noticed that this morning!"

"I like tea. So what?" I shoot back, crossing my arms. "You know what? I'm so sick of your holier-than-thou attitudes. You think I'm the one who baffles the mind? What about the two of you?"

They both smile, clearly liking the challenge. "Yeah, what about us?" Casey asks, taking the bait.

I grunt. "Ok, well, first of all. Explain to me why two guys with more money than they probably know what to do with, two guys who have an entire mall's-worth of clothing options just a personal shopper away, point to the plain, ratty t-shirt and say, 'Yes. That's it. That's what I want.'"

They laugh, and Luke shakes his head. "Again with the t-shirts! You really have a vendetta, don't you?" he teases.

I raise my eyebrows and give them an obvious appraisal. "Am I wrong? You two look identical right now."

Casey visibly braces for the fight. "Well, first of all, if you recall, I'm actually wearing his clothes, so..."

"And, second of all, I thought we already established pink polo shirts weren't my thing," Luke adds.

I deflate with a pout, afraid maybe I'm losing this round. No! I'm not losing. "I didn't say you had to dress like an investment banker, I'm just saying, would a little color or design kill you? I mean, really. It's appalling."

"She just wants us to take our shirts off," Casey teases, and I blush. I don't know why. At this point I've seen both of them almost naked, one of them actually naked, and yet still I blush. Stupid Casey and his sexy smile...gosh, sexy everything. I have to force away the extremely unhelpful memories of him in a towel.

"Whatever. You're just mad because I don't drool over you all the time like you're used to."

"No? Really," Casey challenges, moving around the island. He pulls his shirt over his head, and sure enough my mouth goes dry. I curse to myself. At least I'm not drooling.

"Not even a little interested?" he continues, taking my hand and guiding my fingers over his chest, his abs. His perfectly sculpted tattooed torso. The detailed ink reminding me of every tantalizing picture I'd made the mistake of studying in my earlier search.

I can hear Luke snickering from his seat, and struggle desperately for a witty return. Anything! Just...something!

I swallow. His warm skin feels so good beneath my fingers and I can't get our kisses out of my head. The way his hands moved over me, the way he felt beneath my own. Gosh, I want him so much that I actually hate him right now. I especially hate that he clobbered me in this debate, even if he totally cheated.

"Geez. Put your clothes on. Luke's trying to eat."

"I'm good," Luke interjects, and I glare over at him, but finally manage to pull away from Casey. I grab his shirt from the floor and sling it back at him. He captures it against his chest with that goofy grin that only increases his appeal.

"And also, I don't believe for a second that you can look like that sitting around watching TV and eating bar food, so that makes you a liar on top of everything else."

Casey laughs and mercifully slips his shirt back over his head.

"Of course not. I was kidding about the junk food and stress. Trust me, they keep us on a pretty tight leash." He pauses, and glances over at Luke. "Speaking of which, I was gonna ask if I could borrow your key and go hit the gym later."

For some reason, Luke looks to me first before nodding. "Actually, if you want, I'll just call down and have Mara get you one of your own."

I'm sure Casey's stunned expression mirrors my own, and it's everything I can do to stay calm and not tackle Luke with a gigantic hug.

"Thanks, man," Casey replies casually, but I know he must be bursting inside as well.

"Sure. Thanks for the burger."

Casey nods, and somehow we all sense the universe has shifted.

LUKE SAYS he'll make the call to Mara from his room and disappears shortly afterwards for some time alone. He's had an emotionally exhausting day that jerked him all over the spectrum, so I'm not surprised. You don't shatter glass without drawing blood.

Once we're alone, I glance back at Casey who still seems in shock.

"Guess you're staying?" I say.

"Guess so," he replies with a smile.

"What about your life? I mean, don't you have somewhere else you're supposed to be?"

He grins. "Trying to get rid of me?"

I roll my eyes. "You know I want you here. I just...I don't know. You must have a whole other life. Obligations."

"Obligations," he smirks. "Yeah. But nothing I can't do from here. Don't worry, Mom, I'll be where I need to be when I need to be there."

He sighs. "Anyway, I do have my own place, but it's nothing worth missing. I'm on the road so much I never thought there was any point in setting up roots." He pauses. "I could say the same to you."

I almost laugh. "Please. My life is literally nothing. Talk about a pointless existence."

I feel his gaze and realize I revealed more than I'd intended.

"Sorry, that didn't come out right."

He shrugs. "I don't know. Maybe it did. What does that mean? Who are you? I don't even know your last name."

I look away. "No one worth your time, believe me."

I upset him. I can see it in the way his eyes change, that constant amusement dissolving into anger.

"You do understand you're insulting me, too, when you do that?"

Not the response I was expecting. "I'm sorry. I didn't mean it like that. I just ...I don't know. I just meant I'm no one."

He shakes his head in frustration. "What the hell does that even mean? You're no one? So am I just an idiot then to be wasting entire days and nights with 'no one'?"

My heart starts to pound. "No. That's not what I meant. Of course not."

He glares at me and curses. "No, I know what you meant. I know exactly what you meant. Your face isn't slapped all over the internet and some stupid magazine so therefore you don't count as a person in my life just because mine is. God, Callie, we basically met two days ago and I can't even imagine not having you in my life at this point. Luke didn't know you existed a month ago and now you're his best chance at survival. You're doing what no one else could! You write poetry that cut into me, and have made me laugh so much these last couple days it's actually starting to get painful." He draws in a deep breath, and I can only stare in stunned silence. "So stop with the 'I'm a nobody' bullshit and tell me who you really are!"

I bite my lip and shift in my stool, doing everything I can to sort through the explosion. There's so much there, it's so heavy, I don't know how. I cover my face with my hands and lean my elbows on the counter. He doesn't respond, he's waiting for my decision, and I suck in a deep breath. Is he proving to be my hammer?

"I'm Callie Roland, twenty-three, born and raised in Shelteron, Pennsylvania."

I finally dare to look again, and his eyes have softened. He takes the stool beside me and holds out his hand.

"Casey Barrett, twenty-five, born and raised in Houston, Texas."

"Houston?" I repeat in surprise, remembering Luke's recent journey.

He nods and gives me a sad smile. "Elena Barrett Craven was my sister."

———

MY HEART STOPS. I stare at Casey in shock, not sure what else to do. It can't be...but it almost has to be at the same time.

"I'm sorry to just dump that on you. I thought you should know. Maybe that matters, maybe it doesn't," he says quietly.

"Of course it matters!" I cry, still shaken from the news.

He looks away. "More pieces of the puzzle, huh?"

"More insight into you," I correct, taking his hand. He glances at me, and I see that it was my turn to surprise him. "I'm so sorry, Casey," I continue, my heart breaking as I recast everything I'd understood about the situation into a new light. "And yet you stood by him? Cared for him?"

Casey stares at the floor. "We were both hurting. Maybe I thought we were standing by each other in the beginning. But I wasn't the reason for her downfall, he was. I was able to forgive myself and continue to love her after she was gone. Luke's pain was different."

I hug him then. I can't help it. I don't know how else to explain how he never ceases to amaze me.

"You're a special person, Casey Barrett," I whisper.

He laughs against my hair. "You've only known me a few days. I'll get on your nerves soon enough."

I squeeze tighter, finding that unlikely.

He pulls back and searches my face. I want him to kiss me again, but don't dare to hope lightening will strike a third time. A brief struggle flickers behind his eyes before he finally smiles and sits back.

"So does that mean I've won enough points to continue our *Dead Head* marathon?"

I groan. "Do we have to? Right before bed?"

He shrugs and gives me that look I'll never be able to resist.

"Fine," I concede with a sigh. "But I maintain the Power of the Mute Button."

"Deal. But no fast-forwarding."

I grunt. "Deal."

I CAN'T SLEEP that night. Our *Dead Head* binge turns out to be the least of my problems as I stare at the ceiling of the guest room. Casey took the couch, and part of me wants to wake him up just so someone else can share in my misery. But I realize that would make me an awful human being, so I manage to stay rooted under my sheets. Still, I don't know how much longer I can lie here with my riotous mind.

While thoughts of Luke pound against my skull like always, it's surprisingly Casey's face that keeps me awake tonight. I can't stop thinking about his revelation, about the number of conversations he'd had that he could have made about himself, and didn't. Here I'd been counting on him as my support, Luke's rock, and he'd had as much reason as any of us to need an anchor. He calls himself Luke's brother and I'd been assuming that was figurative.

I think back to all his warnings about me falling for Luke. No wonder he was so sensitive to that likelihood. And here I'd been annoyed with him for being intrusive. For overstepping his bounds. I was the one stomping all over his heart and mocking his fences.

I have to fight the urge to go to him now, to wake him up with a confusing explosion of words and feelings that will make no sense to him since he hasn't been in my head for the last three hours. And that's when I realize I have no choice. I have to do something before I self-destruct. There's only one way I know how to capture what I'm feeling. One thing that helps me turn the chaos in my head into something livable.

I climb out of bed and grab my laptop.

"How was I supposed to know your smile was
only a distraction?

How am I supposed to feel, stuck in veiled
conversation?
Because you never let me in, now I have to
watch you drowning.
Quiet suffering speak!

I'll stay here, don't look down.
There's nothing waiting for you on the ground.
You're stronger than you're feeling now.
I'll stay here.
I'll stay.

How was I supposed to know you wore silence
like some worn out fashion?
How are you supposed to heal, so afraid of our
reaction?
Because you have to let me in, please stop all of
this pretending.
Oh quiet suffering speak!

Quiet suffering, I hear it. Deafening.
Quiet suffering, I feel it. Pounding.
Stop these games, you don't need it. They're
maddening.
Quiet suffering, I don't believe it. I'm waiting.

I'll stay here, don't look down.
There's nothing waiting for you on the ground.
You're stronger than you're feeling now.
I'll stay."

16

DAY NINETEEN

I was sure I'd be the last one up because of my late night, but there's no activity in the main space when I emerge. Casey glances over at me from the couch with a groggy smile, and I know he's just woken up as well.

"Morning, Sunshine," I chirp, motioning him to move back on the couch so I can sit by his legs. He adjusts, and I place my laptop on his chest.

"For you," I explain, giving him a quick kiss on the forehead. "I'm gonna go shower."

I HEAR the music through the door when I exit the bathroom to my room. It doesn't surprise me, at least, not as much as the voices. Luke must be up, too. I dress quickly and comb through my hair, eager to join them and solve the mystery. I've felt queasy since leaving my heart with Casey, knowing he could hate my work as much as love it. Would he even get it? Be offended? My mental journey last night had taken a lot of turns and made plenty of assumptions he couldn't possibly understand.

They stop when they see me, and I feel the heat rise to my cheeks. Casey has the guitar in hand like I'd suspected, but it's Luke who gives me the first smile.

"Wow, Callie, I'm a little jealous that he gets a poem and I don't," Luke teases. At least, I think he's teasing. I can't tell, and don't respond at first. I cover the distance between us and grab my laptop from the coffee table.

"Hey! I wasn't done with that!" Casey whines, and I give him a look.

"I'll give it back in a second."

I turn to Luke. "I did one for you as well, but you weren't awake."

Luke looks surprised, as does Casey.

"Really? You wrote two last night?"

I shrug. "Couldn't sleep." I pull up Luke's verses and go to hand him the computer, but he shakes his head.

"No, you read it."

"What?" I ask, my heart racing.

"I want you to read it. I want to hear it how you intend it to be heard."

I swallow and suck in my breath. That's different somehow. I don't know why, but it is. Maybe because there's not enough distance then.

"I..."

"Read it. I want to hear it, too," Casey jumps in, and now I know I'm stuck.

I glance back and forth between the two of them and sigh.

"Ok." My voice comes out like a squeak. I can't believe how nervous I am. Casey has already seen the one I'd done for him, but this one is different. This is for Luke. It's more personal in a way, more intimate. I'm not sure he'd want Casey to hear it, but then realize if anyone has a right it's his best friend, brother-in-law, and my...I don't know what.

As I start reading the first line, my voice is weak. I can hear it and nearly cringe. This is not how I intended the words to be heard. Not at all. I shake my head, feeling the tears coming, both from the memories and my current failure of the memories.

"No. That's not it. I'm starting over."

I dare a quick glance at them and see Casey's compassion all over his face. Luke looks more contemplative than anything, and then I recognize his expression. It's the classic "Luke Craven braced resolve." He's not testing me, he's testing himself. Can he hear what I have to say? Can he open up to someone else's heart?

I have to do this. For Luke. For myself.

> "I could have told you everything would be
>   alright.
> I could have told you it gets easier the harder
>   you try.
> But I couldn't lie to you, even though I'd die
>   for you.
> And I could have told you instead of just
>   holding you.
>
> But what could I say that my eyes haven't
>   already said?
> And what words could heal the wounds that
>   bleed like this?
> How many tears will it take to drown away the
>   pain?
> I don't know, but I can hold you.

And I could have taken you far way from here.
But where would that leave you? It'd be the
      same even there.
I won't hide you, even though I'd like to.
And I could have spoken instead of just
      loving you.

But what could I say that my eyes haven't
      already said?
And what words can heal the wounds that
      break us?
How many tears will it take to drown away the
      pain?
I don't know, but I can hold you. I can love you.
I can hold you."

No one speaks as my voice fades. I swallow hard again, my throat dry, scratchy. I can't look at them. I'm afraid. Afraid I exposed too much too fast. Afraid it wasn't enough.

"Can I see that?" Luke says quietly after a long, painful pause. I glance at him in surprise before handing him the laptop.

He scans the screen again, and I feel Casey's eyes on me. I'm afraid maybe he's jealous, but when I dare to meet his gaze, it's so warm and understanding that there's no doubt in my mind he's everything I've come to think he is.

"That was beautiful, Callie," he offers, and I notice Luke's absent nod in agreement as he studies my words. No, his words.

"Thanks, Callie," Luke mumbles softly, handing me my computer again. It's a strange comment, considering he follows it by rising to his feet and disappearing down the hall. I hear a door close and know it's too early to be his room. He's escaped to the office.

"He loved it, but it was a lot for him," Casey explains gently as I study the dark hallway.

"I know," I reply, dropping beside him. "He's with The Chair."

"The chair?"

I nod. "He stole it from the café. I think it has something to do with Elena."

Casey blinks, clearly confused. "I'm sorry, what?"

I shrug. "The Chair is how we met. I was sitting at my table one day at Jemma's, and he came in and asked me to move. Apparently, I was in his chair, that chair. He'd go into the café every day and stare at the same one for several minutes. Freaked out the servers and café regulars, but no one asked questions or stopped him. Finally, the day of the party this past weekend he just lost it and basically marched down to the café and stole the chair in broad daylight, right in front of the patrons and staff. I'm surprised there hasn't been more about it in the news."

Casey is staring at me like I'd just recited the *Declaration of Independence* in a made up language.

"Luke...stole a chair. A cheap café chair?" He clears his throat and leans forward on the couch, eyes fixed on the coffee table.

"Yep. Just a chair. He was obsessed with it before he stole it."

Casey shakes his head. "And now what? What does he do with it? I don't remember seeing it."

"He keeps it in his office and sits in it."

"And does what?" Casey cries in exasperation.

I shrug. "Nothing. He just sits there. That's where I found him yesterday when he finally broke down."

I can see the look in his eyes and know I'm about to be tasked with damage control.

He jumps to his feet, and I follow.

"What are you doing?" I ask in alarm as he moves around the couch.

"Going to find out what the hell is going on."

I vehemently shake my head and grab his arm. "No, you can't."

"I can't? You're telling me my unstable friend has some kind of obsessive relationship with a piece of furniture, and I shouldn't go try to find out why?"

I nod. "Yes, that's exactly what I'm telling you. It's not just a chair. It's something else, and he's not ready. If you barge in there now and attack him, you're going to undo everything we've done!"

Casey throws his hands up in frustration before locking his fingers above his head. He begins pacing in front of the couch, muttering to himself, and I know I have to intervene for his own sake. He deserves better as well. I take his arm and pull him back to the couch.

"Please, Casey. I'm asking you to let it go. Not forever, just for now, ok? Let him have this. I'm telling you, he needs this. Can you just trust me?"

He meets my gaze, he has to, I've centered it inches away, and finally lets out an aggravated breath. "This is crazy. I mean, he's always been odd, but a chair?"

"I don't know what the chair means, but I know it's significant. He'll let us in when he's ready."

"And until then?"

"Until then, we keep fighting for the small stuff."

I sense his concern finally dissolving into amusement.

"What?" I ask, suddenly self-conscious.

He smiles and shakes his head. "Nothing. Just you."

"Me? What about me?"

"You're like a cross between a motivational poster and a shrink... And my mom."

Now, I have to laugh. "Your mom? Really? You made out with me...twice...and I remind you of your mom?"

He ducks from my playful swing with a sheepish grin. "I don't know! You're always yelling at me!"

"Ha! I do not!"

"I don't eat enough vegetables. You don't like my clothes. I'm too mean to Luke..."

I roll my eyes, but can't come close to being annoyed at him with the look on his face. Instead, I lean against him and take his hand. He quiets as I trace his fingers and concentrate on the steady rise and fall of his chest.

"You're thinking about my mom now, aren't you?" he asks with a knowing grin, and I shrug.

"Maybe. What's she like?"

He laughs. "She had ten kids. Some say that makes her a saint, others say she's insane."

"What do you say?"

"Probably somewhere in between."

"Do you get to see your family a lot?"

I sense his mood shift and wonder why.

"Some of my siblings. There are two in particular I'm close to."

I glance up at him and note his distant expression.

"What about your parents?"

He shakes his head. "No. Not really. She won't see me unless I see him and that's not happening."

It's then that I remember "Argyle" and almost cringe.

"I'm sorry," I say quietly. "My parents are no picnic either."

"Yeah? What are they like?"

I grunt and stare at the ceiling, settling into him. "Well, I haven't seen my mom since I was twelve. She met some guy at the bowling alley…yeah, I know."

"I'm sorry, I know it's not funny," Casey snickers. "But come on…"

"Total small town cliché, I know. But yeah, she took off, and we never heard from her. Dad…well…I don't know. We functioned, I guess."

"Functioned?"

I shrug. "We kind of just stayed out of each other's way until I was old enough to make my own decisions for my life."

"Which were what?"

"What do you mean? My decisions?"

"Yeah. What are you now that you can choose?"

I swallow and realize I'm clenching my other fist. I think he might notice when he takes that hand, too, and kisses my fingers. It's so sweet it almost hurts, and I want to answer his question. I just don't know how. What am I? I have no idea.

"I don't know, really. I couldn't wait to get out of Shelteron, and then when the opportunity came, I had no idea where to go or what to do. I've kind of just been floating, sometimes treading. Not really sure where to go or what I want. Just avoiding the things I don't want."

"Ok, but you must be doing something to survive here on your own."

I shake my head, not sure he's ready for this part. No, I'm not sure I'm ready for this part. I take a deep breath.

"I'm living off money from a lawsuit settlement."

I have his attention and I'm not sure what to do with it. I think I might care about him too much to finish the story.

"Really? What happened?" he asks, as I knew he would. Only Luke doesn't ask the obvious questions.

I look away, and he must notice me tense, but he doesn't let me off the hook. He's not nosy, he cares, and I draw in a deep breath.

"When I was seventeen I got a job at a large, independent grocery store. The owner took an interest in me and a couple of the other girls."

I quiet, not sure I can actually tell this story. I never really tried. It didn't seem relevant or necessary until this moment, until this person. Casey squeezes my hand as if sensing my hesitation.

"It started off with just some comments, stupid stuff. Completely inappropriate, but whatever. It's not like there were tons of employment options for high school kids in my town. I kick myself to this day because I feel like I should have known. I know it's common for victims to blame themselves, but..." I shake my head. "Well, anyway, one day..." I stop again. I can't tell if this is going well or not. I feel the tears burning low, and I'm annoyed that they're still there after all this time. I thought for sure they would have dissolved by now.

"Anyway, I couldn't prove it, he didn't rape me or do anything that left evidence, just..." No, that part isn't necessary. "But once the other girls came forward as well, and we realized there was a pattern and we had a case, one of their parents said we all needed to press charges. Nothing really stuck from a criminal standpoint since it was only our word against his, but there was enough to make a civil lawsuit a painful experience for both sides. His lawyer urged him just to settle, and so he did. We each accepted a big lump of cash. And that was that. My dignity got a price tag."

"And you came here?"

I meet Casey's gaze, thoughtful, compassionate, gentle.

"I had to. I had to go somewhere. I wasn't me anymore. I was either the slut from the grocery store or a potential payday. To my dad and his girlfriend, I was basically both."

I watch the anger flash across his face and find comfort and security in that for some reason.

"If you were my daughter, I wouldn't have slept until that bastard was in prison or the ground," he spits.

I trace his jaw, warmed on so many levels. "I'm glad I'm not your daughter," I joke, and he returns my smile, but the sadness is still in his eyes. It's so beautiful, and my heart nearly bursts when he gives me a quick kiss.

I try to clear my head so I can return to my story. "So that's pretty much it. I came here, not to make a name for myself in lights, but to disappear. I wasn't running to anything, just running from, and have basically been trying to figure things out ever since." I quiet and meet his gaze, serious this time.

"When I say 'I'm no one' it's not even about self-esteem. I just don't know who I am, what I am. I don't know where I'm going or what I want from life. I just knew I didn't want to be the slut from the grocery store or Kyle and Nora's daughter. I wanted to be no one so I could start fresh and hopefully be someone else one day."

Casey is quiet as I draw my speech to a close. I don't really know what else to say, so now it's just a matter of holding my breath and dealing with the fallout. I can see his mind working as we sit in silence, his ever-present smile tabled for the moment as he considers his response. I love that he considers his response.

"What happened to you isn't right and I'm glad you got some retribution, even though I wish that bastard would have gotten jail time instead," Casey says finally.

He hesitates, and I can't stop my smile. "But..." I continue for him.

He returns it, almost shy. "How do you know there's a but?"

"It's all over your face."

He grins and shrugs. "No, not so much a 'but' as a caution about the ending of your story." He has my attention.

"Oh, you don't like the ending."

He shakes his head. "No. I don't. You make it sound like your value is in your identity, and your identity is something that doesn't exist unless it's concrete."

"Concrete?"

"Definable. I don't like you defining yourself by what you're not, and therefore concluding you're no one. What about what you are?"

"What I am?"

He nods. "Your identity shouldn't be an occupation or a status. Hell, it's not even dreams and aspirations. Those things will flow out of who you are once you embrace it. You have to stop looking at what's missing and focus on what's here."

"Now, who's a walking motivational poster," I tease. I can't help myself, and he tosses back his own sheepish grin.

"Well, you need to hear it, that's all. You know why I'm here?" he asks suddenly. "Because when I was sixteen, Elena Barrett told me that our dad was a liar. That I wasn't a worthless piece-of-shit just because I didn't meet his expectations. That I was smart, and caring, and a talented musician, and even though I was just a kid fooling around with drums in a stupid band with my friend Luke, it was important because I loved it." He quiets, and I can see the emotion rising in him. "That's why I'm here, Callie. Because she told me what I was when everyone else in my life was telling me what I wasn't. Once I started focusing on what I was instead, that's where my identity came from, my dreams, the drive."

"It all starts with believing in yourself," I echo dryly.

His eyes narrow. "No, that's a lie. It starts with accepting yourself. You can't believe in what you don't understand. And if you're still telling people you're no one, then you don't understand yet."

I don't respond. Not because I don't have anything to say, but because I have too much to say. And yet, I realize he's given me even more to think about, and that's what I need to do with his words right now. Tuck them away and consider them with the same care and insight with which they were offered.

"Can we work on our song again?" I ask after a long pause.

He glances at me, clearly pleased. "Which one?"

It's my turn to be surprised. "What do you mean?"

His grin turns mischievous as he picks up the guitar.

"Fire up that laptop."

WE WORK INTO THE AFTERNOON, taking a break for some food at one point when we realize we never even ate breakfast. I choose the meal this time and force him to eat a salad.

"What?" Casey asks, his fork stalling in mid-air as he observes my satisfied smirk.

"Nothing. Just enjoying the moment."

He looks skeptical and shakes his head.

"And what moment is that? Enjoying a meal with a super hot rockstar, or watching me eat vegetables?"

I grin. "It can't be both?"

"You're acting like my mom again," he warns, and I shrug.

"Good. You need it. Vitamins, Casey. You need vitamins."

"There are vitamins in fries."

"What would TJ say?"

Casey almost drops his fork and laughs. "TJ...don't remind me. Please."

"What? You know I'm right."

"Right about what?"

Casey and I glance over at Luke who does his magical appearing act at the presence of food. He grabs the extra salad and joins us at the table. We went formal for lunch.

"TJ would want you to consume a well-balanced meal," I explain, and Luke glances at Casey in surprised amusement.

"TJ Barringer?"

Casey nods and rolls his eyes.

Luke laughs. "How does she know TJ?"

"I don't," I defend. "Only by reputation."

"Oh, really? Interesting," Luke responds.

"She was with me when TJ called about the new tracks."

Luke seems to understand and starts on his salad.

"Not to mention you guys talk about him. I remember stuff."

"Don't we know it," Casey mumbles, and Luke smirks.

"Heard you kids working again," Luke comments, surprising both of us.

Casey nods. "Yeah, Callie has a lot of good ideas."

"Oh, please," I scoff. "I sit there and offer moral support while you work your magic."

Casey gives me a mock glare. "Those aren't my lyrics."

"They're not lyrics, they're verses. It's a poem."

"Not anymore," Luke counters, and I turn on him.

"Wait, whose side are you on anyway?"

Luke shrugs. "Sorry, hon, but poetry set to music is called a 'song.'"

I roll my eyes, but my grin breaks when his does. "Fine, whatever."

"Accept it, Callie. You're a songwriter now," Casey echoes.

My eyes widen. "No, I'm not. Wait. Really? But..."

He just shrugs and gives me that smile that always seems to calm me and excite me at the same time.

"I'm having trouble with the hook into the chorus, though," Casey continues, back to business, and I can see that means more to Luke than it does to me.

Luke nods. "Let's hear it."

I'm sure Casey is as startled as I am at the request, but he does a better job hiding it.

"Ok, yeah, sure." He pushes back from the table and retrieves the guitar.

Luke continues eating but watches Casey intently as he plays through what we have of our mirror song. I can see the music working its way through Luke's head as he listens, concentrating, evaluating.

Casey finishes, and I sense this moment means more to him than I can possibly understand. He rests the guitar on his lap and pretends to pick at a scratch, but I'm pretty sure he's just distracting himself as he waits for the verdict.

After a long silence, Luke nods. "It's good, Case. Really good. I see what you mean about the hook, though. Try throwing the F# minor in after the A and add an extra two beats to the break."

Casey's eyes light up. "You mean, bring the chorus back in late on the offbeat?"

Luke nods. "Exactly. Plus, the minor at the end of the bridge will give it a bigger cut. Hanging on the 4 was fine, but I think the 2 will give you more depth." His gaze turns serious as he studies his friend. "Case, the chorus is killer. Really, really good."

I can't help but smile at the look on Casey's face, the pure relief and joy. The moment is so beautiful, I'm almost annoyed that Luke ruins it by drawing me in. I hate taking anything away from them.

"You, too, Callie. I know those are your words."

"Mostly. Casey changed them around a bit and added some."

Luke shrugs. "Yeah, but you understand that's not because there was anything wrong with the original. They just have to flow with the music. It's all a give and take in the process."

I nod and smile. "Of course. He made it better, there's no question."

Then, suddenly, Luke's eyes change, and I see something there I've never seen before. A light, a spark. I've seen it in Casey many times now, but never Luke.

Surprised, I can only watch as he turns back to Casey and asks for the guitar. Casey is just as shocked and hands it to him, almost reverently.

Luke pushes back his chair and examines the instrument in his hands for a moment. Casey and I watch in awe as he holds it, his fingers touching the strings like they might break if he applies any pressure. I can't even begin to guess what's going through his mind, or Casey's for that matter, but I'm so happy I feel ready to explode.

Finally, Luke seems able to accept the fact that he's holding a guitar again and begins picking out a string of notes that flows into a seamless melody. It's beautiful. I don't know much about music, but I know whatever this is would sound perfect with what Casey just played. Casey seems to understand the significance of that even more than I do.

"Sweeny's lick," Casey murmurs, and Luke nods, raising his eyes to meet Casey's.

"For the bridge. I think we just layer rhythm for the chorus. Maybe some killer reverb on the 'hello' vocal?"

Casey nods. "Definitely. I was thinking even a tight band-pass filter on the second line."

Luke considers that and shrugs. "Yeah, that could work too. I'm hearing it."

They continue like that for a few minutes, and my jaw is on the floor. They're too wrapped up to notice.

I think I'm the only one who heard Luke use the word "we."

"HOW EASY DO you think it would be to get into Jackson Street tomorrow?" Casey asks once they finally seem content with whatever they'd just created in their heads. "I know we haven't used them in a while, but Julian's a pro."

Luke shrugs. "I don't know. TJ might be able to get you in. You want to lay some of this down?"

It's Casey's turn to shrug. "Thinking about it. Why not? It's out there now. Might as well see what it sounds like. Wish we were home and could just use our own stuff, but Jackson Street is cool. Julian has gear we can use, right?"

Luke nods. "Probably. He's got his studio guys, too, if you want to mess around. You might need to give him a heads up though so he can get them in. Send TJ a work tape. He'll lose his mind."

Casey nods, and I can see something change in his expression. He's going to ask. I know it. We all know it.

Luke swallows and shakes his head. At least he's not angry this time. Sad, more than anything. I can see it hurts him to keep letting Casey down. I can see how much he loves him.

"I can't, man. You know that. I just..." He stops and draws in a deep breath. "You've got my support on this."

Casey deflates, and my heart breaks at his disappointment. "Yeah, no, of course," he says with a weak smile. "It would have been...no, yeah." He lets out a dry laugh, but there's no humor in it.

"Good luck, though. I think you have something," Luke

offers as consolation. He clasps his friend's shoulder as he passes, and I watch Casey try to put himself back together.

I'm not sure what to say when we're alone. I don't want to embarrass him, but it also kills me to watch the previous joy siphoned out of him. Hope can be a devastating thing, and when it comes to Luke, it often proves to be even more treacherous.

"I should go call TJ and see if he can set something up.," Casey mutters. I'm not even sure he's talking to me.

"Casey..."

He pushes up from the table and waves me off. "It's fine. Not a big deal." But he's lying, and we both know it. "I'll be back in a few minutes," he says, pulling out his phone.

Alone again, I sigh and study the empty lunch dishes in frustration.

———

WHEN IT RAINS IT POURS. TJ isn't able to get Casey into the studio until Friday, which is four days later than he wanted. The setback also gives me the opportunity to watch Casey sulk for the first time. Luke's rejection, coupled with his frustrated creativity, is apparently more than he can handle at once, and after two hours of watching them pout alone in silence, I finally get sick of both of them.

Casey doesn't seem as upset as I would have hoped when I tell him I'm going back to my place for a bit. I need to check in on my own life, as well as collect some more supplies. Maybe even do laundry. He does little more than shrug and tell me he'll let me know if anything comes up. I'm hurt, but I get it, and give him the space he seems to so desperately want.

It would have been funny, if it hadn't been so depressing, that it's literally pouring when I emerge from the hotel and flag a cab to return home. I'd gotten lost in that little bubble of Suite 403, and if it hadn't been for Casey sending me home to get my laptop, I realize I wouldn't have experienced fresh air in days. I cringe when I consider that's Luke's life now. At least when he had Jemma's, he had some interaction with the world. I decide my next goal has to be getting him out of his room.

It's almost strange being back in my apartment. So much has changed in the last few days, I've changed, and it almost doesn't feel like home anymore. Not that Luke's place does either. Maybe it's that I've realized I don't really have a home, just places I live. Is that how Luke and Casey feel? Always moving, never belonging. What's changed is that the thought doesn't totally make me sad anymore. It's hard to feel lonely when I've just spent days filling myself to the brink with two incredible people. I'm almost exhausted from it, and yet, I find myself missing them already. It's absurd, I know. I'd been so eager for air and space, and now I keep checking my phone in hopes of closing the gap again.

I set to work, mostly to distract myself, and begin tidying up a bit, collecting my dirty clothes, and shoving a fresh supply of travel necessities into a bag for when I return to the suite. There were several items I'd wished I'd had over the last couple days, and I run a mental checklist as I survey my apartment. When I get to my bed, I stop with a sigh, realizing I should probably stay here for the night. I can't actually live in Suite 403, right? Crashing there on occasion is fine, but...

Yeah, I'm staying here. It's settled. I'll give Casey his space, Luke his privacy. Maybe even give them time alone to repair and explore what they can't when I'm there. And goodness knows there's plenty for them to repair and explore.

My phone buzzes and I glance down in anticipation, instinctively grinning at Casey's name. I read his message, a quick apology followed by a silly grin, and know he couldn't have said anything more perfect. It's him in all his glory, and I write back that I'm not upset, just taking care of some stuff here before I go back. I'll see him tomorrow.

My phone rings a second later, and I shake my head with a smile.

"Tomorrow?" he asks, clearly not happy.

"Yeah, I thought you guys should have some time alone. Like I said, I have a lot to take care of here," I lie. He's still quiet, and I glance at the clock. "Besides, it's already three. You guys have been great, but I'm not going to take advantage of your hospitality."

I can feel his scoff through the phone. "Yeah, because that's what this is. Us being nice," he mutters.

"That's not what I mean. I miss you already, it's just... I don't know. It would be weird for me to be there all the time. Remember how freaked out you were when you thought I had moved in?"

He's quiet again, and I wish I could see his face to read his silence. "No, I get it. If that's what you want. Ok, well, I should get going. I'll talk to you tomorrow."

"Casey..." I don't want to part with him upset.

"What? I said I get it."

"I don't think you do."

"I'm not going to beg you to come back," he snaps, and my stomach drops. He hasn't spoken to me like that since we'd become friends. It's my first reminder that he's human, too. Maybe even slightly more entitled than I want him to be.

Even the perfect ones can't be perfect all the time.

"Come on, I would never expect you to. You know that. I'm amazed you even talk to me at all."

He's quiet again. I can hear his sigh through the phone. "Callie, I'm sorry. I shouldn't have said that. It's been...I don't know...it's been a weird day. I know I was acting like an idiot when you left. I know why you did, but I regretted it as soon as you were gone. It's better when you're here. I don't know why, it just is."

I take a deep breath, feeling better for a dozen reasons.

"Thanks, Casey. That means a lot. I miss you, too. I'll be back first thing tomorrow, ok? I really need to do laundry and pay some bills and stuff." I pause. "Just do me a favor and take advantage of this time alone. Try to talk to Luke, ok? You both love each other and are so important to each other."

"I can't do it on my own, Callie. I told you how hard I tried. It's not up to me."

"No, but Luke isn't the same person he was the last time you tried."

More silence. I've given him a lot to think about and am starting to feel good about my decision to separate again. Maybe he's becoming too important to me, too. A little space will do us both some good.

"Good night, Casey."

"Good night, Callie. Bring breakfast with you tomorrow."

I'm not sure if he's joking or not, but at least the smile is back in his voice.

I PURCHASE four new albums after I hang up and download them to my phone. I pop in my headphones and, thirty seconds into the first song, abandon all plans of being productive.

I don't know what I expected. Maybe it's because they've always been just Luke and Casey to me. My friends whom I miss and can't wait to get back to after our spontaneous recess. In the bubble world of Luke's suite, their music was that hesitant strumming on an old beat-up guitar. That was Night Shifts Black. But I was so wrong.

I'd forgotten they are also Luke Craven and Casey Barrett, rock superstars with the awards to prove it, and I actually feel stupid as the saturated music invades my ears. I'm particularly horrified that I let them see my own "art" and even thought for a second I could be in their league. I don't know why Casey is pretending to work with my verses, but the thought that I had even offered to "help" him write music would make me laugh if not for the fact that it's so humiliating.

I'd heard of Night Shifts Black, of course I had, but I hadn't even realized half these songs were theirs. Luke's celebrity appeal probably made them more popular in the mainstream than their style of music otherwise would have invited, but it definitely resonates with me, and I love every second of it. Luke's voice is powerful, beautiful and haunting at the same time. I listen closely to the percussion, blown away by Casey's skill. To think they constructed these songs, created this mastery from nothing. To think that my silly mirror poem might sound like this in their heads.

I can't help myself. I pick up my phone again and find Casey's number. I begin typing.

> Listening to your stuff now.

Yeah? What do you think?

> That I can't believe you even spent two seconds on my stupid poems.

Haha i love your poems

> Why didn't you tell me you guys were so good?

I tried. You wouldn't listen.

I actually do laugh out loud at that one. He has a point, and

I'm so filled with awe, honored that someone who could create masterpieces like this would have the patience for my own bumbling attempts at expression. After our previous spat, I can't possibly return to him right now, but I want to. So badly.

> It's incredible, Casey. Really. I wish I had listened sooner. You guys are legit.

Thanks. Wait until you hear what I'm thinking for your song.

> I don't know if I can wait after hearing this. Is it Friday yet?

I wish. Hey, it's weird here. Hurry back.

> Not going well with Luke?

Does Watching TV together in awkward silence count?

> Are you fighting?

No.

> Then sure.

haha

> You and I spent hours watching TV in awkward silence. Were you texting someone to rescue you then?

It was only awkward because I was trying to figure out the best way to get a kiss. Not the same with Luke.

My heart pounds and I have to force air into my lungs.

> Really? You didn't try very hard.

> You seemed really into Dead Head. I can't compete with zombies.

I grin. I know he is.

> You know, I'm really enjoying all the pictures of you on the internet. Do they not let you wear clothes in the photo shoots? Is that a contract thing or something?

> Funny. You're the first to complain.

> Not complaining. Just wondering why drummers and lead singers can't afford anything but undershirts.

A photo pops up, and I laugh. It's Casey at some formal event with a tux, tie, and signature goofy smile. His tie is loose of course, top button open, hair messy, but he looks amazing.

> Hmm…not sure if I like you better with or without clothing.

> Come back over and we can figure it out.

My blood pounds.

> Tempted. But nope. We're still on break. Hey, did you know there's an actual movement called 'Team Casey'?

> hahaha You should see the t-shirts and hats. They're not bad actually. I give Jessica M. props.

> Jessica M?

> The founder of 'Team Casey.' Cool girl actually.

> You've met her?

Of course. A few times. Thanks to Jessica M there was actually a Team Casey before a Team Luke.

> Your ego never ceases to amaze me.

Ego! These are just facts, babe. Get used to it. Wait...are you jealous?

I realize then that I'm still smiling. I've been grinning like an idiot this entire conversation, and my jaw is starting to hurt. I try to straighten it, but can't. Oh well.

> Maybe. Do you think Luke would be jealous if I joined? Am I allowed to join more than one team?

Kinda defeats the purpose of picking a team don't you think?

> Oh? And what exactly is the purpose of picking a 'team'?

Hmm you know I've never thought about it. ...pre and post-show rioting?

> haha. Casey fans vs. Luke fans?

Something like that.

> Are there Team Eli and Team Sweeny fans too?

Yeah, but not as many. They'd get clobbered in a riot.

> OMG I love this song. I didn't even know this was yours!

Which one?

All Hands. Don't hate me but I actually thought this was a Cartwright song.

Cartwright?????? Ok, I'm putting the phone down now. We're done.

I'm sorry!!! But you have to admit, you guys sound a little bit like Cartwright.

No!! Cartwright sounds a little bit like us. Even though they don't. Like, at all. god Kevin Ramerson is such a douche too.

Kevin Ramerson?

Cartwright's embarrassingly inferior version of Luke Craven. We toured with them four years ago. Never again.

Not on good terms I guess?

Yeah right. Know what that bastard posted for Luke after Elena? 'Karma, Bitch.'

What??? No!!

Yeah...exactly. Total dick.

Wow. Well, I'm sorry. I wasn't trying to make you cry. My point was that I love All Hands.

ha I know. Luke and I actually wrote All Hands in a single afternoon. We'd just gotten back from our Desperate Times tour and swore we weren't going to pick up a guitar for a week and then bam, we had our next hit. It's one of my faves too. You know it almost didn't make the album.

Really?? How's that possible!

The Label thought it was too much of a departure from the other tracks. Didn't fit.

> You mean, it sounded too much like a Cartwright song.

> Shut up. I hate you.

And I miss him so much right then I start counting the hours until morning.

17

DAY TWENTY (MONDAY)

I keep my promise to Casey and grab some bagels on my way in the next day. I'm in such a good mood I even wave to Mara on my journey through the lobby. She's not sure what to do with that and returns some kind of strange hand swipe. Aidan is more accommodating and mirrors my grin.

"Morning, miss," he says.

"Morning, Aidan. And it's Callie."

"Miss Callie."

"No, just Callie."

He smiles. "Fourth floor?"

I nod. "Yes, please."

"Those for Mr. Craven and Mr. Barrett?"

I glance at my box and nod. "Promised I'd bring breakfast this morning. You want one?"

He seems surprised by the offer and shakes his head. "Thank you, but I can't eat on duty. Only on my breaks."

"Got it. Well, have a great day. Thanks!" I hand him his tip and take off down the hall. I'd whistle as I walk if it wasn't nine in the morning and I actually was a decent whistler, which I'm not.

Instead, I stop before the door, suddenly shy. After my interaction with Casey, I'm not sure what to expect, how to act when we see each other again. We'd flirted before, but not like that.

He probably does it all the time, I tell myself, and decide not to take it too seriously. I let myself in and breathe a sigh of relief when Casey glances over at my entrance, a huge smile lighting up his face.

"You came back."

"And brought food as commanded."

"Good, I'm starving."

He joins me at the island, and I lay out my offerings. "I got a few kinds of cream cheese. I wasn't sure what you liked."

"Plain."

"Got that."

I hand him the tub, along with a plastic knife they gave me at the bakery.

"How's Luke?" I ask, as he sets to work on his bagel.

His smile fades, and I sigh.

"Uh-oh," I say, and he nods.

"Yeah. It wasn't a good night. I didn't want you to worry so I didn't say anything, but remember that thing you told me about with the chair?"

I nod, my stomach dropping.

"Well, it hit last night. Freakin' blew up. I've been on the phone since six this morning with TJ, the lawyers, the Label PR people. What a mess."

I shake my head. "I was afraid of this. What are they saying?"

He grunts. "All bullshit. You know how it goes. No one actually knows anything so they all put their own 'hypothetical' spin on it, which then becomes fact. You should hear some of the stuff they're saying. Totally crazy."

I'm not hungry now, and poke my own bagel as my mind wanders. "What kinds of things?"

Casey shrugs, and I can see the righteous anger seeping into his face. "Stupid stuff. That he was high. That he got in a dispute over a bill. Oh, and you'll love this. You're in the story now, too."

My heart stops. "I am?"

He nods. "Yeah, pretty much the main story, actually." He studies me, and I can see the concern in his face. "Just a heads up. Anyone you've ever known, like, ever, is going to be trying to contact you within the week. Better turn your phone off and plan to stay hidden."

I suck in my breath. "Contact me? Why?"

He shrugs. "Hey, just a warning. Trust me, when people think you're worth something to them, you will suddenly be their top priority."

"Worth something?" I shake my head. "What are you talking about? What are people saying?"

He studies me for a moment, and I can't breathe. It's bad. I can tell.

"Honestly, Callie, the main story coming out of it all is that you're Luke's new mystery girl."

I let out my breath in almost a snort. "What? That's crazy!"

He shrugs. "The restaurant witnesses all say you were seen together eating breakfast almost every day. No one seems to know you, and Luke doesn't talk to anyone anymore, so there's no one to counter the story. Not to mention, if they do any investigating, and they will, they'll learn you practically live with him now."

"So do you!" I cry.

He grins. "Maybe the three of us have something going. Lucky girl."

I shake my head in disbelief. "That's insane."

He shrugs. "That's the media. It doesn't exist if there are no stories, so they have to make them exist."

"But it's not even true! It's all just speculation!"

"Yep. Welcome to celebrity life."

I grunt. "Well, I guess it could be worse for me than people mistakenly thinking I'm the girlfriend of Luke Craven."

"True. For now."

My eyes narrow. "What do you mean?"

He softens, and I can see that he truly wants to help me. He's genuinely worried about us.

"They're going to figure out who you are Callie and then it all comes out. Everything, believe me. There are no secrets in our world. We know they're going to talk, so our best bet is to master the art of steering the conversation."

My eyes widen. "Is that why you freaked out about the chair and wanted more information? You wanted to try to initiate damage control before word got out?"

He looks away. "Don't blame yourself. There's no guarantee there's anything I could have done. I might have done more damage to Luke by badgering him at that moment than a few stupid rumors like this will do. This chair thing isn't a huge story. It'll probably blow over."

He quiets, and I suspect there's more.

"Ok, but?" I press, eyeing him from across the counter.

He sighs and studies me. "You're the much bigger story, Callie. Believe me, the people are going to be much more interested in Luke's rebound girl after his wife's highly publicized suicide than some stupid diner chair."

I almost choke. "But I'm not his girlfriend!"

Casey shrugs. "Ok. So prove it. Who are you? How are you going to explain your relationship then?"

"I don't know, but this isn't fair! I don't care about myself, but he shouldn't have to deal with this."

Casey nods and is silent for a moment. I know I've just hit on something significant. Finally, he looks up at me, his eyes searching mine. "This is our lives, Callie. This is the risk we take every day. Every place we go, person we talk to, thing we do, could come back and bite us in the ass. Everything. We never know what or when. Things you do every second of every day without thinking could destroy us if the right people say the wrong things. A receipt falls out of your pocket walking to your car, and next thing you know you're a litterer who hates the environment and wants to murder all the baby seals."

I take a deep breath and drop to the stool beside him. "So what do I do? How can I help?"

"We're working on that. I explained the whole situation, everything, to our people, and they're going to put together a response," Casey says. He takes my hand. "Hey, it's going to be ok. I promise." He squeezes, and I lean into him. He wraps his arms around me and kisses my hair.

"It would so much better if they just thought I was your girlfriend instead," I mutter before thinking better of it. I immediately gasp and pull back. "I'm sorry! I didn't...I meant...for Luke's sake."

He's not smiling this time, just studying me again, and I can't breathe. I'm such an idiot! I cover my face, completely mortified.

"I'm sorry. I...I should go check on Luke," I manage, attempting my breakaway.

He grabs my arm to stop my retreat and forces me to face him. His face is inches away from mine, his eyes searching, so deep. So beautiful.

"You don't actually want that, do you? I mean, do you have any idea how hard it would be to date someone like me?"

Actually, yes, I do have an idea. I also know how hard it would be not to date him after everything I've come to learn and love about him. But I don't say any of that. In fact, no words seem to come out at all.

He looks away. "I'm sorry, Callie. I know you didn't mean it like that. I just wanted to make sure...I mean, even if I really liked you, and I do...I wouldn't be able to live with myself if I hurt you and I'm afraid I would."

I nod. Numb. Then, completely heartbroken.

"Yeah, of course," I reply as casually as possible. But there are tears close to the words. I'm afraid he can hear them as the weak syllables come out. "Um...Yeah, I should go. I..."

I pull away, and he lets me go this time. As I head toward Luke's room, I'm almost sure I can hear him curse.

———

I FIND Luke in his room. I had checked the office first and was relieved that at least he wasn't with the chair. I try my best to brush off my fiasco with Casey, determining to sort through that later, and focus on being strong for Luke. He's the one who needs me. Casey's proven I'm nothing more to him than a temporary distraction. I grimace. I know that's not remotely fair, but I'm hurt and irrational at the moment.

"Hey," I say, moving into the room.

He's propped up in his bed watching some spy thriller. His eyes are red, his hair's a mess, and I wonder when he last slept.

"Hey. Casey said you went home last night."

I nod. "Just to get some stuff and take care of errands. Still have rent and laundry," I explain with a forced smile.

He returns a fake, polite one of his own, and I sigh. I can't do this. Not now. Not after what just happened with Casey.

"Move over," I command, pushing him to his left so I can settle in beside him.

"You hear what happened? What they're saying?" he asks. He seems concerned, certainly apologetic, and I find it funny that we're both more worried about each other than we are about ourselves.

"I did. Girlfriend of the great chair thief, Luke Craven. I've been called worse."

He smiles over at me, and I hate how exhausted he looks. He's tired of life. I can see it in his expression, his manner, every pore of his existence, and it terrifies me.

"Yeah. I'm sorry about that. They'll fix it, though. They always do. Casey's working on it."

I nearly flinch. Strange how I counted the seconds until I could see him this morning, and now I can't even stand to hear his name.

"I'm not worried. More concerned about you. You ok?" I ask.

He shrugs. "I've been called worse," he repeats with a smile.

I laugh and take his arm, leaning against his shoulder. "We're gonna be ok, Luke. You know that, right?" I say.

He nods, but I'm pretty sure it's for my benefit, not his. He stopped believing that a long time ago.

"Watch some TV with me?" he asks, and I smile, squeezing his arm.

"Of course."

He lifts the remote and resumes the movie.

IT'S a good two hours before I finally venture back to the main room. Casey is gone, and I'm strangely relieved and disappointed at the same time. I grab a bagel for Luke and am about to return to his room when the main door clatters. Casey turns the corner, dressed in workout clothes, a towel slung over his shoulder.

"Hit the gym?" I ask as nonchalantly as possible.

"Had to work off some steam," he replies with a weak smile.

I nod. "Ok. Well, we're watching spy movies in the back." I start walking again.

"Callie, wait! Please."

I stop and turn to him, my heart racing, but doing everything I can not to let it show.

"I'm sorry about earlier. I just need you to understand that it's not you. Please know that."

"Yeah. It's not you, it's me. Got it," I reply, turning again.

"Stop! Will you just stop?" he pleads, grabbing my arm. He pulls me toward him, and I'm almost angry that he looks like he's about to kiss me again. I yank my arm away and take a step back.

"What is your problem, Casey? What do you want from me? You want to fool around for a bit before you head back on tour with your real model girlfriends? I'm not interested in that, ok? I was pretty sure you were smart enough to pick up on that."

His face falls. I can see I'm hurting him but I don't understand how. It was his choice, not mine. It's his life keeping us apart.

"It's not like that, Callie. I...I don't know how to explain it. I just don't want to hurt you. I'm afraid I'm not what you think. I'm afraid I can't live up to your expectations. I mean, I'm not... At the end of the day, I'm just a guy."

I almost laugh. "My expectations? I didn't even have any! I

wasn't interested in Casey Barrett, the rockstar. I don't know him! I was interested in Casey Barrett, the seventh son of Mr. and Mrs. Barrett of Houston, Texas. The guy who would stand beside his friend when no one else saw any reason why he should. The guy who didn't shy away from someone else's puke, or late nights, or fights with a powerful Label because they were hurting someone he loved. The guy whose smile literally got me through the last few days of emotional hell, and who's been nothing but a rock for all of us." I stop, the tears brimming now, and I swat at my eyes. "I was interested in the guy who was finally starting to make me believe in myself. So if you're not actually that guy, then I guess you're right. We can just end this, whatever it is, now with a clean break."

With that, I turn and retreat before he can stop me again. I can't face him. Not now, maybe not ever at this point. Because the truth is, I'm more than interested in that guy. I'm falling hard for that guy.

"YOU OK?" Luke asks when I make my way back into his room.

"Fine. Why?" I say, handing him his bagel.

He's studying me, I can feel his gaze, but I can't meet it. My drama is the last thing he needs in his life right now.

"You were crying," he says.

I shrug. "Just allergies," I lie.

He smirks. "Yeah. Sure. Is this about the rumors?"

Now, I actually do manage a smile. "No. Not at all. I'm not worried about that. I don't have a life to ruin. Just worried about you."

He quiets, and I don't like the way he's looking at me. "Is this about Casey?"

My throat constricts as my brain goes into crisis mode. "Casey? What do you mean?"

He scoffs. "Please. It's obvious there's something going on there."

I look away and shrug. "Not according to him. Look, can we just watch the movie?" I ask, dropping to the bed.

"He said he's not interested? Really?"

I glare at him now. For all the times I've respected his privacy over the last few weeks, he can't drop my crap for once? He holds up his hands in surrender at my look.

"Ok! Sorry! It's just..."

My gaze continues to bore into him, daring him to finish that sentence.

"Casey Barrett thinks it's best that we keep our distance," I explain, but the bitterness is too pronounced. I had been going for matter-of-fact.

Luke grunts. "Ok. Then Casey Barrett is lying to you."

I glance at him sharply, and he shrugs. "Well, sorry, but it's true. I've known the guy for half our lives. He's crazy about you. I told him on Day One you two were perfect for each other. He knew going into that first breakfast meeting what to expect. I'm not at all surprised you guys hit it off. I called that from the beginning."

Luke isn't helping my broken heart, and I can feel the tears hovering again. Just under the surface. Just one more reminder of what I can't have away from being a full-on episode. It's not going to happen.

"Are you starting the movie or what?" I snap, and he shakes his head.

"Whatever. You two are making a huge mistake."

I glare at him. "Luke, I'm begging you. Start the movie!"

He rolls his eyes, but finally presses play.

A KNOCK at the door at minute 17 interrupts our showing, yet again. The hero was just about to embark on his epic journey through the rugged wastelands of some fictitious third-world country to rescue some important politician from...I don't know. I'm way too distracted to actually follow the action. I'm only here so I don't have to be out there.

Which is exactly why Casey's face is the last thing I want to see poking around the door at the moment. But here he is, freshly showered and hoping for another change of clothes.

"Dude, you really need to send for your stuff or go shopping," Luke mutters, and Casey gives him a look.

"What are you watching?" he asks as he rifles through Luke's drawers.

"*Absolute Descent*," I answer. He glances at me quickly, then returns to the drawers.

"Any good?"

"So far it's fine," I return. "Just started fifteen minutes ago."

"Can I sit?" he asks.

I want to say no, but it's not my call. It's Luke's, and I can feel his questioning gaze, which is why I realize I'm completely screwed because Casey Barrett is my problem, not his.

"Sure, man. We can go out to the living room if you want."

Casey shrugs. "No, this is fine. There's room."

I almost openly glare at him when he chooses my side of the bed instead of Luke's. I have to suck in my irritated grunt as I adjust so he can sit beside me. Again, I can feel Luke's satisfied smirk on my other side, and now I want to smack both of them.

"Are we finally settled?" Luke asks.

"All good," Casey assures him, and I don't like how close he is. I gave him plenty of room to give me plenty. Instead his arm is resting against mine, his leg, his hip, the heat of his body spreading through me, the clean scent of his shampoo filling my head with brutal images of him in the shower. I'm so angry I'm sure I'm scraping enamel from my teeth.

The movie hasn't resumed for more than two minutes before it happens. Suddenly, my hand is brushed by his. Gently at first, so I think maybe it was an accident. But his gaze turns on me, I can feel it, then a more intentional touch. Furious, I finally blast him with a look that contains all the fire raging inside me.

He doesn't shrink, however, instead only grabbing my fingers, holding firm as I instinctively try to pull away. His eyes continue to stare into mine, searching, waiting for me to calm down. To forgive him. To understand something.

"If you two need to be alone..." Luke teases, and I flinch, my face on fire. I don't know what to do. I'm so confused. I'm still mad at Casey. No, I want to be mad at him, but I'm not. He has me burning with a different kind of fire again. The kind that will get me in trouble if I don't temper it with reality. I don't understand why he's doing this to me. Why Luke is encouraging it.

I yank my hand away.

"I'm going to go get a drink," I say, sliding off the far edge of the bed.

"Callie..."

I don't hesitate this time, and exit into the hallway just in time to hear, "I don't know what you did, but you need to go fix this."

I know Casey is following me. I can hear him, sense his presence, and when I get to the living room I spin around to confront him. But my angry words catch in my throat at the expression on his face.

"I'm sorry, Callie...I..."

He shakes his head and curses to himself. Clasping his hands above his head, he begins that distracted pacing he does, and my inevitable compassion begins to creep back in, ever so slightly.

Finally, he clenches his eyes shut for a second before focusing back on me, a desperate look on his face.

"I don't date, Callie," he blurts, and I squint at him in surprise.

"Not ever?"

"Not seriously."

He sighs and drops to the couch. I follow, but stay a safe distance away. I trust him, just not myself.

"My whole life has been spent witnessing one endless string of bad relationships. I grew up watching my dad beat my mom, older siblings getting dumped, older siblings wrecking others by dumping them." He quiets and sucks in his breath. "Then the finale of Luke and Elena."

He shakes his head again, deep in thought.

"Luke was my best friend, Elena my closest sibling. When they started dating, I wasn't surprised, but I was terrified. I knew Luke. I knew he couldn't be what Elena needed and I knew Elena couldn't handle what he was. I tried to warn them! I..." He covers his face with his hands, and my heart starts to shift as it starts to understand.

Still, I don't react as he collects himself. I can tell he's not finished and I want to hear him. I want his story and I want it told his way. Finally, he clears his throat and dares a look at me again. I want to reach out to him, but I don't. It's not time.

"Anyway, they wouldn't listen to me. They were both so crazy about each other, it didn't matter what anyone said. There was nothing I could do but brace myself and watch the disaster unfold." He closes his eyes again, and I can see the pain rushing back. "And that's what I did. Watched for three years as the two people I loved most in this world absolutely destroyed each other and themselves."

He meets my gaze, his eyes searching, pleading. "Do you know what that's like?" he whispers, tears in his eyes. "It killed Elena, and now it's killing Luke, and I swore I'd never do that to someone else! I would never, ever, hurt someone I loved the way they hurt each other. The way my dad hurt my mom. I don't know how else to do that except to stay away from them." He quiets and rests his head in his hands, and I can't take it anymore.

I close the gap between us and touch his arm, forcing him to look at me. He does, and I grasp his hand.

"You're not Luke. I'm not Elena."

He shakes his head, the tears spilling to his cheeks. "You don't know that. You...what if I am?"

I shrug and give him a direct look, firm, confident. "You know what? Maybe you are, but you're worth the risk to me. You just need to decide if I am. You've told me many times I have to start trusting myself. Trust who I am. So do you."

He seems touched. And conflicted.

Suddenly, he pulls away and shakes his head again. "We can't, though! Don't you get it? I've got maybe three to four months, then I'm gone again. I'm on the road all the time, and even when I'm not, I've got obligations and expectations that take me everywhere and..."

"Casey, stop!" I cry, jerking his hands.

He blinks, and I shake my head in exasperation.

"I'm not asking for a ring, here!" I laugh. "I'm talking about just letting whatever this is develop while it can. We can decide later what to do with it." I take a deep breath. "You can't force yourself to be alone forever just because other people made some poor decisions. What happened to Luke and Elena..." I sigh. "I can't even imagine what that was like for you, but that's not going to happen with us."

"But..."

I silence him with a look and gaze hard into his eyes. "Casey, even if you break my heart you will not break me. You won't."

I can't tell if he believes me, but I can tell he's sincere, and that's all I've ever wanted from him. I believe him.

This time it's definitely me who initiates the kiss. He wouldn't have dared, which is yet another reason why I want nothing more than to be close to him at that moment. Will he break my heart? Maybe. Probably. Just like I will break his at some point, too. But I also know it would absolutely shatter mine to move on without even giving myself the chance to get close to this amazing, talented, beautiful person. I have to try, despite the pain, and I think maybe he's starting to understand that as well.

He pulls me hard against him and I can sense the desperation in his kiss, how much he wants this. How much he wants me. How hard it must have been to keep me at arm's length in his misguided attempt to protect me from the person he's not. Just the fact that he would try is all the evidence I need that he's everything I've come to believe he is. I want him so much it hurts as he guides me back on the couch, our kisses, our bodies, trying to make up for lost time. I pull at his shirt, my hands gliding along his back, his arms, locking him against me while his lips trace my neck, my cheek, and back to my own. I can't breathe. I can't think. I just know that I've never felt so wanted, so satisfied.

"Casey?"

"Yeah?" he breathes.

"We're going to be ok."

He stops and focuses on my eyes, that grin I so crave suddenly slipping back to his face.

"You think?"

I nod. "Yeah."

I reach up and run my fingers along his jaw, staring into his incredibly complex soul. He lowers his head and gives me another solid kiss before straightening and helping me up.

I'm not done with him yet, though, and slide my arms around his waist as his tighten around my shoulders. I just want to stand there forever, even though I know reality is going to slap us in the face soon enough. For now, however, I let myself feel safe, at peace, and yes, maybe even the slightest hint of love.

"Would you be upset if I tell them to fix the PR mess by reporting that you're my girlfriend instead of Luke's? No one would care then and they'll leave you both alone."

I lean back and glance at him in surprise. "I don't know. It depends. Is it true?"

He seems flustered. "Um...I don't know. Do you want it to be?"

I almost laugh. "You're kidding, right?"

His smile is shy this time. "Well, I didn't want to assume...I mean after being such an ass the last couple days..."

"You were," I tease, before growing serious. "You have my permission to call it whatever you want, but *you're* my choice, Casey, not Luke. Any rumors floating around about me should revolve around you."

He bites his lip and nods, and I can tell that means a lot more to him than I can even know. I can't imagine what it's like to constantly live in Luke's shadow. To love him and have to fight the nagging temptation to be jealous of him at the same time. To watch him get everything you deserve as well but will

never have because labels matter. Then again, I'm not so sure
Luke has anything Casey wants.

"Should we get back to the movie?" I ask, taking his hand
and loving the fact that it's mine now, too. I can't wait to cuddle
up with him without questions. No more wasted brain cells
and heart beats on hesitation and speculation.

"Not yet. I have something for you," he says, pulling away.

"Huh?"

His sheepish smile is accompanied by a casual shrug this
time as he grabs the guitar.

"I got bored of the chair drama last night, so I wrote one for
you." He laughs. "Luke even helped, although he mostly just
made fun of me. It was late so it's totally stupid, but it's all
yours," he laughs.

I freeze. Tears spring to my eyes as I stare at him in
disbelief.

His face falls. "Are you upset? I'm sorry...I..."

I shake my head with a vehemence that brings back his
smile, and wipe my eyes.

"Of course not! I just...thank you."

His grin returns in full force as he lowers himself to the
couch and does a quick tune. "Might want to wait on the gratitude. You didn't even hear it yet."

I don't have to to know I'll love it.

But then he starts to play the incredibly sweet and goofy
song, leaving no doubt.

"They say I'm a rockstar, baby
But that's just what they made me
Ignore my wall of Grammys, right now I'm
    only yours.

I'm a superstar or pathetic cover, it's all in your
    power, lover
You're everything I need to know, let me be
    yours

I'm no titan, hon, a liar, maybe
I'm no one else you need to know
You unravel my maze, the light in my haze
You're everything I need to know

You may drive me crazy
But when I'm with you I'm just Casey, and
    that's how I know, that's all I need to know,
I'm yours"

CASEY and I return to Luke, different, better, and he gives us a knowing smile when we enter hand-in-hand.

"I didn't pause it. You'll have to just figure out what's going on," Luke mutters as we take our places on the bed again, but I can tell he's not nearly as annoyed as he's letting on.

I grin and shove him a bit with my shoulder. "Thanks," I whisper, leaning close and giving him a quick kiss on the cheek.

He seems surprised, but not upset, almost pleased. He returns my smile before focusing back on the screen, this time with a content expression I've never seen before.

CASEY SPENDS several more hours on the phone that night, pacing throughout the suite, arguing with invisible opponents, nodding, cursing, shaking his head.

Luke and I order some food and watch with a mix of amusement and pity as he battles the world on our behalf. His "people" seem to be confused about why he didn't just explain I was actually his girlfriend, and not Luke's, the first time they talked, but he covers it well and they seem to buy his story. The rest is just a long list of warnings and instructions, repeated several times, from several consultants, in several ways.

My heart goes out to him as I see the frustration and weariness settling into his features.

"Still questioning his loyalty?" I shoot at Luke as Casey unleashes yet another exasperated iteration of the same story.

"He's a saint, no question," Luke agrees.

"He's doing this for you."

Luke shrugs. "I don't know. You're his girlfriend," he teases, and I give him a mock glare.

"Seriously, you're ok with all of that? I know maybe it's weird."

Luke almost looks annoyed. "Am I ok that two of the best people I know have found happiness in each other and someone they deserve? I think I'm good."

I roll my eyes. "You could have given your approval without the sarcasm," I mutter, and he grins.

"Hey, you got it, didn't you? Anyway, if anything, my approval is more selfish than anything. It guarantees I get to keep both of you in my life."

I squeeze his hand, wishing with all my heart he could be as happy as I am at that moment.

Then Casey hangs up the phone with a curse and slams it down on the table. I try to be appropriately sympathetic, but it's just too insane not to laugh.

"Oh, I'm glad you guys think this is funny!" he quips.

"Eat something," I say, pointing to a chair. "It's bar food. Not a single vegetable."

He sighs, and I know there's a smile in there somewhere that wants to come out. There always is.

"I'll get you a beer," I continue, half serious and half teasing him about the last time I owed him a "thank you."

It works, the smile breaks, and I can't help but squeeze his arm as I pass. I'd do a lot more to cheer him up if Luke wasn't sitting right there.

"What'd they say?" Luke asks, and I listen closely as I retrieve the beer and pop the cap.

Casey sighs again, and I hand him the bottle.

"Alright, so here's the deal. Lawyers are pretty sure there isn't much legal risk. The leaked footage clearly shows the restaurant manager giving you permission to take the chair. The only person endangered was Callie when you took a swipe at her, and I'm going to assume she doesn't intend to press charges." His face changes. "Really, man? You swung at Callie?"

Luke looks away. He seems like he might be ashamed which is a good sign. Maybe he's starting to understand what he is when he loses control of himself.

Casey shakes it off. "Anyway, legally we're good. Publicity-wise, they actually think we're good, too, as long as nothing else comes out and we lay low. While the blow up part with the chair isn't great, we can spin it as a painful outburst of a hurting icon on the mend. With no laws broken, the public is going to like that Luke is back out of hiding and clearly reconnecting with people again, even if it is with his best friend's girlfriend." He turns to me. "Which, for the record, now means you have to be seen with me at, at least, two high profile events in the next month. Sorry, but it was non-negotiable. We need to prove that you and Luke were just hanging out as friends, and you and I are madly in love. If they see the three of us together, even better."

He stops and surveys us like we're his second-grade class. "Any questions?"

I raise my hand, and he rolls his eyes.

"Yes, Callie."

"Are you going to finish those mozzarella sticks?"

Luke laughs, and I duck as Casey throws one at me.

18

TUESDAY

Casey and I fall asleep on the couch that night after being up late talking. I learn a lot more about him, all minor compared to the game-changing character traits I've gotten to witness over the last several days, but still worth every second. I can't believe it hasn't even been a week since all this started. It feels like a lifetime. Casey doesn't seem as concerned with the timeline, and I wonder if it's because the pace of his life doesn't allow him to be overly cautious. Once he let go of his fear of getting close, he seemed to have no problem abandoning his soul completely to me. It's an amazing feeling to have someone's trust, their heart. I accepted the gift with reverence and offered the same in return, revealing things to him I thought I'd tucked away forever. We laughed a lot, cried a little, and I realized there was nothing about this person I didn't find fascinating.

When I wake the next morning, still resting against him, I don't want to move. My body gets in the way, however, and eventually I force myself up as quietly as possible. He stirs, but doesn't wake, and I make my way to the bathroom. I decide to shower and dress while I'm there, never sure what the day will bring with these two.

I'm glad I did.

I can hear voices when I turn off the water, multiple voices, actually, and realize we have guests. There's a lot of laughter, so I can at least assume they're welcomed guests.

I'm startled by a knock on the bathroom door and wrap the towel around myself.

"Yeah?" I call through the door.

"Hey, it's Casey. Can I come in for a sec?"

I swallow, excited and terrified at the thought that I'm naked five feet away from him. That's normal, right? I'm still getting used to this whole boyfriend thing.

"Um...sure. Hang on, I'm coming out."

I wrap the towel more securely, just in case. I'm not concerned or anything, this just isn't how I pictured our first intimate moment as a couple.

I open the door and brush past him into the guest room to get dressed.

He stops. "Wow."

I roll my eyes, but can't help the smile. "Don't get too excited. It sounds like we have guests."

"Yeah but...wow..."

I laugh and shake my head. "You knew I was showering. What did you expect?"

He nods, but I'm not even sure he hears me. "Yeah...um..."

"You came in here for a reason?" I remind him, helping him along.

He clears his throat, and I'm tempted to completely unhinge him with a peek, but have mercy.

"Yeah, so, ok." He shakes his head and actually looks away to regain his thoughts. "The guys are here," he explains finally.

"The guys?"

"Sorry. Sweeny and Eli."

His shy smile makes an appearance, and I immediately brace for whatever triggered it.

"Ok..."

"Yeah, so TJ told them we were hitting the studio Friday."

"Hitting the studio?"

"Recording."

"They're recording?"

"Songs? Music?"

I give him a look. "I get that. I mean, I'm surprised they're here to record. I thought you were just going down by yourself on Friday to fool around."

Casey cringes. "Yeah, about that...So TJ pretty much wet his pants when I sent him the work tape. The Label went nuts and is sending a trailer with our gear."

I stare at him. He's clearly not finished explaining what that means.

"Ok..."

"Well, so, basically they booked the studio for the day and want us to track the entire song."

"The song? What song?"

"'Greetings from the Inside.'"

My eyes widen. "Wait, our song? You're going to record our song? Your actual band. Night Shifts Black."

Casey grins and nods. "Yeah. I think we are."

I let out my breath, stunned. I don't even know what to think, let alone say. "But, I thought...we were just messing around, right?"

He shrugs. "Maybe at first, but it's really good, Callie. Even Luke thinks it's worth a shot. The guys are here now and we've got three days to work on it together. By Friday we should have something worth laying down."

I shake my head, amazed, terrified, confused. "Won't they be upset?"

"That we're actually moving again?"

I shrug. "I don't know. I mean, they don't even know me and now I'm butting in?"

"Butting in?"

"Lyrically speaking."

He laughs. "Is that even a thing?"

"I don't know. Is it?"

"If it's good, they won't care. Luke and I do most of the writing anyway. We're the ones getting our toes stepped on. Ok, well, I should get back to them."

I nod. "How's Luke with all of this?"

Casey shrugs. "Good, actually. I'm surprised, but he's with them now. It's almost noon so we're having some food sent up."

"And how are you with it?"

He looks confused. "What do you mean?"

I shrug. "I don't know. You're about to introduce your controversial new girlfriend to your band-mates?"

He grins. "I'll be fine as long as you don't let them see you like that."

I laugh and swing at him, but he ducks away, suddenly pulling me toward him instead. My blood starts to pound as his eyes meet mine with a breathtaking intensity. He's going to kiss me again. Right now. Right here, and I almost gasp at the fire ripping through my body when our lips collide. I reach into his hair, pulling him against me with a greedy abandon that surprises both of us. I've never wanted anything so much in my life.

"Casey..." I breathe, eyes closed as his lips caress my neck, his hands gripping my towel, dangerously close to starting something we both know we can't finish right now.

"I know," he groans. "I know."

But he just feels so good. My own fingers are on the waist of his jeans, instinctively pulling at the clasp. I almost hate our guests for taking this from me. I don't care, I don't want to let him go, and allow our kiss to take on an urgency I know he won't be able to resist. Especially when I undo the top button of his jeans and pull his hips into mine. It's not fair, but I want him to suffer as much as I am right now.

He breathes a curse, pausing as he rests his forehead against mine. We hover like that for a minute, momentarily paralyzed by our mutual denial. When he finally manages to pull away, I can see the longing all over his face. We're both breathing hard, staring at each other, wondering if there's some way to alter Time so we can have this moment we both so desperately want.

He takes a deep breath and shakes his head with a wry smile. "You did that on purpose," he charges.

"Did what?" I ask with a mischievous smile of my own.

He gives me a mock glare, but his return grin betrays him. "Come out when you're ready, you vixen."

I SPEND a little extra time on clothes and makeup after Casey leaves, still burning from our heated encounter. I almost regret trying to stir him up, since I'm paying just as high of a price now. I can still feel his firm body pressed against me, begging to be explored, to give itself over completely. He was mine for a second, and now I'm addicted. I suck in a deep breath, willing my racing pulse to calm itself, and finally manage to focus on reality and the unnerving prospect of meeting the rest of the NSB "family."

I glance at my reflection again and sigh. There's no hope for my hair, which is soaking wet, so I comb through that and hope for the best. At least my casual look will prove Casey, Luke, and

I are close enough to be past the "trying too hard" stage. If only they knew.

I brace myself and draw in a deep breath, nervous for some reason. It's not that I care what the others think for my sake, but for Casey's. Obviously, his life will be a lot easier if they like me.

The conversation dies the second I come into view, and I plaster a warm smile on my face.

"There she is!" Casey cries, jumping up from his stool before anything can get awkward. "Guys, this is Callie."

"Callie, this is Eli and Jeff, but everyone calls him Sweeny."

I wave. "Nice to finally meet you," I say.

"You look great," Casey whispers, kissing my cheek. It's sweet, but I can't tell if he's sincere or acting for his band-mates. My guess is they need to believe our relationship is legit, too.

"Thanks," I say with a genuine smile once I conclude that Casey's is also. What a weird situation, pretending to date my actual boyfriend. He gives me a knowing look that indicates he's still reeling from our bedroom scene also, and my blood starts pounding again.

I swallow. "You guys just came in this morning?" I ask, somehow managing to ignore the throbbing in my veins.

"Yeah, as soon as we could," Eli says. "Had to once we learned this guy rejoined the planet."

Luke gives him a smirk, but only shakes his head.

"Heard you guys have been working on some stuff. Can't wait to hit Jackson Street Friday," Sweeny continues.

Casey grins and slings his arm around me. "Actually, yeah. Thanks to Callie. She got me writing again. We can drop some ideas over the next few days and see if any stick."

Their expressions change a bit, and I wonder what they're thinking. Are they annoyed that I've invaded their turf or impressed that I got the ball rolling again? I decide it's best to just smile and stay out of it. I certainly didn't expect what actually happens.

"Callie's for real, guys," Luke chimes in. "You'll like her stuff. It's good."

Casey and I both stare at Luke in shock. The others seem to visibly relax at his approval.

"Looking forward to it," Eli says.

"You're a writer?" Sweeny asks.

I almost laugh at the ironic question and catch a subtle glance from Casey.

"Apparently," I reply, and Sweeny looks appropriately confused.

"She is," Casey clarifies, squeezing my shoulders.

"Cool," Eli says. "Oh hey, it's still downstairs, but we brought some of your stuff, Case. TJ said you were looking for a few things to prepare for Friday."

"My gear?" Casey asks as though Santa himself just offered him the pick of the North Pole Warehouse.

They return his infectious grin. Apparently, he has that effect on everyone.

"What we could anyway. Just your small controller and the acoustic. Don't get too excited, we weren't going to mess with the amp, so we didn't bring your electric."

Casey doesn't seem concerned. "What about my recording stuff?"

"Assuming you've got your laptop and drives, but the interface, mics, and boxes are in the case with the controller. No kit though. You'll have to wait for the trailer on Friday," he adds with a smirk.

"Come on. You couldn't spring for an extra carryon?" Casey teases. He looks about ready to run from the room in search of this mysterious cart of gifts.

I'm not entirely sure what any of this conversation means, so I remain silent and keep my ignorance to myself.

"Just go, Case," Luke mutters, but seems amused more than anything.

Casey nods and gives us an apologetic look. "I'll be right back. Gonna go find my stuff."

"They said they'd bring it up as soon as someone was available," Eli explains, but clearly that's not an option.

"It's fine. Be back in a minute!"

With that, Casey is gone, and it's just the rest of us staring after him in amusement.

"Good call, guys," Luke observes to the other two. "He deserves to catch a break for once."

They seem confused, but not enough to ask. "How are you doing, man? We heard what's going on."

Luke shrugs. "Fine. I have my girl Callie here to keep me from going completely nuts."

The other guys are no more surprised than I am by Luke's comment. I glance at him, but he's not looking at me. In fact, his tone is so casual, so nonchalant, I almost missed the significance of that statement.

"Is she your girlfriend or Casey's?" Eli snickers, and Luke only gives him a mischievous shrug.

"She was mine first. He stole her," he teases, and I shove him.

"What? It's true!" Luke cries good-naturedly.

The others laugh. "Yeah, right. Barrett stole a girl from Luke Craven. That'll be the day."

I shrug. "It's kinda true," I return lightly, and Luke and I exchange an amused look.

"Man, next you're going to tell us this whole thing with Jackson Street was all Casey, too."

Now, Luke and I laugh. "And that's a hundred percent true," I respond, totally proud of him.

They shake their heads.

"What is happening to the universe?" Sweeny mutters.

"I told you guys you've always underestimated him. Not all drummers are idiots," Luke jokes.

"Our Baby Casey is all grown up, I guess," Eli laughs.

I raise my eyebrows. "Baby Casey?" I ask, and Luke nods with a smile.

"He was fifteen when we started. He never really outgrew the name," Luke explains.

Eli nods. "Yeah, Sweeny and I are both 30, then there's Little Luke who's, what are you now, 27?"

Luke nods.

"Which leaves Baby Casey at the bottom," Sweeny confirms.

I laugh at the nickname. The thought of Casey as "Baby" anything, especially after the way he just took care of us this past week, is so ridiculous. I can't help it.

"So how long have you two been together?" Eli asks me. "It's not like our boy to settle down."

Luke and I exchange a careful look, and I'm not sure what to say. I don't know what Casey told their manager, what the official story is. We didn't think we'd need it so soon.

"Not long," Luke says. "But when you know you know, I guess. It was obvious to me before it was to that idiot," he adds, and the others grin.

I give him my own grateful smile, which he returns with a slight wink.

"So what, you three just shack up here together now?"

Luke shrugs. "Sorta. Callie's got her own place also. Casey's just hanging out for a while. So how did the tour finish up?" Luke asks quickly, changing the subject.

It works, and the other two launch into more stories about people and lingo I don't know. I start to tune out, counting the seconds until Casey returns. Baby Casey. Even his nicknames make me smile.

CASEY DOES RETURN SOON ENOUGH. We hear the clatter of the door, and I rush to hold it as a porter maneuvers through the opening with a cart containing two huge cases.

The guys pause their tour conversation, and I can't help but melt at the childlike joy on Casey's face as he tips the porter and thanks him. Maybe I do understand the nickname after all. He stands motionless for a minute, as though he can't decide where to start. One case is clearly a guitar, the other's just a large rectangular box framed in steel.

Luke comes over and slaps him on the back. "You want to set up the keyboard in the office or at the table here?"

Casey glances around the room.

"Here, probably. If we're going to be working together."

Luke nods. "Makes sense." He bends down and opens the rectangular case while Casey opens the guitar.

I'm surprised at how small the keyboard is. I don't know much about instruments, but I know a piano is a lot bigger than whatever this thing is. I'd just assumed keyboards would have the same number of keys as the piano, but this one clearly doesn't. I'd be surprised if it were half the size. I would have asked Casey about it if we were alone and I thought there was any chance he would have heard me. The way he cradles his guitar and gazes at it like a child he hasn't seen in months, I'm not sure he even remembers any of us exist.

I catch Luke's quick grin and headshake to himself as he observes the same thing I do. He doesn't comment either, however, and only places the small keyboard on the table. He begins unloading the other equipment from the case, which includes two small boxes with knobs and holes, a foot pedal, and two microphones. Finally. Microphones I recognize. There are also several coils of cables that he stacks neatly beside the rest.

By now Casey has his acoustic guitar assembled and slung over his shoulder. He's picking and strumming, and even I can see and hear the difference between this one and the one he's been playing in the suite. He seems much more at home now, more comfortable, and the clean, rich tone makes it obvious how much the inferior instrument was holding him back. I find myself getting excited to hear this guitar do our song justice.

"So do we get to hear this new masterpiece or what?" Eli asks, and Casey almost seems startled from his rendezvous with the guitar.

"What? Oh. No, not yet. I want to do a quick scratch track for you. I'll record something right after we eat." He thinks for a moment. "Actually, yeah, sorry, I'll set up in the office," he directs to Luke who nods.

"So secretive," Sweeny teases.

Casey shakes his head. "Nah, it's not that, it's just, we're further than concept, and what we've got is too complex to get the feel from the acoustic alone. I want to layer in the keys and some strings and pads, too. Oh! Plus, Luke wrote this awesome lick for you, Sweeny. You're gonna love it."

Sweeny seems impressed, and Luke shrugs.

"Now, I wish we'd brought the Les Paul," Sweeny mumbles, and Casey gives him a smile.

"It's fine. This is fine. I can layer in an electric and some percussion samples so you get the idea."

I'm trying desperately to follow their conversation and keep the baffled look from my face. I look again at the table, which has one tiny keyboard and two small boxes. There can't be more than 50 keys on the thing, and yet Casey's talking about recording a whole orchestra in the office. There seem to be more buttons and levers on the keyboard than actual piano keys, so maybe that has something to do with it, but I doubt it. I'm so confused.

"Can I help?" I ask, more to remind him of my existence than anything.

He smiles and starts toward the table. "Yeah, great! Grab those boxes and cables and put them in the office. I'll get my laptop and the controller."

"Controller?"

"The keyboard," he explains, and I nod. That makes sense. I guess. Or not.

I can hear the other guys resume the conversation without us, and focus on my assignment. I gather the equipment, as requested, and follow Casey toward the office.

He's already begun arranging the keyboard on the desk and has his laptop fired up to the right.

"Can you pass me the USB cable?" he asks. "Yeah, the little one there."

I nod and hand him what looks like a cable I'd use to hook up my printer.

He plugs it into the keyboard and connects it to the laptop. I see that he also has an external hard drive hooked up. Next he takes the pedal and plugs that into the back of the keyboard.

"You've been calling it a controller more than a keyboard. Why?"

He continues his setup as he answers. "Because that's all it is. It actually doesn't do anything on it's own. It's like a mouse or keyboard for your computer."

"Huh?"

He stops and waves me over. I can see it's taking incredible patience for him to stop his eager preparations to explain, but I really want to understand.

"Listen," he says, and starts pressing the keys as though he's playing a song.

I see that the display on the keyboard is lit and numbers are flashing, but I don't hear a sound.

"I don't hear anything," I say, and he smiles.

"Exactly. It doesn't make any sounds. All the sounds are generated by the computer. This thing is just a fancy joystick really." He laughs. "These days you have to be more of a computer programmer than a musician to make music."

I stare at him in awe. I had no idea.

"Can you show me?" I ask, fascinated.

He seems excited again, and I love watching his passion come to life. He navigates around his laptop, and soon I'm staring at a program that covers the screen with lots of small boxes and even more empty space. I still don't understand what's happening, but wait patiently as he clicks and moves around with a casual expertise.

"Ok, hang on a sec." He glances around the desk as if searching for something, and then grunts. "Do you have head-phones? I'd let you use mine but they're custom for my ears so you won't be able to hear very well. I was hoping they'd have external speakers in here but they don't and the built-in speaker won't do it justice."

I nod. "I do in my bag. I'll go get them."

"Ok, great. I'll load some stuff for you to hear and get this set up."

I grab my headphones from my room and return as quickly as possible. When I do, I see him hard at work, one hand on his laptop and the other playing the keyboard. I can see he has headphones in his own ears now and I'm not even sure he's noticed I've returned.

I wave my hands to get his attention, and he pulls one out of his left ear.

"That looks like a high-tech hearing aide," I comment, observing the molded earpiece dangling around his neck.

He grins. "It kind of is. Only a million times better. They're called in-ear monitors. They're custom fit to my ear so they fit perfectly. These babies have twelve drivers!"

I smile, knowing I'm supposed to be impressed by that, but I don't know what a driver is.

"Ok," I say. "These probably don't."

He laughs. "No probably not. It's ok. You'll still be able to hear this."

He waves me over, and I hand him my headphones. He plugs the end into the laptop stereo jack, and I put the buds in my ears. My jaw drops when he starts playing. That tiny little machine on his desk has transformed into an entire band in my head.

I can tell he loves my expression, and his eyes are wild with excitement. He's trying to talk to me again, so I pull out one of the headphones.

"Tell me an instrument you want to hear," he repeats, and I think for a moment.

"Violin," I say, remembering his other talent.

He nods, clearly happy about my choice, and I watch him move around his screen, adding things to boxes and blank space.

"Ok, now listen."

I put the headphone back in, and he starts playing. The beautiful, simple melody ringing through my ears sounds exactly like a violin, down to the vibrato and hit of a bow on a string.

My eyes widen. "I can even hear the vibrato," I whisper.

He laughs. "Tremolo, but yeah. How about this?"

He clicks more buttons and starts playing again. This time the sound is fuller, another stringed instrument has joined in a duet. He clicks some more, and next thing I know I'm listening to an entire strings section playing a steady, syncopated riff that changes its rhythm as he moves a button on his screen.

"That's amazing," I exclaim. "It sounds just like an orchestra!"

He nods. "And check this out."

He clicks some more buttons, and now I hear an acoustic guitar strumming along. I glance around the room, still unable to believe he's doing all of that with this little keyboard.

I laugh. "You don't even need an actual band anymore, do you. You could record an entire song with just this thing!"

He shrugs and grins as I pull out my headphones. "A lot of people do that actually. There's a huge advantage to recording in midi. You're basically converting sounds to data, which allows you to do anything you want with them. I can record a riff on the keys and make it sound like a trombone. Then decide I want it to be a cello, instead. Then decide I want to turn it into a loop and copy and paste it a hundred times, or just have it play once and tell it to repeat. I can quantize it, level volumes, even alter specific notes if I don't like the way something modulates without re-recording anything."

"So what does this box do?" I ask, tapping the other rectangle on the desk.

"That's an interface. It's going to allow me to hook up the mics and my guitar to the computer so I can add vocals and live guitar to the recording as well."

"This is crazy."

"I know. It's awesome. And see all these buttons and faders?" he asks, pointing to the knobs and sliders on the keyboard. "I can program all of these to control anything I want to. It's especially valuable when playing live because it allows me to change sounds and trigger what I need right from here instead of messing with my computer."

I look at him. "But I thought you're a drummer."

He smiles. "Yeah, I don't do this for NSB. Just on my own projects."

I shake my head in disbelief.

"What?" he asks, suddenly shy again.

I smile at him. "Nothing. You just keep surprising me, that's all."

He laughs. "Hopefully, good surprises," he teases, pulling me toward him.

"Oh yeah," I assure him, sliding onto his lap. It's so natural, so easy, and I kiss him without even thinking. He kisses me back, and there's that sudden urgency again. I feel so secure, so sure, in his arms, and wish I'd been bolder earlier in the guest room after my shower. I want him. That much is obvious to both of us. Gosh, right now if I could. I can't get enough, grasping his collar as I press into him. He seems just as determined, and I love the way his hands hold me against him. It's pretty obvious how much he wants me, too.

Finally, he pulls back with a grin. "Wow, computers really turn you on, don't they," he teases, and I smack him lightly before smothering his easy smile with another kiss, this one completely abandoned.

THE FOOD ARRIVES SHORTLY after Casey finishes setting up, so we're forced to take a break from our recording session, not that I was allowing him to get much done anyway. Casey seems disappointed at the interruption, and I'm sure he wouldn't have stopped to eat if I hadn't made him.

"So Callie, what's your story? How'd you and Casey even meet?" Eli asks.

"Uh-oh," Casey mutters, and we exchange an amused glance.

I rub my hands in anticipation and lean forward. "Well, like I said earlier, it actually started with Luke. Luke and I met at a café and started a breakfast club which Casey crashed one morning."

"I didn't crash!" Casey cries, holding up a potato in protest.

"Oh my gosh, Casey, you crashed so hard," I reply, and the others laugh.

"Dude, you literally crashed it by storming off," Luke reminds him, and Casey grunts.

"Fine, yeah, but only because you were being a jerk."

Luke shrugs. "True. But you basically told me that to my face. I mean, you crashed in all its definitions."

Casey rolls his eyes. "Whatever."

I wave my hand. "Anyway, he eventually came back to hang out, we hit it off, and here we are."

Eli gives us a skeptical look. "Hang on, breakfast club?" he asks.

Luke nods. "Yup, we met at Jemma's Café pretty much every day for breakfast."

"Jemma's? Isn't that the place where you stole that chair?"

"I didn't steal it!" Luke defends. I give him a look, and he shrugs. "Ok, fine. I kind of stole it. Yeah, that place."

"So what's with the chair?" Sweeny asks, and I instinctively know that question crosses the line. Luke has been much improved lately, but that's too far.

He shrugs. "Long story," he mumbles.

"What about you guys?" I ask quickly, changing the subject, and Luke gives me a grateful look. I return a quick smile, before focusing back on our guests. "I know all about

Luke and Casey, but not the mysterious Eli and Sweeny. Are you from Houston, too?"

They shake their heads. "Austin, actually. We hooked up with Luke and Casey about eight years ago."

I nod. "Gotcha. So Sweeny, you're lead guitar and Eli...?"

"Bass."

I nod. "Ok."

They're looking at me the way Casey and Luke looked at me in the beginning. Who am I kidding? The way they still look at me half the time.

"She didn't actually know our music, or anything about us, before she met us," Casey explains with a snicker.

I roll my eyes. "You're still hung up on that, huh?" I grunt.

"You tried to convince me you were royalty."

"Yeah, well, you tried to convince me that I should kiss your feet because you happen to bang buckets with sticks pretty well."

The others laugh, and Casey gives me a dirty look.

"All drummers think they're God's gift. Don't worry, sweetheart," Eli assures me.

Casey straightens. "Yeah? Try playing any of our songs without drums. I could track your part in an hour before the show," he returns, and now it's Eli's turn to glare.

"Whatever."

"Ok, children," Sweeny jumps in. "You both are super awesome. Can we let this go?"

Casey winks at me, and I shake my head with a smile.

"Ok, so tell us about this song. We're dying to know what's got poor TJ all hot and bothered," Eli says.

Casey's eyes light up as he leans forward. "Alright, so crazy story. Callie and I were talking the other night, and I saw some poetry she was working on. I'd been playing around with some chords in my head for a while and when I saw her stuff, I just felt it. I don't know, I knew it was going to work for some reason. Anyway, we've been working on it ever since, and I think we've got a pretty good start."

"Yeah?" Eli asks. I can't read his reaction. "What's it called again?"

"'Greetings from the Inside,'" Casey says.

"And what's it about?"

Casey turns to me, and I swallow at the unexpected spotlight.

I clear my throat. "Um, well, I guess it's about depression and how you let yourself see a distorted reflection of yourself that becomes reality. It traps you and you can't overcome it until you learn to recognize the lie."

They nod, considering my explanation.

"Ok, right on," Sweeny says, nodding in approval and relaxing in his seat. He turns to Casey. "So is this getting off the ground or what?"

"I'm working on it! I still need a minute. I'll have something for you by dinner."

They nod.

"Well, then get to work!" Eli cries shooing him away, and Casey mutters something as he pushes himself up from the table.

I DON'T LIKE that Casey leaves me alone with the others, but realize there's no way around it. He has work to do, and I'd only be in the way if I followed him. Thankfully, I'm spared the fifth wheel awkwardness when Eli and Sweeny announce they still have to settle into their rooms on the 2nd floor. Luke and I say goodbye and promise to let them know when Casey is ready for his big unveiling later that night.

"So what do you think?" Luke asks me once we're alone.

He drops to the couch, and I follow, leaning against the other armrest so I can face him.

"They seem cool. I mean, it's not like we could really get to know each other in such a short time."

He shakes his head with a smile. "I meant about Casey in his native habitat. You guys were in there for a while. I know how he gets with his toys."

"It's pretty remarkable," I confess. "I had no idea about any of that stuff. He's so talented."

Luke scoffs. "You haven't even seen him play drums yet. Honestly, people don't realize that, in a lot of ways, he's more important to the band than I am. I was just the face. He's the heart. Our producer would grab him for collaboration before me."

"He said they almost kicked him out when he refused to do the cable special on you."

Luke sighs, and I can tell he's not thrilled about me recalling old memories, but at least he's letting them surface now.

"They figured out pretty quick that wouldn't have been good for them. They need Casey a lot more than he needs them. You know he's got a whole other side project going. Has he told you about that yet?"

I shake my head, and Luke nods. "Oh yeah. He dove in even harder after I left and things slowed down for NSB. Casey Barrett is also the genius behind Penchant for Red."

My jaw drops. "Wait, the band that does 'Untouched' and 'Closer to the Edge'? That's Casey?" I cry.

He grins and nods. "Yep. Penchant is totally his baby. They released their first album six months ago and have already sold almost a million copies."

I'm in shock. I don't even know what to say next. "So does

he tour with them also?" I ask, suddenly concerned. Maybe that's why he was worried. I had assumed "being on the road all the time" was a figure of speech. What if it wasn't?

Luke shakes his head. "No, not really. They play a few shows, but don't do a formal tour. He can't do much because of his commitment to NSB, but don't be surprised if one day Penchant for Red eclipses anything we've ever done."

"'Closer to the Edge' is so different than what you guys do!" I reason. "How could it be him?"

Luke laughs. "It's much more contemporary and mainstream for sure, which is why Penchant will explode one day. You know he's a classically trained musician, right? His parents wanted him to be a violinist or something. He knows more about music theory than any of us. He's a freakin' genius with all the production and computer stuff." Luke stops and glances toward the hallway. "Wait until you hear what he's putting together now with that little controller. I'm sure it will blow your mind."

My heart is swollen with pride. In Casey. In Luke for his humility in demonstrating how much he loves and respects his friend.

I shake my head, still in disbelief. "Wow, I had no idea."

Luke grins. "You snagged a good one, Callie...then again, so did he."

I return his smile. "I knew that long before I knew any of this," I say, and I can tell Luke appreciates my response. "I saw who he was the night of your party."

My words have an effect on him, but I'm not sure of the result.

"Should we go see how he's doing?" he asks, and I'm on my feet as he finishes the question. I'd been counting down the seconds.

We make our way to the office, and it suddenly occurs to

me that the same room Luke uses to escape and fall apart, Casey is now using to grow and create. I wonder if Luke sees the irony as well.

I'm surprised when he doesn't knock, but simply opens the door as quietly as possible and peeks around the corner. Casey must wave him in because he then shoves it the rest of the way and moves inside.

"How's it going?"

Casey smiles and stretches. "Well, it's been all of ten minutes so not much to show so far. Basically got the tempo set and first midi track lined up. I did one pass with keys but I think I'm going to run it on guitar, too, and see what that sounds like. I could use some input. Do you have your ears?"

Luke nods. "Yeah, in my room. Just a sec."

He leaves us, and I move around the desk so I can see the screen.

"So Penchant for Red, huh?" I comment casually without even looking at him.

I can see his grin break out of the corner of my eye as he shakes his head. "Luke told you."

I face him, and this time don't even bother hiding my awe. "Is there anything about you that isn't going to make me swoon? What else is there? You also have a PhD in physics and founded a franchise of orphanages?"

"Swoon! There's my old lady. Love it," Casey laughs.

I roll my eyes and shove him.

"Want something to drink? What can I do to help? Anything?"

He shakes his head. "No, I'm fine. Just need time."

"And silence," I conclude.

He smiles and shrugs, but I can tell I'm right.

"Not a word. Promise."

"Well, it doesn't matter much for this part. Just when we track the vocals. Minus the distraction element, of course."

"Oh, so I'm in your way. Got it."

He gives me a sly grin. "I didn't say that. I said distraction. You can be very distracting."

"Oh really?" I ask, leaning toward him. I know Luke is going to return any second, but every cell in my body wants to be alone with Casey right now.

His eyes meet mine, and it's useless. I can't stop myself. He pulls me against him, and our lips meet in a brief, but saturated collision. It's not nearly enough, but we hear the door move, and I straighten.

Luke shakes his head with a smile.

"I can come back," he jokes, and I grunt.

"No, it's fine. Somehow I think Casey would pick you over me right now anyway," I tease, although I'm pretty sure based on the look on his face, I'm right. He's already back in "artist mode," and I'm not entirely positive he heard a word I said.

Luke gives me an apologetic smile, but I only laugh.

"Have fun," I say, moving toward the door.

Luke surprises me by stopping my retreat. "Where are you going? You should stay. You cool with that, Case?"

Casey shrugs and nods, barely even adjusting from his focus on the screen.

"Fine with me. Hey, so here's the first take at the keys. Before I clean it up, I just wanted to see what you thought of the general direction."

Luke nods and pulls a set of the same type of custom headphones Casey has from a solid black case. He puts them in his ears and hands the other end to Casey to insert into the laptop.

Casey makes a few keystrokes and waits while Luke listens. We both watch his face, and I find myself nervous for Casey for some reason. It's obvious that Luke's opinion means a lot to him. Finally, Luke must finish and pulls an earpiece out.

"It's good, Case. Maybe a little aggressive on the verses. I love the intro, though. I can totally hear the piano riff followed by the band coming in with the crash of the drums and guitars."

Casey nods. "That's what I was thinking. One pass of piano for that first progression, and then all-in hard on the second."

Luke agrees. "Yeah, I like that."

Casey quiets and stares at the screen again before turning back to Luke. "I'd love if you could help me with the vocal. You'd kill this one. You know you would."

I hold my breath. The look on Casey's face. The look on Luke's. I don't know if I can handle watching Casey's hopeful expression shatter again. Or Luke's pain at causing it. I almost want to flee from the room rather than be forced to witness either.

There's a long silence that's painful for all of us.

Finally, Casey looks away and nods, and there it is. The heartbreak I didn't want to have to see. I swallow, my own heart aching for him.

"Yeah, sorry," Casey mumbles.

Luke draws in a deep breath, and I see his fist actually clench in distress.

"Casey..."

Casey doesn't look at him and waves his hand. "No, I know. Sorry, it's fine. I shouldn't have asked." But we both know he's hurt. Again.

Luke shakes his head and steps forward. "No, it's not fine, Casey. It's not fine."

Casey glances at him in surprise, as do I. Luke's face is a mess of regret and love and sadness, and a host of other things I wasn't expecting and can't start to explain.

He draws in a deep breath and picks up one of the microphones, examining it with an eerie mix of awe and fear. There must be a hurricane thrashing around his head right now. And Casey's. I don't speak, trying not to move for fear of ruining whatever miracle might be occurring at the moment. Finally, he closes his eyes for a brief second before focusing back on Casey.

"Can you run through it with me a few times first?" he asks quietly. "I only heard it that once, and I know you changed some of the melody anyway."

Tears spring to my eyes when I see the glisten in Casey's. Then Luke's.

Casey clears his throat and blinks back at the screen. I can tell he's trying not to let the tears take hold. "Um, yeah, of course. Just..."

Luke nods, and places his hand on Casey's shoulder. Casey glances up at him still in shock, and I almost choke when Luke pulls him to his feet in a solid embrace.

I slip through the door and close it quietly behind me.

I FORCE myself to leave them alone the rest of the afternoon. I can hear enough to know that whatever they're creating is something I want to witness more than anything, but I manage to restrain myself and give them their much-needed time alone. What happened, what's happening now, is historic, and I'm not about to risk any kind of interference. Still, I'm dying for more than the muted sounds of laughter, debate, and Luke's iconic voice filtering through the door. I consider hovering right outside, but convince myself that acting like a creepy stalker fangirl after all of this is not the way to go.

Instead, I lie on the couch, staring at the ceiling, smiling like an idiot to myself as I listen to what I can of the magic.

After about three hours, the door finally opens, and I bolt up to greet them.

Casey almost looks startled when he sees my head pop up from behind the couch and laughs.

"What are you doing?" he asks, and I rest my arms on the edge to face them.

"Not distracting you," I tease with a grin that he returns.

"Oh really?" he says, and I love the light in his eyes.

"I'm gonna go chill in my room for a bit. Nice work, Case," Luke says, slapping his arm before disappearing back down the hall.

"Want a beer?" Casey asks me, heading toward the fridge.

"Sure," I answer, and he grabs a couple bottles. "Sounds like it's going well," I continue after he pops the caps and hands me one.

He nods and drops beside me. "We're both pretty happy with the direction. It's going to sound awesome with our actual gear in the studio."

"I can't wait to see you play drums," I say.

He glances at me in surprise, then laughs. "That's right. I guess you haven't even seen me play yet."

I shake my head. "Just violins and that weird string-choir-air sounding thing."

"Pads."

"Huh?"

"That sound. It's called a pad."

"Oh." I lean against him, and he puts his arm around me as I'd hoped. "How's Luke?" I ask quietly.

"Good," he says. "Better than I've seen him in a long time. It was like..." he stops, and I can hear the emotion rising in his voice again. I reach up and interlace my fingers with his. He squeezes and lets me pull his arm tighter around my shoulders.

"It's going to be slow, but it's going, Casey. I think it's finally going."

He nods and kisses my hair. "You're amazing, Callie. I don't know how you got through to him, but you did."

I almost laugh at the absurd comment. I'm amazing. Yeah, right. I'm still not even sure what I am exactly, but I'm pretty sure it's not amazing.

"All I did was force myself into his life and refuse to let him hurt me."

"Yeah, well, no one else managed to do that."

"How many people really tried besides you?"

He quiets, and I sigh. "It was timing, too, Casey. It was a lot of things. Sometimes it takes a stranger. Friends know too much."

"True. You hold on too tight with friends."

I nod. "Although, let's be honest. I'm the one who got the best deal out of all this."

"Oh yeah?"

"No question."

I turn to him and gaze into his eyes. His expression softens, and I love the smile that spreads over his lips. I kiss him gently. I have to. That smile...

"Promise me one thing though, Callie."

I grow serious when he does.

"No matter what happens with the two of us, we will always be there for him. I can't lose him, too. I can't."

I squeeze his hand. "Neither can I."

He seems to relax, and the mood lightens again. "Want to hear what we've got so far?"

"Are you kidding? Since the second I left the room."

He grins and pulls me to my feet.

CASEY KEEPS HIS PROMISE, and by early evening we've all assembled in the main living room. He's converted his afternoon's work into an audio file that he can play through the entertainment unit's surround sound system, which only adds to the dramatic effect of the big reveal. He hooks up his laptop, and we all settle back on the couches in anticipation.

Eli and Sweeny have a look of stern concentration as Casey pushes play, but I can see Luke's smirk. It's good and he knows it. He's not worried.

Even though I had an earlier preview, I'm still not prepared for the blast of sound that pours out of the speakers into the room. I can't believe Casey did all of this in an afternoon on that little keyboard, but instead of being smug and arrogant, he seems contemplative more than anything. I can see his mind considering each note, each sound, as he studies the air with the same concentration as the others who have never heard the song before.

Only Luke seems relaxed as we listen, each person lost in their own journey with the sound swelling around us. I'd love a glimpse into their heads as they decide the fate of Casey's efforts, and find it fascinating that even after all these years together, all their success, all the hundreds of reasons why Casey Barrett should be bursting with confidence, he still waits with such nervous tension for the evaluation of his work.

The music dies, and I hold my breath for the verdict.

"Play it again?" Sweeny asks, and Casey clicks a few buttons to replay it.

This time I can sense the change in their engagement with the music. I see the involuntary movement of their fingers as they seem to work out their own contributions to the composition.

"There! Right there! Stop it!" Sweeny cries. Casey obeys,

and Sweeny closes his eyes, reviewing something in his mind. "You're going to hit the kick hard on that build, right Case?"

Casey nods. "On the bridge into the chorus? Yeah. Definitely a fill, too, at the end. I was thinking Eli would come in hard with some killer run, too."

Sweeny nods. "Ok. Yeah. That lead guitar riff is sick. Wanted to make sure we were supporting it."

"Absolutely. You can thank Luke for the riff."

Sweeny seems impressed, but Luke only shrugs.

"It's nothing. Casey did everything else."

"And Callie," Casey corrects.

"And Callie," Luke echoes with a direct smile to me.

I'm pretty sure I'm blushing, but hope it's not obvious in the dim light.

"Love it, Case. Really," Sweeny says. "You know, I like that for an album title, too. *Greetings from the Inside.*"

"*Greetings from the Inside*," Casey repeats, then nods in agreement. "Yeah. I like that."

"Luke, you slayed the vocal," Eli adds, and I have to agree. I love Casey's version, but Luke's voice transformed the song into something entirely untouchable. Casey seems to agree, and I wish I could bottle the look on his face.

"You sound like a rockstar or something," Casey jokes, and Luke rolls his eyes.

"What are you doing?" Casey asks as Eli starts dialing his phone.

"Calling TJ," he answers.

Casey seems startled. "TJ? Why?"

"To see if he can get our trailer here by tomorrow instead. I want my bass."

CASEY AND LUKE make good on their promise to take me to 49th & Finch for dinner. I'm just thrilled to get Luke out of the suite. Eli and Sweeny join us as well, and the five of us slide into a booth that looks more like a lounge. When they said "bar food," I had expected bowls of peanuts and pool tables. I don't know why I would. Nothing else is ever as I expect with them.

Based on the reactions of the host and staff, it's pretty obvious they're immediately recognized as high-priority guests. There are bottles and glasses on our table before we even have our jackets off.

"And I thought I got VIP service at Jemma's," I mutter to Luke.

He smiles over at me. "Just wait."

"Shit..." I hear Casey mumble, and glance over at him in alarm. He's staring across the restaurant at another table of glossy patrons, one of which looks very familiar. Luke must notice as well.

"Oh, man. Sorry, Case. You want to leave?"

Casey sighs and shakes his head. "Nah, it's fine. Maybe she won't see us."

Luke scoffs. "Jana Furmali? That woman has a freaking radar for you."

Casey glares at him. "Yeah. And thanks for inviting her to your little get-together, by the way. She practically tackled me."

Luke gives him a look. "Of course I didn't invite her! She must have come with Davis and Kane."

Casey grunts and fingers his napkin. I reach over and grab his hand, which seems to startle him out of his daze. He gives me a weak smile that tugs at my heart.

"Sorry. She's just..."

"Persistent," Eli finishes for him, and Casey sighs again.

"Yeah, persistent. We went out a couple times a few

months ago and she will not let go. I told her it wasn't going to happen."

"I picked up on that at the party," I comment. He seems concerned as he searches my eyes, but relaxes a bit when I squeeze his hand. "I'm not worried," I assure him, and he gives me a quick kiss.

"Dude, she just saw you," Sweeny warns, leaning close.

Casey curses under his breath, and now we're all staring at her as she squints through the restaurant. Her face ignites when she concludes it's him, and she starts moving toward us.

"Can I kiss you?" Casey whispers. "Please?"

I almost laugh, and pull him into me. We put on a pretty decent show, and I can feel Luke's amusement to my right.

"Hey, guys! So good to see you!" a voice interrupts, and Casey and I pull apart.

"Jana, how's it going?" Sweeny asks in a flat tone.

"Great! Good. Casey, how have you been?"

Casey glances at her and forces a polite smile. "Fine." He holds up my hand clasped firmly in his. "Hey, did you get a chance to meet my girlfriend Callie at Luke's place last week?" he asks, and we can all see the moment when her world crashes down around her.

"Um...no, I don't think so. Hi," she says in a painfully unconvincing greeting.

"Hi," I respond. "I love your dress."

I can sense the guys holding in their laughs.

"Thanks. It's a Bella Amberosi."

I nod. I don't know what that means.

"I like your..." She hesitates, unable to even vaguely disguise her disgust and confusion at my existence.

"Boyfriend?" I finish for her. "Yeah, I know. He's amazing. I don't blame you."

She almost chokes. I can feel the others' shock, but know I

guessed right when her eyes narrow and she mutters some unintelligible retort. Finally, she spins and marches back to her table.

"Oh man, that was awesome!" Sweeny laughs.

"You're my hero, Callie!" Eli echoes, slamming his fist on the table.

I grin, and steal a glance at Casey who is still shaking his head in amused disbelief.

"Dude, she is it," Sweeny continues, pointing at me, and I squeeze Casey's hand.

"Thanks, Callie," he whispers, his face broadcasting everything I need to know.

I nod, then grow serious.

"What exactly is a Bella Amberosi?" I ask, and they laugh.

CASEY AND LUKE order what seems like the entire menu of appetizers, and I'm blown away by each one. I can still feel Jana's hostile gaze from across the room, but I don't let it poison the incredible food.

The guys weren't kidding about 49th & Finch's bar food. The wings, the pretzels, sliders, everything I try is a familiar flavor, but completely different at the same time. I realize I was right on with my joke that they've simply upgraded the same food they ate when they were a poor garage band crashing in cheap motels.

Casey orders a couple bottles of that champagne I liked at Luke's party, and I love that he remembers my reaction to it. He pours a glass for all of us, and we toast Friday's return to the studio.

As the night wears on, I settle into my seat and study each of them in silence. Sweeny and Eli seem like good guys, down-to-earth and passionate, but clearly not in the same league as Casey and Luke. There's no question in my mind where the heart and soul of Night Shifts Black is. It makes sense, given the band's history I'm starting to piece together.

Based on the clues I've assembled, it seems that Casey and Luke started playing together when Casey was fifteen and Luke was seventeen. Whether they were serious or not, or had other band-mates at that time, I don't know, but Sweeny and Eli would have come into the picture two years later. They've put out four albums together since then, and I remember the first one being dated seven years ago, with the second one the following year. Several of the songs were the same on both, but the newer one sounded much fuller and more professional to me. I'm guessing that's when they signed with their mega Label. Since then, they'd done two more albums, the last one going platinum and winning them a Grammy. I remember something about an Academy Award for a song in a movie as well, but I can't remember which song or what movie. I never pay much attention to all those award shows.

My stomach flutters when it suddenly occurs to me I might have to start. I glance over at Casey and realize I may even have to attend one. I'm still pretty sure I'm sleeping, and yet, at the same time, it's almost like the rest of my life was the dream. Casey credits me with bringing Luke back to life and Luke credits me with inspiring Casey again. But what about what they both did for me?

I feel alive for once. Awake. I have hope, purpose. Value. Not because I'm the girlfriend of a rockstar, but because I'm somebody who can love enough to make an impact. Because I can create. Because I'm a whole person even if some of the parts are broken. I'm Callie Roland, friend, counselor, inspiration. Writer. I'm Callie Roland and I'm someone.

AFTER SEVERAL MORE BOTTLES OF alcohol, and way more food than we should have eaten, we eventually lose Eli and Sweeny to a table of single women.

Casey excuses himself to the restroom, and Luke leans back in his seat.

"So..." he says, glancing over at me with a smile.

"So..." I answer, returning it.

"We've come a long way since breakfast club, huh?"

I laugh and lean back as well. "I'd say. Although Jemma's made a killer cup of tea."

Luke grins. "I'll find you a suitable replacement. I promise."

"You better since you got me banned."

He laughs and shakes his head. "Yeah, sorry about that. Not one of my finer moments."

I squeeze his knee and let go. "I've got you, Luke. Always, ok?"

His eyes change as he studies me, and I let him look. I have nothing to hide. I mean every word.

Finally, he gives me a weak smile. "I know. I don't take that lightly." He quiets and stares off at nothing for a minute. "You know, a year ago I was pretty sure I'd be dead by now. Two months ago I knew it. I was hoping." He glances at me again. "I'm not supposed to be here, Callie."

My chest starts to burn at his words, the look in his eyes.

"Well, I need you here. So does Casey," I reply, leaning against him. "You're not allowed to leave us."

I can feel his gentle laugh as he hugs me.

"Casey is a special person. One of a kind. What that kid has been through..." Luke shakes his head. "Anyway, I don't deserve him."

"You mean, with his dad?"

Luke nods, and I pull away so I can face him. "His father, his sister. He was one of my first friends after I moved here. My parents pretty much decided they were done being parents when I was fourteen and sent me from Johannesburg to my aunt in Houston. I was completely alone, scared, and literally had nothing but my guitar and a few changes of clothes. I met Casey a year later and he became my best friend. He was my brother long before my brother-in-law."

He laughs at the memory. "You would have loved it. Wish I had pictures with me. He was this scrawny little kid with a violin, dressed like a punk rocker. From the second I saw him I knew I had to figure out what was wrong with this dude."

I laugh, not surprised for some reason.

He grows serious. "We both lived through hell. We needed each other and supported each other over the years more times than I can count."

A light bulb goes on, and my eyes widen. "Is that where you found your music? Is that what 'Argyle' is about?"

Luke seems pleased that I put it all together and offers a sad smile. "Yes, exactly. The music started ten years ago when he was fifteen. His father was going after his younger sister one day and he jumped in. Took a hell of a beating for her, but didn't back down once. It was the bravest thing I'd ever seen. Even I was too scared to do anything but get his sister out of the way. He stayed with me for a week afterwards to recover, and because he was scared to go home. That's when we started writing. I had my guitar, he had his passion for music, and that was that." He quiets, and I can see the pain in his eyes. "Elena, his big sister, found him an old beat-up drum set that my aunt let us set up in the basement. Casey came over almost every day to take out his frustrations and heartache on that kit."

He clears his throat, and I don't miss any of the significance of the gift he just gave me. I also have an overwhelming urge to hug Casey. Which reminds me...

"Where is Casey anyway?" I ask, suddenly concerned.

Luke furrows his brow, and I follow his gaze across the restaurant. Jana isn't at her table either. My heart starts to constrict.

"You should go check on him," Luke says.

I swallow and nod. "You don't think..."

Luke almost seems annoyed I'd even ask. "Of course not, but he's probably trapped and could use the help."

I want to believe him. I know I should. Casey's done nothing but prove over and over again that I should, and yet...all I can picture is Jana Furmali in her slinky little Bella Amberosi.

I give Luke an apologetic look. I hate to leave him right after finally opening up about his past, but if I know him at all, he probably wants to be alone for a few minutes to process what just happened anyway. And I need Casey.

I slide from the booth and make my way toward the restrooms. Sure enough, I'm not surprised when I peek into the alcove and see him tucked against the back wall, literally cornered by Jana.

I know I shouldn't, but I have to know. I have to, and pull back into hiding so I can listen.

"I just don't understand! What did I do wrong?"

"You didn't do anything wrong!" I can hear the exasperation in Casey's voice and immediately relax. I feel guilty for even doubting him for a second.

"But we had such a good time!"

"Yeah, and that's all it was. Look, I don't want to be a dick, but I have to get back. To my friends. To my *girlfriend*."

"Just give me one more chance! I'll get you that meeting with Reese Aster!"

He lets out a bitter laugh. "Are you actually bribing me to go out with you? Come on, Jana. Don't. You don't need that. For the hundredth time, I'm seeing someone. You need to let go."

"No, I don't believe that! There's no way you're seriously dating that little country slut."

"Don't ever talk about her like that! You don't know anything about her. Get out of my way."

"Casey!"

"Let go of me! It's not happening, Jana. Ever!"

I round the corner, and Casey freezes in alarm. I feel terrible at the petrified look on his face, the fear that I'm going to think he's anything but the prince that he is.

"Callie...I..."

"I think he's made himself pretty clear," I direct to Jana. "Even a 'country slut' like me can understand his message," I quip, and I see Casey visibly take a breath.

His relief only lasts a second. Jana's glare turns violent as she spins and smacks him hard across the face.

I gasp, and would probably have hit her back if she doesn't run from the scene while we stand paralyzed in shock. I quickly recover and rush toward Casey, touching the fresh red mark on his cheek. His jaw is clenched, fire in his eyes, but I can tell he's trying to gain control of himself.

"Hey, are you ok?" I ask softly, trying to soothe the burn with my compassion.

He curses and closes his eyes. "Fine."

"Casey...It's definitely not you...it's her," I joke, and he cracks the slightest of smiles.

"Yeah, I know. I saw that coming after our third date. That's why there were only three."

I laugh. I can't help it. "Well, I'm sorry if part of that was my fault. Ironically, I came to find you to give you this."

His gaze shoots to mine in surprise, and I wrap my arms around him. He relaxes and pulls me close.

"Thanks, Callie. I needed that."

"Me, too," I whisper. His heart is still beating fast, but I don't know if it's from me or Jana. Probably both. "Let's go home," I say, even though it means I have to let go of him.

"Yeah. I'm definitely ready to get out of here."

I squeeze again before letting go. "At least the food was good," I offer, and am thrilled to get my grin back.

"Yeah. But definitely takeout next time."

"Totally agree. Let's go make sure Luke picks up the check."

LUKE not only picks up the check, but has already taken care of it by the time we return. His intuition regarding the people he cares about never ceases to amaze me, and he hands Casey his jacket as we approach the booth.

"You ok?" Luke asks.

Casey mutters something, but doesn't look over at the table across the room. I do, and notice it's emptier than before.

"She stormed off," Luke explains, reading our interest. "What happened?"

"She hit him," I hiss, and Luke's face darkens.

"No way. Seriously?" he asks, scanning Casey's face. He curses when he catches the red tinge of his cheek. "Man, I'm sorry. At least that means she gets it now."

Casey sighs and shakes his head. "Let's just get out of here. Where's Eli and Sweeny?"

Luke smiles. "They left, too," he says.

Casey almost seems relieved. "Ok. Let's go home."

THE THREE OF us crash on the couch when we return to the suite. Luke grabs a drink, but Casey and I pass. It's then that I consider the reduced flow of alcohol into his system lately. Sure, there's still a steady trickle, but it seems as though he's cut back considerably.

I lean against Casey, and Luke faces us from the other side of the couch. We're all quiet for a while, enjoying the silence after the chaos of the bar, or club, or whatever 49th & Finch considers itself.

"I told her some things," Luke confesses, breaking the long silence.

I can feel Casey stiffen, and glance up at his face. He doesn't seem angry, just concerned.

"Yeah?"

Luke nods. "About how we got started, about that time with your father and Molly. Just thought you should know."

Casey doesn't respond at first. "Fun story," he mumbles finally.

I take his hand and lace my fingers with his. "I want to know all the stories," I say. "Fun or not."

"I don't talk to him anymore," Casey replies, and I'm not sure he even heard my response. He's back there again. I can see it in his eyes when I look up at him. "I'm the only one who doesn't, but he always hated me more than the others. I wasn't as afraid of him as he wanted."

Luke nods, and I can see the understanding all over his face. The friendship, the history, the connection that explains their incredible music.

"He hates that he was wrong about you, Case. He hates your success. I saw him when I went home a few weeks ago. He's a bitter, miserable man," Luke says.

"You went home?" Casey asks, surprised. "Why? Why didn't you tell me?"

Luke flinches, and we can tell this wasn't supposed to be part of the story. I remember his trip. Clearly. I'd been so worried about him when he suddenly disappeared for a week without a word.

The way his eyes are shifting now, I know it's bad. What I don't know is if he's finally ready to share it with us. I don't think we were supposed to know any of this. I doubt anyone was, which is all the more reason why it has to come out.

He draws in a deep breath and concentrates on the floor.

"I was... putting things in order. Preparing for..." Luke stops just as my heart does.

I stare at him in horror, unable to speak. I don't know what to do with that sentence. It's too heavy, too important, too awful, too expected, too full, to process. I can't see Casey's face but I can feel his sudden tension behind me and know he's having a similar reaction.

Luke's eyes venture toward us again, searching, clouded this time. "A month ago I was ready. I was done. That's why I started visiting Jemma's. The chair. To say goodbye with one final punishment for what I was. What I'd done. To force myself to confront my failure. A month ago was supposed to be the end."

I jump up from my seat and rush toward him. I don't care. No. It's too real now. Too close. I throw my arms around him and feel his tighten around me in return. We both are thinking the same thing, filled with the same sickening questions. What if I hadn't butted in? What if I'd ignored his crazy behavior like everyone else? What if I'd done the right thing and been polite? My inexplicable rudeness saved his life. Started mine.

I hold on. I know Casey understands what's happening. That he's not jealous, and he waits in silence as Luke and I put each other back together. Luke finally pulls away and swats at his eyes, a haunted look on his face. I know something's happening in his head and sit back to let it breathe.

He closes his eyes and starts speaking so softly, we can barely hear him at first.

> "It's a perfect day for candlelight, let it cast its
>   shadow.
> It's a perfect day for apathy.
> It's a perfect day for tragedy, eclipsed by a
>   moment in time.
> It's a perfect day, why not today?
>
> It's a perfect day, don't wait up for a tearful
>   goodbye.
> It's a perfect day for illusion.
> It's a perfect day for solace, I'll make this easy
>   on you.
> Don't you worry, it's a perfect day, why not
>   today?
>
> Can you hear me, screaming some lie,
>   disguising the truth
> Can you see me, bleeding, I'm unraveling
> Shattering
> Do you remember what you told me, 'Every-
>   thing has its place and time?'
> Well, that's fine, you can look away, you're just
>   proving it's the perfect day."

He stops, and I'm certain none of us is breathing. We can't risk changing the silence, the significance of the moment. We just absorb it, Luke's devastating words echoing around us, reminding us how close we can be to pain without feeling it.

I manage to inch back to Casey and lean against him. As soon as we touch, his arms encircle me and pull me close with an urgency that breaks my heart. I can feel him bury his face in my hair, and I clasp his hands to my chest, gripping hard. I can't tell if he's crying, but I know he's a mess, too. We all are. But for the first time our disaster is out in the open for us to pick through together. I also know it's finally time.

"What's The Chair, Luke? What's its power?" I ask gently, somehow sensing he needs to tell us.

He nods in response, almost as if he'd been expecting the question. I can feel Casey's attention shift back to Luke as well, and we are both holding our breath, bracing for the ghost.

"Things were really bad with Elena," Luke begins, quietly. "They had been for a long time, but...I loved her... God, I loved her so much...I just couldn't stop hurting her!" Luke's voice is suddenly violent, "saturated with the self-hatred" Casey had described that one night. The tears come again, to all of us this time, but there's nothing we can do but watch. Luke has to finish shattering.

"We'd talked that day," he continues after a long, painful pause. He wipes his cheeks with a rough hand. "She couldn't take it anymore, the way things were. She wanted to try to work things out. I agreed to meet her that night at a little café called Jemma's. One last shot to fix things."

A sob escapes him and he presses his fists to his eyes, shaking his head in disbelief. Finally, he looks up again, his eyes so full, so haunted, I'm completely paralyzed.

"I didn't show..." he whispers in horror. "No, worse than that. I ended up in a hotel room getting wasted with two girls I didn't even know. I just...I just left her there! Fucking abandoned her!"

His hands are shaking as he suddenly pulls out his phone. He scrolls through it with a delicate violence and stops suddenly, his eyes filling again. After a brief pause, he closes them and passes the phone to us, almost dropping it from the trembling. I glance at the screen and gasp, my pulse pounding.

It's a photo from Elena. Just a simple picture. Innocuous to anyone else, but horrifying to those who recognize that ugly, battered, vacant diner chair.

I choke at the caption below it:

> Guess I'm talking to a ghost tonight? Fuck you, Luke. I hate you.

"I left her there to die," he whispers, tears streaming down his cheeks. "She killed herself shortly after she gave up and left." His eyes turn hostile as he shakes his head. "No, sorry, wait. No! I killed her that night," he hisses. "I was supposed to be there! I should have been in that chair! But I'm not, am I! I'm not there!" he cries, furious. "If I had, if I'd just..."

He breaks down completely, and this time it's Casey who closes the gap. He embraces Luke, and my heart explodes in my chest at the sight.

"I need you to forgive me," Luke sobs. "Forgive me for killing her. Please!" he pleads, his eyes wild, desperate, and Casey nods, tears drowning his own.

"I do," he whispers. "You know I do. Just come back to us, ok?"

We don't move for a long time. Casey holding Luke, me serving as a witness to this latest miracle, all of us thinking about the ghost chair locked in the office down the hall. I want to destroy it. Crush it into the unrecognizable pile of garbage it is, but it's not my demon to kill.

"She called me, too, that night," Casey says quietly.

We both stare at him in shock.

He nods and draws in a ragged breath. "Obviously, I didn't know what she was planning to do. I thought it was weird that she called just to say she loved me and was proud of me. But I didn't ask. I didn't understand until after...until they called and said... And then..." He stops and meets Luke's gaze. "I'm the last person she spoke to. Me! I had a chance to help, and I didn't. Maybe it's just as much my fault for not stopping her. For not loving my sister enough to recognize a suicide note when it slaps me in the face."

"Casey..." Luke says, but Casey pulls away and wipes his eyes.

"I blamed myself for a long time, too, but now I know that blaming only helps if it has the power to change us. To make us better." Casey meets Luke's gaze, almost pleading with him, yet gentle at the same time. "Elena's death made us better, Luke. And now we have a chance to make it matter. To make her matter!"

Luke clenches his jaw, and I can tell Casey's words struck hard. He stares at the far wall, his mind clearly taking off in many directions at once.

"She matters, Case," he whispers, looking up at him again. "So much."

Casey nods. "I know she does. I know." He squeezes Luke's arm, and glances at me. I smile through my tears, so full of compassion and love I can't even speak. He seems to understand anyway as his eyes soften and he returns a weak smile of his own.

We're silent again. All of us, but it's different this time. It's softer, more comforting. We're exhausted from what just happened, and I finally force myself up from the couch. I don't know why, but suddenly, I can only think of one thing. One ending to this incredible, horrible, impossible night.

"I'm going to make some tea," I announce.

I'm met with two shocked stares that quickly transform into perfect grins.

"Tea sounds great," Luke sighs.

LUKE TAKES his tea to his room, and I place a second steaming cup in front of Casey who's perched at the island.

"I can't believe you're getting two jaded rockers to trade in their whisky for Earl Grey."

"Lady Grey," I correct.

"Lady Grey?"

"Lady Grey. It's milder."

He gives me a skeptical look. "You're making me drink a tea called 'Lady Grey'? You realize this could ruin my career, right?"

"And you will love it," I assure him, rounding the counter to his side.

"Oh, will I?"

I nod with a sly grin and force his stool around to face me.

"Oh yeah."

I slide my hands around his waist, forgetting all about the tea. "Besides, you still owe me a research study," I tease, gripping his shirt and pulling him off the chair.

"Huh?"

"You know, an empirical investigation of whether I like you better with or without clothing?"

His expression turns mischievous as it clicks. "Hmm...that's right. Well, you know me. I'm all about science," he returns.

"Good. I was counting on that," I reply, moving my grasp to the waist of his jeans.

I pull him against me, forcing our bodies together, loving

every desperate ache of the mounting tension. His eyes intensify, tracing me, searching me. When his addictive grin breaks, every cell in my body erupts. I wonder if that smile will always make me this crazy.

I can feel the violent thump of his pulse, the hard pressure of his muscles, his hips, braced against mine. I want him so much I can't concentrate on anything else.

"So, which is it? On or off?" he whispers, torturing me with a long, hungry kiss that leaves me gasping.

"Off. Definitely off," I breathe, pulling him toward the couch.

19

WEDNESDAY & THURSDAY

I wake up beside Casey in the guest room several hours later. Slivers of light are peeking around the seams of the curtains on the window, so I know it's well into the morning. He's still asleep, and I study his peaceful face for a while.

I can't believe last night happened. Even more unbelievable is the fact that I don't have to lie here regretting it, aching over a euphoric anomaly. Last night could be tonight or tomorrow night or the next night, or all of those nights. We're Casey and Callie now, however, whenever, whatever, we want. It almost doesn't seem fair to the rest of the world.

I trace his hand resting by my pillow, part of me wishing he'd sleep for hours so we could stay like this. The other part missing his smile, his laughter, and counting the seconds until he wakes.

Apparently, he's a light sleeper because a second later I'm staring into those dark, playful eyes.

"Morning," he mutters.

"Morning," I return with a smile.

His own smile breaks through his sleepy expression, and he turns to his back, stretching.

"What time is it?" he asks, and I realize I have no idea.

"I don't know. Does it matter?"

"I guess not." He glances back at me. "How long have you been awake?"

"Not long."

He nods. "Hungry?"

"A little. I should shower first, though. I'm sure Eli and Sweeny will be up here any minute, if they aren't already."

Casey grunts. "Good point. I forgot about them." He gives me a sly look. "Like I said, you can be very distracting."

I laugh and take a swing, but he catches my arm against his chest. I try to pull away as he holds firm, but quickly realize I like this position a lot better and settle against him.

"We could just tell them we're sick and stay here all day," he suggests with a glint.

"Nice plan, genius. They'd be right outside the door!"

"We could be quiet!"

"Ha! Yeah right. Nice try," I smirk, although I know if I don't move soon, I will be the one constructing conspiracies to stay. I will never understand how someone can look so good first thing in the morning. I'm sure I don't. I force myself to pull away, and he finally lets me go. It almost hurts to separate from him, and I have to fight the urge to climb back into his arms. There's no way I'd be able to leave then.

Shower. That was it. I was going to take a shower. Maybe a very cold one.

"Shower's big enough for two..." he says as if reading my mind.

I roll my eyes and laugh when I see he's not serious.

"The shower's big enough for five. We could all fit," I return, sliding off the bed.

He makes a face and tosses a pillow at me.

ELI AND SWEENY are in the kitchen, along with Luke, when I emerge from the guest room, but Casey's missing. They must notice my confused search and tell me he went to get us breakfast. I force a smile, hating that a ridiculous part of me is actually disappointed, that I can't be apart from him for twenty minutes without missing him. Of course, they didn't spend last night with him.

I can feel Luke's gaze and wonder what he's thinking. Can he tell I'm falling in love with his best friend? Can Casey? I wonder if Casey feels the same way. If not, I'm going to have to get control of this train before it crashes head-on into a wall. I had promised Casey he couldn't break me and I intend to keep that promise.

"So are you guys working on the song today?" I ask, mostly to make conversation as I move to the stove to start a pot of water.

"That's the plan," Sweeny responds. "Our trailer is supposed to get here by 3PM so we can get really serious after that."

I nod. "Does anyone else want tea?"

I can feel Luke's amusement and cast him a quick glance.

"You and your tea," he teases.

"What? Don't even pretend you didn't like it," I warn.

He smiles and leans back in his stool. "Actually, it wasn't bad. I'm man enough to admit that."

"What, you're a tea-drinker now? What happened to you, bro?" Eli asks.

Luke shrugs. "Yeah, it's true. You've got to watch this girl.

She may be small, but she will uproot your world before you even know what's happening."

"She certainly got to Casey," Sweeny smirks, and I shake my head in disbelief.

"Yeah, because a shy poet from Shelteron, PA is going to be able to boss you superstars around. Please," I mutter. I can feel their humor behind me as I set to work on my tea.

"Ha! You've done nothing but boss us around since the day we met," Luke counters.

I spin around with a mock glare. "Oh, like you didn't need a good kick in the ass," I quip, and the others laugh. Even Luke grins and shakes his head.

"I didn't say I didn't. Just that you excel at it," Luke defends.

Eli laughs. "Man, Baby Casey's got his hands full..."

"You know our boy. He'd have it no other way," Sweeny returns, and I roll my eyes at all of them.

"So was that a no or a yes to the tea?" I ask.

They smirk, and we all turn toward the door when it crashes open. I rush to help Casey as he shuffles inside, hands and arms full of bags and drink carriers.

I almost choke when I catch a glimpse of the logo.

"Jemma's?" I ask.

He grins, and as usual his sweet gesture threatens to unravel me.

"Thought we could all use some French toast, and since you two are banned from the premises..."

Luke laughs while Casey drops the rest of his load on the counter and begins distribution.

"Coffee. Coffee. Coffee. And...tea." He kisses my cheek as he hands me my cup, and my heart just about bursts in my chest. There's just no way he's real.

"I'm assuming there's a story here," Sweeny interrupts, eyeing his container of French toast with suspicion.

"Breakfast club was at Jemma's Café," Luke explains. "It's how we all met."

"This is so sweet, Case, really," I say, not wanting to embarrass him, but unable to hold it in any longer. His grin is priceless, and I can't stop my arm from wrapping around his waist. He gives me a quick squeeze back, and I let go.

"Aww, you want a kiss from me, too, Case?" Sweeny teases, leaning forward with puckered lips.

"Shut up," Casey snaps, shoving him away. "Eat your food."

I laugh, just as my teapot starts to whistle. "I was going to force them all to drink tea," I explain, removing the pot from the burner. "They owe you for rescuing them."

"This actually isn't bad," Eli comments through a mouthful of bread.

"It's the powdered sugar," I explain, and I can see Luke and Casey trying not to laugh.

"Huh?"

I can feel their amused looks, and it's too much.

"I'm kidding," I say to Eli when my smile breaks. "We talked about the powdered sugar for a good five minutes the first time we had it. Long story."

"Oh, hey! I was thinking about the intro to 'Greetings,' and I think Sweeny should do that lick after the piano," Casey announces, all business.

"The bridge lick?" Sweeny asks, and Casey nods.

I can see their minds working. "Before the rest of the band comes in?" Eli asks.

Casey shakes his head and cuts into his French toast. "No, no, at the same time. With the drums, bass, and rhythm."

Their eyes change, and I can tell they like it.

"Yeah, ok. Maybe. What do you think?" Sweeny asks Luke.

Luke shrugs. "I think it would work. It's a pretty in-your-face song so why not hit them early."

"You said the trailer is here at 3:00?" Casey asks, and Eli grunts.

"Supposedly. They're supposed to call the second they roll in."

Casey nods. "I talked to that Mara lady on my way out. She said they have a room we can use."

"Private?" Luke asks. "We don't need any of this leaking out."

"She says yes. In the basement."

Luke nods. "Ok." He turns to me. "Can you stand watch just to make sure?"

"Can I have a black 'Security' t-shirt?"

Luke rolls his eyes and shoves me.

EVEN THOUGH THE equipment hasn't arrived yet, the guys want to scope out the rehearsal space and make sure it will work. They seem impressed with the size and seclusion of the storage room Mara shows them, and her tight face actually appears to approach an outright smile at the fact that Night Shifts Black is working on their new single in the basement of her hotel.

"Let us know what you need, if there's anything else we can get for you," Mara gushes.

Luke glances around the room. "This is great, Mara. Probably just a small table and some chairs, I guess. Maybe a few bottles of water?"

She nods. "Absolutely, Mr. Craven. I'll take care of that right away."

She hesitates for another moment, as if still trying to piece together this incredible development in her head.

"Thanks, Mara. We appreciate it," Luke says, guiding her toward the door.

She even smiles at me on her way out, and I can't help but snicker.

"I think she's starting to warm up to me," I comment after she's gone. "At the very least, accepting the fact that I will continue to exist."

Luke laughs and shakes his head. "You're too hard on her. Do you have any idea how many people she has to thwart on a daily basis?"

I hadn't thought of that. "Fine. Good point," I concede with a sigh. "Ok, well, I guess I'll go wait for your chairs and water while you work," I say, moving toward the door, but Casey grabs my arm.

"Not a chance," he barks, surprising me. He smiles to lighten his tone. "You're not our road manager, Callie. It's not going to be like that, got it? We pay people to get us water and chairs. Not you."

I swallow, slightly embarrassed, but mostly touched more than anything. "I know, I just..."

"You like to take care of people, and I love you for it, but we need you here, ok? This is as much your song as ours."

I stare at him in disbelief, speechless, and then my eyes flicker to Luke who only shrugs with a grin of his own.

"He's got a point," Luke agrees. "Besides, our security team needs to stay with us. Things could get dicey."

I laugh in exasperation. "Ok, ok. But I'm going to be the best darn bootleg-recording-thwarter you've ever seen."

Casey extends his hand. "Deal. But only if you promise to work on more songs while you're waiting to thwart."

I grin and squeeze his hand. "Deal. But only if you promise to make-out with me on your breaks."

The others roar, and Casey looks stunned before shooting me a mock glare. I'm pretty sure he's actually blushing.

"I knew there was no way you could handle her!" Sweeny laughs, smacking him on the back. "Called that."

Casey rolls his eyes but rewards me with a grin.

THE TRAILER ARRIVES a few hours later, and the band and small crew who delivered it get to work unloading its contents. I can tell this is second nature to them, and suspect I'll only be interfering if I try to help, so I stand back, holding doors for the most part. Casey looks like a little kid again as he moves his toys into the storage room, and I love watching him unpack his drums from their cases. He sets to work with an expertise that shouldn't surprise me, and yet does, once again. One day I'll get used to his brilliance, but I think it will probably take a while.

Eli and Sweeny work on their own equipment, and even Luke joins the effort. I had wondered if they were going to send his stuff, and am happy that he seems happy they did. I can't believe how much that trailer held, and am in shock that the large storage room now seems tiny, crammed with instruments, stands, and monitors. Eli, Luke, and Sweeny connect their guitars to large boards which are lined with smaller boxes and connected to amps.

"It's a pedal board," Luke explains as I study the little blinking lights and buttons. "Listen."

He starts to play, and I notice all kinds of changes to the sound depending on what he hits with his foot.

"Got it," I say.

He returns to tuning and playing with his boxes as I

maneuver toward Casey. Casey has his kit fully assembled now and is in the process of adjusting it when I approach.

"So this is it. You in your native habitat."

He grins, pointing his sticks at me.

"Be prepared to be amazed."

"I already am," I laugh, loving his expression.

He takes a pass at his drums, and I shake my head in disbelief. If this is the warm up, I can't even imagine what's coming next.

Mara had kept her word, and Casey has his computer and keyboard set up on the table near him. There are also several chairs and a cart with water in a bowl of ice, as well as, fruit, crackers, and an assortment of other snacks.

I had retrieved my own laptop from the room and intend to keep up my end of the bargain as I take a seat by the door.

"So you ready to do this, or what?" Eli asks. "Sweeny and I listened to the track a bunch last night. I think we're ready to go."

Casey and Luke exchange a glance and a nod. "We're ready," Luke replies with a shrug. "Let's run through the intro and get a quick sound check."

Casey nods and counts off.

FOR THE FIRST twenty minutes I don't move. I'm sure my jaw is on the floor, although I try to disguise it as much as possible. They start and stop dozens of times, discussing and debating changes to things I thought sounded amazing. But of course, after the debate, it sounds even more amazing. I still can't believe I'm here, witnessing history. No, being a part of history. It's my words Luke is belting into the microphone, even though I know I never would have dreamed they could have an impact like this. Luke and Casey have turned my little poem into a masterpiece, and I can't stop the chills coursing through me at each new surprise. I hadn't understood Casey's initial demo the way the others had. Now, engulfed in the real song, I'm completely speechless. And yet, Casey still doesn't seem happy when we break for dinner a couple hours later.

I had ordered food for them, at the risk of Casey's wrath, but I didn't think they'd want to break long enough to go out. I guessed right as Casey comes over with a weak smile.

"Thanks, Callie," he says, grabbing a sandwich from the cart. "You didn't have to do this."

"Just don't yell at me," I tease, and he shakes his head. "You guys sound amazing," I add, sensing his frustration.

"Yeah?" But I can tell he doesn't agree.

I nod. "What is it? What's wrong?"

He shrugs, and glances over at the other three who are laughing and talking. They don't seem nearly as upset as he is. He sets down his plate and leads me outside the room.

He's quiet for a moment, and I'm filled with concern.

"Casey, what's wrong? Are you not happy with the song?"

"No, it's not that. I mean, the song is going well, great actually, it's just..." he stops, and my heart breaks at the way his face falls. I instinctively squeeze his arm, and he looks back at me, almost haunted. "This is killing me, Callie," he whispers.

I stare at him in shock. "What is? What do you mean?"

He sucks in his breath and waves back at the door. "This. Having Luke back. What if it's not for real? What if this is it? I don't think I can handle losing him again. I don't want to do this without him anymore. I can't."

I hug him. I have to, and his arms tighten around me. "Do you think it's not?"

"I don't know," he says quietly against my hair. "He seems sincere, like he's happy to be back, but what if...I don't know.

What if we wake up tomorrow and learn this was it, all we're getting?"

"You need to tell him this," I say, pulling back and searching his eyes. "He needs to know how important he is."

Casey bites his lip and nods, gazing back at the doorway. "He just needs to come back."

THEY GET BACK TO WORK, and I continue on my own project. I'm haunted by Casey's words, and watch the next session from a different vantage point this time. I can see Casey's concerned glances at Luke, almost longing, and feel awful for never even considering how hard this must be for him. To get a brutal reminder of what was, a small taste of what could be, and yet, know there's a chance this is the end. That after tonight they go back to the empty shell of what they should be.

I remember Casey's harsh critique at breakfast the first time we'd met. When he'd blasted Luke for leaving them and sentencing them to a fraction of what they should have been. I hadn't really understood then. I didn't know what music meant to them. I'd thought it was about money and fame and the fact that Luke's absence meant no more big stadium concerts. But now, watching Casey's expression and knowing everything I do about him, about both of them, I realize there is nothing shallow about Casey's pain at losing Luke. It's not about any of that. It's about a broken connection that removed a piece of him and the chance to reach his own potential as an artist. They are both brilliant, but together they are untouchable.

I can't help but think about what it must be like to watch someone you care about so much, your brother, your best friend, self-destruct so completely. My own broken heart is only a flesh wound compared to what this last year must have been like for Casey. To lose his sister, his friend, his music, and the enormous chunk of his identity wrapped up in those things. I feel my own heart constricting at the thought, the chills from what this exact moment means to Luke, but especially Casey. I can't even imagine how hard it must be to have Luke back only to know there's no guarantee it's real, that his other half won't follow him out of this room. And then the emotion starts to swell within me, that painful throb in my chest that can only be relieved one way.

I stare at my blank screen and start to write.

———

WE ALL WORK late into the night. The guys on their song. Me, on the spewing of my heart. By the time they call it quits, I can tell they're happy with their efforts and feeling good about Friday's recording session, especially given the fact that they still have tomorrow to work.

Eli and Sweeny want to go out and celebrate, but the rest of us aren't up for it. They leave us at the lobby, and Luke, Casey, and I continue the journey to 403.

"Saw you working like crazy. Looked intense," Casey comments with a smile as we exit on the fourth floor.

I blush a little and nod. "Yeah, I had some stuff I had to get out."

"Can I see it?"

"Once we get inside."

He understands, and Luke opens the door.

"You guys sounded great. Unbelievable, actually," I say once we're inside.

"You think?" Luke asks, and I nod.

"Absolutely. As a psycho fangirl, totally impressed."

He laughs and shakes his head.

"Well, good. Thanks for guarding the door."

"Any time."

"So what's this new piece?" Casey asks, and I can see I have Luke's interest, too.

I swallow, the mood immediately shifting. It's a hard one, painful, and I'm not sure we're ready for it. But maybe we don't have a choice anymore.

I offer a weak smile as they sit at the stools, studying me.

I open up my laptop and stare at the screen, scanning the words as my heart races.

I glance up and meet their expressions, suddenly captivated by the same overwhelming feelings that gripped me downstairs during the rehearsal.

"Watching you guys...together, how incredible you were, and yet, thinking that it was almost lost...I was...I don't know. So full of love and fear and regret at the same time." I feel the tears coming again out of nowhere and try to blink them away. "Do you two even know how amazing you are? I mean, not just individually, but together. I had no idea. It was breathtaking and so sad at the same time."

I can tell they have no idea how to respond to my unexpected outburst, and Casey especially looks affected after our earlier conversation.

"I wrote this for both of you," I say quietly. I draw in a deep breath. "It's called 'Laughing Stock.'" I turn the laptop around on the counter so they can read, and grip the edge of the granite.

> "It's not funny how far you've strayed, I'll say it
>   one time
> I can tell by your smile you know I'm right, still
>   you hide behind the lie.

It's not funny how far you've strayed, I'll say it
    this time.
I can tell by your eyes you know what I mean,
    still you find a reason to fight, but you'll
    never cry.

How can you believe it's easier to be alone than
    feel loved?
You fear the embrace of a friend, yet welcome
    your enemies' hands as they beat down.
You listen for proof that no one understands
    you, but we do
And it's killing me.

It's not funny to see how well you ignore the
    signs.
By the pain in your eyes I can see you're fading.
Still you try, you're losing the fight.

You're no better for falling apart
Being alone won't make you stronger
You'll fall harder the more space you put
    between us
But I'll catch you, oh I'll catch you.

How can you believe it's easier to feel alone
    than feel loved?
You fear the embrace of a friend, yet welcome
    your enemies' hands as they beat down.
You listen for proof that no one understands
    you, but I do
And it's killing me. It's killing me!

It's not funny how far you've strayed, just listen
    this one time
Look in my eyes and see how I love you."

They're quiet for a long time. I'm not sure how many times they read through my words, but I can tell they're not sure how to respond. I don't know if it's because they love them or hate them, but when I notice the tears in Casey's eyes, I have a pretty good idea.

Luke's jaw is clenched as he glances from Casey, to the screen, to me, and back to Casey. He gets it. I know he does, I just don't know what it means to him. What he's willing to do with it.

"Is it true?" he asks finally, his voice barely above a whisper, but he's not talking to me.

Casey sucks in his breath and nods, his eyes pleading with Luke to understand. It breaks my heart as I watch them, and I almost sob when Luke pulls Casey in for a hug. They hold on to each other, and I have to wipe the tears from my own cheeks. I had no idea words could do things like this. I never understood their power. How had I minimized their value all these years simply because they weren't attached to a paycheck? It seems absurd now, sitting here watching two broken souls repair themselves because of the way I formed a string of letters together. This is what words do. So often they tear apart, but they can also form miracles.

They finally pull away and focus their awe on me this time. I'm surprised when it's Luke who speaks first. "Can we use these, Callie?"

My eyes widen, confused. "What do you mean?"

"I..." He stops, and glances at Casey quickly before turning back to me. "For the EP. We still need two to three more songs."

Casey almost chokes. "Wait. Seriously? You're in?" he asks in shock, barely able to complete the thought.

Luke meets his gaze and nods. "If you'll have me back."

I practically scream as I run around the counter and throw my arms around him. He laughs, returning my embrace, and I can feel Casey joining behind me. I've never been so happy in my life.

"Of course you can use it!" I cry. Then, search his eyes. "But only if you use 'Perfect Day,' too."

Luke visibly flinches. "Really? I don't know," he replies, skeptical. "I didn't write that for anyone else."

"Neither did I," I point out.

Casey's eyes widen with that inspired look I've come to admire. "Dude, she's right. Think about the journey those three songs would represent. After everything we've been through, that's some epic comeback shit right there."

"You just need to add a good breakup song," I suggest. I was joking, but based on their expressions, I don't think they care.

Casey grins. "I think I can handle that one."

I glare at him. "Oh really?" I say, crossing my arms.

"Not for you, silly! The crazy psycho who hit me."

I laugh. "You could call it 'Bella Amberosi.'"

He smiles. "Hey, maybe. I have some ideas." His expression changes as he grows serious again and turns to Luke.

"Really, man, you have no idea...I mean..." he can't even finish the sentence, and Luke claps him on the back, completing the thought with another hug.

"I know, brother. I do."

20

FRIDAY

Casey actually sets an alarm Thursday night, and we all agree to meet in the lobby at 8:30 the next morning to head to the studio as early as possible. Apparently, the Label is shelling out a decent sum to book it, although I suspect the band is so excited at the prospect of recording again that they wouldn't have needed any additional encouragement.

I have butterflies in my own stomach as I get ready, and all I'll be doing is watching. Their equipment had been loaded and transported to the studio last night after they finished their final rehearsal, so this morning it's just a matter of getting the artists to their canvas. TJ arranged for a vehicle to pick us up, and we all pile into a large SUV.

"You ready?" Casey asks, once we're comfortable in the car.

"Me? Are you ready?" I ask with a smile.

He shrugs, but I can see his excitement mounting.

"Hard to believe this is happening," he replies, and Eli and Sweeny nod in agreement.

We all instinctively cast a glance at Luke, but he's staring out the window. I can't tell if he's paying attention to us or not, and can only imagine what's going through his head at the moment. I reach over and squeeze his hand, drawing a startled look. He returns my smile, and I let go. Casey puts his arm around me, and I lean against him, completely content for one of the first times in my life.

Sweeny and Eli chatter most of the way to the studio, but Casey and Luke are lost in their own heads. I can see it in the way they stare off, vacant, but only because they're focused on something no one else can see. They seem content too, however, and I let myself relax for once.

We arrive at the studio, and I'm surprised by the underwhelming exterior of the building. I've passed this storefront before, many times actually, but I had no idea what magic it contained. We pile out of the car and move inside.

A middle-aged man stops his conversation with a woman behind a reception desk, and his face ignites. He rushes toward us with a huge smile, hand out-stretched.

"Hey, guys! Glad you could make it!"

"Julian," Casey greets, taking his hand first.

"Julian" then moves to the rest of them, but hesitates when he reaches Luke.

"Luke, good to see you, man," he says, and I can tell his emotion is genuine.

"Good to be back," Luke replies, but I'm not as sure about his.

"Julian, this is Callie," Casey introduces, and Julian smiles a greeting and takes my hand.

"Callie, nice to meet you."

"She's one of the writers," Casey explains, and Julian's expression changes, clearly impressed.

"Really? Well, glad you could make it," he says, and I'm sure I'm glowing. I can't even begin to believe this is happening. Julian turns and starts heading toward a hallway behind the reception desk. "Ok, well, Jon is ready for you. I've got the lounge stocked, but let me know if there's anything else you need. Michel is overseas and couldn't make it today, but Jon will take good care of you."

"We worked with Jon on 'Collide,' didn't we?" Sweeny asks.

Casey nods. "Yeah, that was it. Cool guy."

I try to listen to their conversation as we shuffle through the building, but I'm more interested in everything else around me. It's nothing like I've ever seen before. Definitely not the type of environment I'm accustomed to, and I'm not sure how to describe this place except "vibe-y." There's mood everywhere, art, color, lighting, and I can feel the "coolness" seeping into me the further we venture into the building and absorb the artistic aura.

I notice a few frames containing gold records on the walls in the hallway, and am surprised by some of the well-known artists I see listed. I'm sure there must be one or more of these for Night Shifts Black somewhere, and wonder which studio gets to display those.

"That's the lounge," Casey explains as we pass a room of couches. There's even a couple pool tables and very inviting wet bar. "It's going to be a long day, so feel free to hang out here whenever you want."

I nod, loving the lounge's calming and modern décor. The room appears to be encased by a short wall of pebbles, and I realize there's a trickle of water moving over the rocks. It looks like a place where an artist would want to relax and be artistic.

We continue on to what they call the control room, and this one looks more like the "command central" I expected. I feel like I'm entering a spaceship cockpit as we suddenly face a giant console with countless knobs, faders, and buttons. I glance at the walls and ceiling, which are covered with the foamy-looking geometric art I'd seen in other places throughout the building.

"Those are diffusers," Casey explains, following my gaze. "For controlling sound."

I nod and stare past the console through a window into another room. It's a gorgeous space made up of shiny wood and glass, and I can see a line of doors leading to smaller rooms beyond.

"And that's the tracking room," he says.

"That's where you actually play?" I ask, and he nods.

"Yup."

"Why are there other rooms?"

Casey grins as though he's giving me a tour of his childhood home. "Well, that's the main tracking room there, and then those are iso booths."

"Iso booths?"

"Yeah, so people like Sweeny can lock themselves in with their cabs and blow their eardrums out without killing anyone."

"I heard that!" Sweeny grunts.

"Am I wrong?" Casey returns, and Sweeny makes a face.

"And what are those little walls? They look portable."

"Those are baffles. They're on wheels and help absorb the sound," another man interjects. He must be Jon. "Hey, guys. Good to see you again."

They all shake hands and conduct their greetings.

"This is Carl. He'll be assisting me today. So what's the plan?" Jon asks, and I'm not surprised when he addresses Casey before anyone else.

"Well, we want to track the entire song, if possible, so we'd like to get started right away."

Jon nods. "Great. Your stuff is already in there and ready for you. Get setup and we can start laying down the scratch. Who's up?"

"Casey's going to play keys with my vocal," Luke says.

"No acoustic?"

"Nah, just keys," Casey confirms.

Jon seems satisfied and moves toward the console. "Ok, great. You guys can get setup in the main room and the rest of you can hang out."

"I'm grabbing some coffee," Eli announces. "You coming?" he says to Sweeny who agrees.

"What about you, Callie?"

I shake my head. "I want to watch," I respond, to no one's surprise.

"First time in a studio?" Jon asks after we're alone.

"Pretty obvious, huh," I answer, and he glances at me before turning back to his work. His smile isn't condescending, however, and I decide I like him.

"Yeah, but it's ok. I'll take genuine interest over whiny arm candy any day."

I laugh. "Well, I can promise you, there will be no whining from this arm candy."

"Casey said you're one of the writers."

I nod. "Yeah, it's kind of a long story."

"Well, it's definitely got to be a good one to get your name in the credits with Casey Barrett and Luke Craven."

I shrug. I hadn't even thought of that. "Yeah, no kidding. They're pretty much the most talented people I've ever met."

It's his turn to laugh. "I could probably say that, too, and I've met a lot of talented people, believe me. It was a sad day for all of us when Luke Craven walked away from music. Seeing him back in a studio...man, you have no idea."

Actually, I think I have a pretty good idea, but there's no way I'm getting into that. Right now, that's a story for only three people.

"I promise not to bother you once we start, but for now, can you explain what's happening?"

Jon doesn't seem to mind my questions and continues working on his console as he talks.

"Sure. We're going to start by laying down a scratch track, which is basically just a rough run-through of the entire song."

"With just Luke and Casey?"

He nods. "Yeah, not the full band. Just keys and vocals. The scratch isn't part of the actual recording. We just use it as a guide for them to play along to when we're tracking their parts. After the scratch, we'll get Casey's drums, then lay down the bass so we can lock it in with the kick. Then guitars, synths, and finally vocals. We won't get to mix and master today, though."

My eyes widen as I absorb everything. "So wait, they don't actually play together at any point?"

He shakes his head. "No, not today. We're going to track separately. Then after all of that we'll mix and master everything to polish it up as the final version of the track."

"Wow."

I stare through the glass and see Casey fooling around with a keyboard, although this one is much bigger than the one in our suite and actually looks like a piano. Luke is standing in front of a microphone, and Carl is hovering nearby, waiting for instructions. They all have large headphones over their ears.

"How's it going?" Jon says into a short microphone on his console.

The guys look up from their place behind the glass and signal him.

"We're ready," Luke replies into his mic.

"Ok, let's get a quick sound check. Casey, I've got you going through a DI so we just have to check the gain. Give me something."

Casey gives him a thumbs up and starts playing. We can

hear the piano, but also a heavy buzz, and Jon holds up his hand.

"Ok, hang on. Carl, I'm getting a hum. Can you flip the ground switch on the box?"

Carl jumps into action and makes an adjustment to the little metal box on the floor by Casey's keyboard.

"Ok, play again, Casey...Ok, great. Luke?"

Luke leans toward the mic. "Check 1, 2...hey hey 1, 2."

"Ok, good. You guys hear each other and the click, ok?"

"Yeah, we're good."

"Great. Alright, whenever you're ready!"

Casey counts off and starts to play.

I'm not sure I actually breathe the entire time they're recording. Even though I've heard the song countless times now, it's different for some reason. Maybe it's because they're different. Casey and Luke have an energy, an aura, to their music I hadn't heard before. It's beautiful, and I have to keep reminding myself to re-oxygenate.

I think the recording sounds great when they finish, but after listening back, Casey and Jon both agree they have to run it again because of something that was happening on the "turns." They do, and this time, seem more optimistic after the take.

Luke and Casey give each other a congratulatory punch, and Jon leans into his talkback mic.

"Ok, I think we got it. Come on in to listen back, and if you're happy, we'll get Casey's kit setup to track the drums next. Carl, I'm going to want 421's on the toms and throw up a couple 81's for the overheads. I need the room mics back in place for the kit, too."

Luke and Casey join us in the control room, and I rise to greet them. I expected Casey to be euphoric with excitement, but instead he seems serious, contemplative. He still has enough playfulness to give me a quick kiss that I treasure, however.

"So what'd you think?" he asks.

I shake my head. "It's amazing. I had no idea."

"We haven't really even started yet," he chuckles. "Let's hear it," he says to Jon. The engineer plays back the recording, and all three of them have a stern look on their faces as they listen.

"Yeah, it's good," Luke says in approval at the conclusion of the song.

Jon nods. "I agree. Ok, Casey. Let's get you going."

Casey nods, and gives me an apologetic smile before retreating back to the tracking room.

"Luke, you can take a breather. We've got a while until we need you again."

Luke smiles. "Thanks. I'll stick around for a bit."

He slings his arm around me and gives me quick hug.

"Good to be back?" I ask, looking up at him.

He nods. "Yeah. I'm not gonna lie, I was nervous. But, yeah, it's pretty great. I missed this."

"You sound great," I say, squeezing him back.

"Yeah? Thanks. That wasn't the real vocal though."

"Oh, right. You don't use that one for the final version."

"Exactly."

"Hey, so what's a click?"

"The click track? It's that steady ticking you heard while we were playing."

"Oh ok, that metronome-sounding thing?"

"Yep. Keeps us all together." He gives me another smile. "You ready to see your boyfriend do his thing?" he asks, and I suck in my breath. Now, I'm the one who's nervous.

"Definitely. I'm excited."

"Alright, Casey, give me quarter notes on the kick," Jon says to the mic, and Casey starts pounding a slow steady rhythm on the big bass drum. "Carl, back off the outside mic a bit? Tiny bit more...ok...good. Casey, give me the snare next."

Casey moves to the smaller, horizontal drum and starts the same simple rhythm. They repeat the drill for the "toms" and "hi-hats," and then Jon has him play the entire kit to do a check on the "overheads" and get the full mix. He finally seems happy with what he's hearing and makes sure Casey is ready.

Casey signals him, and Jon triggers the scratch track.

I'm not sure I actually blink during the five minutes that follow. My eyes are glued to Casey, my ears ringing with an incredible barrage of percussion. I never in a million years would have guessed the cute little song Casey played for me that first day on that beat-up guitar would have this as its base. I can't believe Casey heard this in his head when he read my poem.

Casey wipes his face with his t-shirt when he finishes, but doesn't seem happy.

"Can we run that again?" he asks.

"Yeah, no problem. Sounded like a decent first take out here, but we can run it again."

"Thanks."

They do, and it sounds no different to me, but I know it is because everyone else seems much happier. Casey joins us in the control room.

"That was good, man. Great take. What'd you think?" Jon asks.

Casey shrugs. "I don't know. I'm still not sure about the bridge. Can we hear it?"

Jon nods and starts the playback. I watch Casey's face closely as he listens and notice him cringe a couple times. When it finishes, he moves back toward the tracking room.

"Yeah, we need to run the bridge again. I don't like the build."

"You need a bigger fill, Case," Luke says, and Casey nods.

"Yeah. I also came in too early on the chorus."

"Ok. Let's take it from the turn after chorus two," Jon says, and Casey returns to his kit.

He seems much happier the third time through.

"Killer!" Jon calls into the mic, and Casey salutes him.

"Yeah, I think we got it that time," Casey replies.

By the time Casey makes his way back to the control room, Sweeny and Eli have joined us as well.

"Still tracking drums?" Sweeny smirks. "Why? They're just gonna replace it with samples anyway."

Eli laughs, and Casey gives him an annoyed look. "Hilarious. Hey, how about you do something besides stuff your face with donuts?"

Sweeny seems surprised. "We ready for guitars already?"

"No. Bass," Jon says, pointing to Eli.

"You want my cab in an iso booth?" Eli asks, and Jon shakes his head.

"No, you can set up in the main room. We're crunched for time, so we'll just go direct."

Eli's face falls. "You want to go direct?"

It's Casey's turn to snicker. "Dude, we have an entire song to track in a day. No one cares about making angels cry with your bass tone. Direct is fine."

"Look, man, I promise. It's going to be killer. If it's not, we'll setup your cab, ok?" Jon soothes.

Eli grunts, but moves into the main room and removes his bass from the stand. Carl hands him a cable, and he plugs it into his guitar. He then adjusts the headphones on his ears.

"Alright, go ahead," Jon says, and Eli starts to play. Jon moves some buttons around on the console.

"He's checking the gain and compression," Casey whispers to me.

I nod as though that explains everything. I can tell by his smile he knows I have no idea what that means.

"What was he talking about 'going direct?' Why was Eli so upset about it?" I ask.

Casey grins. "Eli wants to control his tone with his own amp. To really do that, they'd have to set it up in one of those smaller rooms there called iso booths like we're going to do for the guitar cabs and vocals. Problem is, Eli is never happy, so we could spend the rest of the day trying to get his tone right. Jon is saving us a ton of time by having him go direct and controlling it himself."

I nod. "Are they really going to replace your drums with samples?"

I can see Luke and Sweeny snickering, and Casey rolls his eyes at them.

"No. Not on this one," he says.

"What does that mean?" I ask.

"Remember that software I showed you on my computer in the office?"

"With the keyboard?"

He nods. "Exactly. We could basically use that instead of what we just recorded. Makes everything perfect."

"They would do that?"

Casey shrugs. "Honestly, if TJ hadn't sent my own kit, I probably wouldn't have minded. But since we got a really good take, we'll use my track. Right, guys?" Casey challenges with a dark look.

They shrug, still grinning, and hold up their hands.

"You ready?" Jon asks Eli, and the rest of us quiet.

Eli says he is, and this time the song coming through the monitors has Casey's drums added to the original keys and vocals. Eli plays along, but I don't find this part as exciting. The bass makes a big difference to the sound, but it's not as flashy as the drums, and Eli needs four takes until Jon is happy. I suppose that makes sense since he'd only started working on the song Wednesday.

"What do you think?" Jon asks Casey who joins him by the console.

Casey sighs. "Honestly, he's gonna hate me but I think we need to run the last chorus again. I just remembered this sweet run he played last night when we were rehearsing. I'd love to get that in there."

Jon nods. "You want to talk to him or should I?"

"I'll talk to him."

Casey leans over the mic. "Hey, killer. Nice work on that last one. We're close. You sound great. One thing, though. Remember, that run you played last night on the final chorus?"

Eli looks confused for a minute and then raises his hand. "Right on! Forgot about that!" he says into his own talkback mic.

"Sweet. Let's just get that in there and then we're good."

"You couldn't remember that two takes ago?" he fires back.

Casey grins and shrugs. "Better now than on the way home!"

JON TELLS us to take five and grab a bite once we finish with the bass track. We still have to do guitars, synths, and vocals, but the guys seem happy with the progress, so I assume we're making good time. Personally, I'm exhausted, and I'm just watching. Every step seems so meticulous, and I struggle to tell the difference between the "killer" takes and the complete failures.

Casey and I opt for a sandwich on a bench, while the other three go for something more formal at a restaurant the next block over.

"What do you think so far?" he asks, after we settle on our bench.

"Pretty amazing. I'm tired, though!"

He laughs. "It's a long day for sure. We still have at least another six or seven hours."

"Really? You're finished with your part, though, right?"

He shakes his head. "No, I'll help with the synth work after we get the guitars down."

I let out my breath.

"I don't understand, though. If you're playing drums, who plays the synths and keys at the shows?"

Casey shrugs. "We'll usually get someone to play a lot of it live, but we run some in tracks, too. You just can't get everything you want live."

"And I thought music was just a few guys strumming guitars."

He smirks. "Yeah, maybe fifty years ago."

"I can't wait to see you play live," I say, glancing over at him.

He smiles back. "It might be sooner than you think."

My face falls. "I thought you didn't have to tour for a few more months."

He shakes his head. "We don't. But we're still going to play some shows before then. With Luke's return, the Label is going to want to explode us back into the spotlight. I'm sure we'll do some high profile stuff to build up for the tour."

"And you think I'll be able to go?"

He gives me a silly look. "You better go."

"Well, I want to be there, of course, but I don't know. I don't want to get in your way. I mean, with Luke just getting back into it, I don't want to mess with the band chemistry or anything."

He studies me for a moment and sighs. "Seriously? Is that really what you think? Look, maybe now isn't the best time to talk about this, but Luke and I had a long conversation last night after you went to bed. He's serious about coming back, but he wants you to come with us. He needs you, Callie. You're his rock, his support, at least for now. He doesn't believe he would have gotten here without you, so he's not ready to let go."

I stare at him in shock. "Wait, what? Are you serious? He said that?"

Casey shrugs. "It's true. Anyone who's seen the two of you together can see how important you are to him."

I shake my head in disbelief. "Wow...and you think the guys will be ok with that? The Label?"

Casey laughs. "Are you kidding? To have Luke Craven back on the bus? They'd let him bring an entire psychiatric team if he said that's what it'd take. One girl from Shelteron, PA is nothing."

I swallow. "What about you? What do you think?" I ask, searching his eyes. "I mean, I know this whole thing is strange. Luke and I have a very complicated relationship, but you know I'm crazy about you."

Relief floods through me when he smiles. "Hey, look, this whole thing is totally screwed up, I know that, but I also think I understand it. I really do. What you and Luke have is very different than what you and I have, and I think the two can co-exist."

I take his arm, and lean against him. "It's true. But even for the whole touring thing? Are you sure you're ok with me being there?"

He kisses my hair. "To be perfectly honest, I'm thrilled that Luke is taking the hit in demanding your presence, because then I don't have to look like the wussy boyfriend who wants his girlfriend along."

I grin and kiss him. "So that means you do want me along?"

"Well, I mean, we need our best writer, right?"

I LAUGH. "I suppose. I'll need something to do while you guys are busy signing bras and whatnot."

After lunch, Luke tracks the rhythm guitar next, then Sweeny on lead. Casey does the synths and his computer stuff last, and they're finally ready for Luke's vocal.

They set him up in an iso booth, and Jon tells Carl to make sure he gets a Neumann vocal mic or something like that.

"He's clipping," Jon mutters to himself during the sound check, and makes some adjustments on the console. "Hey, Luke, I think we got it now. You ready?"

"Ready."

For the first time that day, the entire band is gathered in the control room to watch. I'm not surprised, and can feel the anticipation in the air. Most of us thought this day would never come, and if they knew half of what Casey and I do, they'd understand the full extent of this miracle. There's a ghost in that iso booth, stealing magic from a second chance he never dreamed he'd have. A month ago, sure he wouldn't. I promise myself I won't cry, but when Casey grabs my hand and squeezes, I know it's going to be a difficult battle. He's thinking the same thing I am, and I can't look at him out of fear I'll lose it.

Jon starts the track, and Luke takes over. From the second he starts singing, the song becomes his. It doesn't matter that Casey and I wrote it, Luke now owns it, and I finally have to steal a glance at Casey's face. He looks mesmerized, completely transported to a different time and place, and it melts my heart.

"That's it, isn't it?" I whisper when the song finishes. "That's what was in your head."

He almost seems dazed and meets my eyes.

"That was it."

Luke and Jon are exchanging words, but I can't even hear them. I'm too caught up in the moment, thrilled for Casey, for Luke, for the world that's going to be blessed with this additional contribution to its rich tapestry of art. This piece of history that had no business being created, but has now somehow transformed several lives.

"You did this, Callie," Casey whispers, tears in his eyes. "Don't ever tell me you're no one."

Speechless, I swallow hard, and gaze back at the booth.

IT'S a long day for them, but completely overwhelming for me. Every second, every experience, was so rich and saturated that my brain seems ready to explode by the time they wrap up the session.

Jon plays the track one last time for us, and I think it sounds amazing, but apparently it's not even done. They still have to mix and master it, although not today. The guys want to celebrate, and even my exhausted brain can appreciate why that would be a necessary conclusion to this incredible day.

"We don't have to stay long," Casey assures me as the car pulls up to the entrance of a club. There's a long line snaked to the door, but Eli and Sweeny don't seem deterred in the least as they saunter toward the entrance.

"You sure you're up for this?" I ask Luke as we climb out of the car, and am surprised when he smiles at me.

"No, probably not, but it's kind of mandatory, huh?" he asks with a knowing glint. He understands I'm as (not) excited about this as he is.

The bouncers let us in without even a second of hesitation, and I wonder how everyone else on the planet is able to recognize these guys except for me. No wonder they found my ignorance so amusing.

Casey seems uncomfortable for some reason, and I see him constantly glancing at Luke. I do as well, and notice he's stiffened quite a bit, a huge change from his smile just a moment ago.

"It's not the same club as that night," Casey whispers, leaning close to my ear so I can hear him. "But it's similar."

I meet his gaze, concerned, then look back to Luke. "Should we go?" I ask Casey, suddenly terrified for some reason. "Is he ready for this?"

"I don't know. We need to keep an eye on him."

We're both studying Luke now, and relax a bit when he requests a table. The club is packed, so I'd be shocked if they have any available, but the hostess consults with some colleagues, and before I know it, we're being led past more security and up a set of stairs to a secluded balcony. There are maybe five other tables surrounded by couches up here, and the hostess shows us to the empty one.

"Please let us know what you need," she says, and Sweeny recites a surprisingly extensive list.

She smiles and promises to have that sent right up.

"You good?" I ask Luke, dropping beside him.

He gives me a weak look. "I don't know yet," he says, staring through the railing at the packed dance floor below.

I loop my arm through his and lean against his shoulder.

"We got you, kid," I say, and can feel him relax.

I sense Casey's gaze and reach over with my other hand to

grab his. He squeezes back, and the three of us sit in silence while Eli and Sweeny take off to one of the other tables.

"You know them?" I ask, and cringe at Luke and Casey's amused grins.

"Do you not have any relationship with pop culture? Like, at all?" Casey asks in disbelief.

I shrug with a sheepish smile, and he shakes his head.

"That's Andis Carver and Kendra Malkin, hon," Luke explains, his expression mirroring Casey's.

My jaw drops. "Wait, the real Andis Carver and Kendra Malkin? Like, the moviestars?"

Luke laughs. "Yes, the moviestars."

"Wow. I can't believe I'm ten feet away from them!"

I can feel Casey and Luke's looks of disbelief and turn to them defensively. "What?"

"What?" Casey asks in exasperation.

Luke is laughing so hard now, I don't know what to do except stare in utter confusion. Casey is just shaking his head, obviously just as confused by me.

"What?" I repeat, totally lost.

"Callie! You're best friends with Luke Craven, freakin' dating Casey Barrett, superstars from rock sensation Night Shifts Black, and what finally impresses you is that you're at the same club as Andis Carver?" Casey cries.

I laugh, finally starting to understand, and shrug with a grin. "I suppose I can see your point..." I grab a napkin and hold it up. "So does that mean I'm not allowed to ask for an autograph?" I tease, and Casey pulls me down and kisses me instead. I giggle and settle against him.

"No autographs," he mutters, and I can actually feel the moment when he rolls his eyes.

LUKE, Casey, and I spend our entire time at the table laughing and talking. It actually turns out to be a fun night, definitely more than I expected when we pulled up, and despite the potentially awkward start, even Luke seems relaxed and in good spirits when we leave. As usual, we lost Eli and Sweeny somewhere along the way, so the three of us return to the suite alone.

"How you feeling, rockstar?" I ask Luke, after we're safely back in 403.

He smiles at me. "Good. Better than I thought I would, if I'm honest."

"Yeah? Good. I'm glad."

I give him a quick hug, then take Casey's hands.

"And what about you, my super famous and disgustingly talented boyfriend?"

He shakes his head with that signature Casey Barrett grin. "Knock it off. We get it. You. Don't. Care."

I shrug. "Well, I mean, maybe I would if you'd been in a few B movies and almost got nominated for an Oscar a decade ago."

"I have an Oscar, sweetheart," he returns, and I laugh.

"Point, Barrett," Luke calls from the fridge. "You two want anything while I'm here?"

I squeeze Casey's hands and lead him toward the couch. "Just water for me. How about a movie, guys?"

Casey nods. "I'm in. Luke?"

"Depends. You lovebirds aren't going to make-out the whole time, are you?" he mutters, and I smirk.

"I don't know. Casey's mad at me, so you're probably safe."

Casey shakes his head, and I laugh as he wrestles me to the couch.

"Yep, that's what I thought. I'm out," Luke jokes as he rounds the corner to join us.

"Oh, stop and sit down," I bark, patting the cushion beside me.

He smiles and hands me my bottle of water while Casey and I adjust to more practical positions. I pick up the remote, but hesitate when I sense there's more that needs to be said. Luke has that far-off look again, but there's something different about it this time.

"You ok?" I ask, studying him for any of the usual signs.

He surprises us when the wistful look spreads into a content smile. "You know, a year ago I wouldn't have been able to do what we did tonight without getting wasted and making a dick of myself. Six months ago I wouldn't have been able to even make it through those doors at all. And then tonight..." He looks at me, and my heart swells. "I think I'm a different person now."

"We all are, man," Casey says quietly.

I nod, and search Luke's eyes. "We are. You don't have to be a ghost anymore."

21

THE NEXT DAY

We all fall asleep on the couch this time. I know because I wake up a few times during the night to see Luke asleep on the vertical side, while I share the horizontal piece with Casey. But by the time I get up the following morning, Luke is gone. I wonder if he moved back to his room, since I don't see him anywhere in the main area of the suite.

I force myself up and stretch, feeling nervous for some reason, but not wanting to totally give in to such an irrational feeling. We had a great night. We'd found an Andis Carver classic, and Luke was in good spirits throughout the movie, joking and laughing with us. So why is my heart pounding in my chest just a few hours later?

I almost laugh out loud to myself at this ridiculous rush of adrenaline as I move to the hallway. The guest room is empty. The office. The extra bathroom. Of course they are because Luke is in his room. Asleep, maybe showering, and I'm going to disturb him because I suddenly can't breathe and feel like I'm suppressing a scream. I swallow and knock.

No answer.

I knock again.

Nothing.

My hands are shaking now and suddenly I know why. My heart stops as the alarm takes over. What did Elena do with her last breaths? Remind the people she loved most how important they were.

No. No!

I shove through Luke's door, completely frantic now.

"Luke!" I cry, sudden tears burning my eyes. "Luke, where are you?"

His bed is empty, still made from room service the day before. His bathroom is dark. I turn the light on, but it's empty, too.

"Casey!" I cry, running from Luke's room back to the hallway. My frantic screams have startled him awake, and he bolts up from the couch, rubbing the sleep from his eyes.

"What? What's wrong?"

"It's Luke! He's gone!"

Casey looks confused. "What do you mean he's gone?"

I shrug helplessly, not even sure where to start. "I don't know. He's not here! I was worried about him and went to check on him and he's not in his room, not in the office!"

"Ok, calm down. Maybe he just left to get breakfast or something," Casey says, but his own voice is wavering.

He puts his arms around me, and we hold each other for a moment, trying to piece together what's happening and what to do with it.

"Oh, god, Casey. What if he was saying goodbye last night?" I whisper, the words oozing out like venom on my lips. I'm having trouble breathing.

I can feel Casey tense, and hold him tighter.

"No, he wasn't. He's fine. He has to be fine."

I nod, completely numb.

"I'm going to call the front desk and see if they can give me any information. Callie, it's going to be fine, ok? I'm sure there's an explanation."

I can't even muster a nod this time as he gently pulls away and moves toward the room phone. While he's doing that, I call Luke's, but I'm not surprised when it goes straight to voicemail. I try a text, but that doesn't go through either. His phone must be off.

"Hi, this is Casey Barrett from Room 403. We're trying to get in touch with Luke and are wondering if he mentioned where he was headed this morning on his way out...sure, yeah, I can wait..." He glances over at me. "They're going to ask the lobby employees if any of them saw or spoke to him." His face changes and he turns back to the phone. "Yeah, I'm here...uh-huh...yeah...wait, what? Really...did he say where he was going or what he was doing? Ok...thanks...um, no, that's ok...thanks for your help."

He hangs up the phone and stares at me. There's nothing I like about the look on his face.

"What is it?" I ask, my voice barely audible.

He clears his throat. "They said they saw him leave about an hour ago carrying an old chair. He didn't talk to anyone."

I pale. I can feel the blood draining from my face and instinctively rush toward the office. I throw open the door and, sure enough, The Chair is missing. All that's left are four small indents in the carpet serving as a grotesque monument to its powerful presence. And now, devastating absence.

"It's gone," I whisper as Casey comes up behind me. The tears start to fall now, and I inexplicably find myself getting angry more than anything. Furious at Luke for making us love him, coming so far, only to give up at the finish line.

"Callie..." Casey's arms wrap around me again, and I turn

to settle into him. We stand in silence for a long time, having no idea what to say, what to do. We don't know where to start looking for a suicidal man with a chair, and the cops would just laugh at our "emergency." So we do nothing because after everything we've done over the last month, there's nothing left to do.

Then, suddenly, a crash.

I straighten, and Casey and I exchange a shocked look before running toward the kitchen. Our door is opening, and before he can even get through it, two roommates are tackling Luke in the entryway.

He laughs at us and almost drops the cup carrier and bag he's holding.

"What's this?" he asks, but I'm not ready to let go.

"You were gone," I whisper. "We were so scared."

He shakes his head in disbelief. "I went to get breakfast," he gasps, holding up the evidence for our review.

His face changes as he studies us. "Wow, you guys were really scared."

I nod and wipe the tears from my eyes. Now, tears of relief.

I step back and search his face. "The chair was gone. The lobby employees said you left with it."

He almost seems embarrassed as I let him go, and he drops the food on the counter.

"Yeah. I returned it."

I stop. "You returned it?"

He nods. "To Jemma's. I shouldn't have stolen it in the first place."

"But..."

"I don't need it anymore, Callie. It's not who I am, like you said."

I close the gap and give him another giant hug, this time

making sure he knows that no matter how bad things get, he is never going to be allowed to leave us. That he is loved too much to be a memory. I still can't speak, but Casey can.

"Dammit, Luke. Can you leave us a freaking note next time?"

22

THE REST

I wish I could say the three of us live happily ever after that. That Luke and Casey (and I) go on to win countless awards. Casey and I get married, have three photo album children, twelve grandchildren, and die as happy old people holding hands in the house we built under a quilt I made. That Luke eventually finds peace and love, and none of us ever has to visit that dark place behind the mirror again.

But that's not the way things work.

I don't know what will happen. I know it probably won't be all, or any, of that. All I know is what's now, and that I have to embrace it, because you can't define yourself by the future and what you're not. Because sometimes we make bad choices and sometimes the evil chooses us, and that mirror is always there, waiting for the moment when we give up and relinquish power.

So, here's what I know.

I'm Callie Roland. Twenty-three, and I'm a great friend. I'm an ok writer who got incredibly lucky and will soon have writing credits on an EP put out by rock superstars Night Shifts Black. I'm crashing in a ridiculously expensive hotel with my incredible boyfriend whom I'm pretty sure I'm in love with, and my other friend I love like a brother.

I know Casey Barrett is inspired again and writing like a fiend. He's already finished his "break up song" called "Too Late," which he continues to swear is inspired by brief fling Jana Furmali, and not me whom he's crazy about. That doesn't stop me from teasing him, of course. Anything to see that magnetic grin as much as possible.

Here are the lyrics we worked on together.

> "Isn't it obvious our feelings fade away
> Isn't it obvious it's too late to make a change
> So I wait for the innocent moment of truth
> You want a sign, demanding your proof
>
> It's too late for answers
> Too late for questions
> Too late for telling lies
> Too late for pleading
> Too late for reason
> You know it's time, oh it's time
>
> Isn't it obvious amidst our cold embrace
> Isn't it obvious there's too much to erase
> And you wait for the shadow of a memory
> Here's your sign, you barely saw me leave
>
> A picture's worth a thousand words
> Let's leave them as memories..."

Thanks, Jana.

Which brings us to Luke Craven. He's still sad, quieter than he should be, but no longer decimated. He participates in life more often than not, and has finally agreed to let us finish "Perfect Day" for the EP. He even had some input on "Too Late" and "Laughing Stock," and openly admits the final set will be an epic comeback that'll make the Label and fans happy. He's also seriously talking about sobriety and promised to seek counseling for his depression. He's cut back on the alcohol to maintenance levels, although he's still stuck in dependence and needs professional support. Casey and I made a compelling case for counseling, encouraging Luke with confessions of our own experiences letting the pros guide and support us through our journey out of the darkness. We're setting a goal of getting him help prior to the tour, which is currently scheduled to kick off on September 12.

And yes, I also now know that I'm officially going with them. Don't laugh, but somehow I've ended up with this crazy image of being Luke's guardian angel. Casey finds the whole thing hilarious, the way everyone treats me like I'm some holy psychiatrist, but he's not complaining, and thinks it will be good for me to be around as support for both of them. Luke needs that extra boost to get through what's going to be a very difficult transition back to the life he fled, and I think, deep down, Casey knows Luke needs more than the ancient friendship Casey can provide. He needs a rude, impolite, busybody who will refuse to let him imprison himself. Someone to fight that damn mirror and keep it from claiming another victim. He doesn't need a fan, he needs a supporter. An anchor, not a dreamer, and that's me.

Callie Roland, hammer.

FOR UPDATES AND ANNOUNCEMENTS, subscribe to Aly's newsletter.

EXPERIENCE the original song "Greetings from the Inside," along with the rest of Aly's music, wherever you stream music.
    Spotify
    Apple Music
    Amazon Music

MORE FROM ALY

From angsty and dark to snort-laugh funny, Aly writes romance from her soul to yours.

THE SAVE ME SERIES

RISING WEST (available on audiobook)

FALLING NORTH

BREAKING SOUTH

CRASHING EAST

GUARDING SHADOWS

CHASING RIPTIDES

THE WRECK ME SERIES

ASHTON MORGAN: Apartment 17B

CAMDEN WALKER: Apartment 8C

TRISTAN & ISABEL: Apartment 11F

THE HOLD ME SERIES

Available on audiobook.

NIGHT SHIFTS BLACK

TRACING HOLLAND

VIPER

LIMELIGHT

AN NSB WEDDING

SMARTYPANTS ROMANCE
STREET SMART
PLAY SMART
LOOK SMART

STANDALONES
YOUNG LOVE

PARANORMAL/SUSPENSE
GIFTED (Gifted, Vol 1)
CURSED (Gifted, Vol 2)
SÖREN (Gifted, Vol 3)
HAUNTED MELODY
TRAITOR

STAY IN TOUCH

Thank you for taking this journey with me. I would love to hear from you! For updates, reveals, and more subscribe to my newsletter and join my fun, laidback reader group on Facebook: Aly's Breakfast Club.

You can also follow Aly's original music wherever you stream music:
Spotify
Apple Music
Amazon Music

Find Aly here:
Amazon
Facebook Reader Group (Aly's Breakfast Club)
Newsletter
BookBub
Spotify
Apple Music
Facebook (Author Aly Stiles)

Goodreads
Website
Instagram
YouTube
Pinterest

Mail:
Aly Stiles
PO Box 577
Trexlertown, PA 18087-0577

NOTE FROM ALY

Depression is a serious illness that can go unrecognized by the victim and surrounding loved ones.

If you, or anyone you know, have plans to harm yourself, or you just need someone to talk to, help is available. Dial 988 for the Suicide and Crisis Lifeline, which is a 24-hour, toll-free hotline available to anyone in suicidal crisis or emotional distress.

Please know you are not alone, you are important, and you are loved.

Sincerely,

Aly

Printed in Great Britain
by Amazon

30685019R00195